PRAISE FOR *VICK'S VULTURES*
UNION EARTH PRIVATEERS BOOK ONE

"*Vick's Vultures* is a lot of fun, and premise. It subverts a lot of our ex, stronger, more enjoyable story."

"*Vick's Vultures* is a fast-paced thrill ride through a galaxy packed with scores of unique alien empires. Our hero, Victoria 'Vick' Marin, is a tough-as-nails lady that knows how to handle a crisis. Read and enjoy!"

—Robert E Waters, author of the *Devil Dancers* Military SF series

"A richly-imagined universe, three-dimensional characters, and a fast-moving plot give the reader a novel that is as interesting to the lover of hard science fiction as it is exciting to the lover of adventure. *Vicks Vultures* is a scientifically creditable, swashbuckapingly exciting tale from a talented emerging author. Read it . . . while I wait for his next book."

—H. Paul Honsinger, author of the *Man of War* Series

"*Vick's Vultures* shines a light on the dirtier side of space. The crew of the Condor will pull you into this gritty space opera and open the doors to a new sci-fi universe."

—Bob Salley, creator of *Salvagers* comic book series

"[A] fast-paced, at times breathless story that makes for a compelling reading while laying the background for the author's vision of the future, one that is quite believable in its lack of glamorous technological advancement for Earth, whose people try to carve their own niche in the grander scheme of things, despite the obvious disadvantages they started out with."

—*Space and Sorcery*

TO FALL AMONG VULTURES

UNION EARTH PRIVATEERS BOOK TWO

SCOTT WARREN

PARVUS
fantasy + science fiction

www.ParvusPress.com

Parvus Press, LLC
PO Box 224
Yardley, PA 19067-8224
ParvusPress.com

Parvus Press supports our authors and encourages creatives of all stripes. If you have questions about fair use, duplication, or how to obtain donated copies of Parvus books, please visit our website. Thank you for purchasing this title and supporting the numerous people who worked to bring it together for your enjoyment.

If this book weighs the same as a duck, it is purely a matter of coincidence. This book is not a witch. Please do not burn it.

ISBN 13 9780997661354
Ebook ISBN 9780997661347
Cover art by Tom Edwards Concepts
Designed and typeset by Catspaw DTP Services
Author photo credit by Rebecca Shelton and Taylor Loy

Union Earth Privateers Book 2:
To Fall Among Vultures

When a Samaritan as he traveled came upon the stricken man who had fallen among robbers he was moved with compassion. The Samaritan came to him, and cleansed his wounds with oil and wine. He set the man upon his donkey and carried him to the safety of an inn.

—The Parable of the Good Samaritan

THE STORY SO FAR

U NTOLD AGES AGO, WE witnessed the gods create fire through lightning and brush, and from then on we thought of little else but stealing it for ourselves. Through peace and war we discovered the engines of steam and combustion, of automobiles and aircraft and then rockets capable of carrying three men to our nearest neighbor: the Moon. Ionic and electromagnetic propulsion followed. Though slow, these engines burned steady and carried us to the red planet we named for the god of the wars that spurred our expansion.

Then we expanded farther to the moons of Jupiter and Saturn and we discovered the keys great minds pondered and lusted after. Matter with the exotic properties required to hoist the Alcubierre designs for faster-than-light travel from the ideas of geniuses to the forges of the governments of America, India, and China. A new space race began, and within a quarter century the speed of light and the petty differences between the two greatest world powers that Earth had ever known became distant memories . Humanity embarked on the greatest exploratory struggle they had ever undertaken as a species: the journey to another star.

Less than a decade after we discovered the secret to interstellar travel, we also discovered that our journey was not at all unique. The stars were jealously guarded, and we learned to our regret that those xenos established among them had little regard for human life and even less respect for the territory humans claimed.

But in the ashes these aliens made of our first interstellar pioneers, the raiders from the stars left a gift of untold value: a tear in the fabric of space near the core of the system. A *second* way around the threshold of light speed, a mystery of physics so utterly alien to human minds that the discovery of the horizon drive shattered our understanding of the natural world. And like fire before it, humanity could think of little else until it was ours.

As the astronauts of Earth flung themselves ever farther across their corner of the Orion Spur, that narrow bridge between the Perseus and Sagittarius arms of the Milky Way, it became clear that we could not survive Earth's discovery. So the Union Earth government elected to withdraw, to colonize planets in secret or cohabitate with other xenos as desperate as we. Until fleets from Earth could stand against the threat of interstellar war, humans would be as ghosts in the darkness between stars. To reach that day, to close that critical technological gap we needed a new method of advancement.

The Union Earth Privateers were founded five decades after the first Alcubierre module pushed itself past light speed on a torus of compressed space. Granted almost unilateral authority, the Privateers had a single directive: Gather advanced technology from every corner of reachable space. Some forged diplomatic bonds, others turned to salvage or piracy. Some became rescuers in an uncaring galaxy, trading safe passage for scraps of xenotech. Through the tireless work and sacrifice of the Privateers, humans began creeping ever closer toward the day when they could stand among the other races in the stars.

n in space. A tricky e lack of gravity not- s opposite the locals' ed as the perforated r screen. Mauled let- e *Kreshna*, which the nimal from the Vau- the destroyer's dorsal the particle cannons stem and main reac- e cleaned up after the

ting that long. Either battle and scuttle her o fleet assaulting the and mop up. But be- out, the destroyer was nough to human un- rs which could bring to force parity among the stars.

Victoria thumbed her tactical team's communication circuit. "Red, we're two minutes out, what's your status?"

"Go for vacuum, Vick. I'm about to cycle the forward airlock," Red answered. His voice was tinny and muffled by the helmet on his armored vacuum suit.

Those laser batteries could still be seen in the distance, even without the computer highlighting their energy signature. Human lasers were still limited to terrestrial warships and planes firing at terrestrial ranges of a few dozen miles. They wouldn't even scratch the paint of xenotech hulls.

As the *Condor* drew close the navigator, Huian Wong, slowed the ship with shielded thrusters. With the heat hidden by shutters, a xeno would have to look pretty closely to notice their approach, vectored as they were to slip between the stars. Someone must have been looking very closely indeed, because a new shortwave frequency appeared on Victoria's command repeaters, accompanied by a red flashing alert from Avery in the sensor shack aft of the conn.

"Shit, is that the *Kreshna?*" asked Victoria.

"Aye Ma'am, a handshake protocol, someone over there wants to get our attention," said Avery.

"Us and every other xeno in this goddamn system. He's turning up the volume, too. We better open the damn channel before he gives us away."

Victoria completed the circuit, a section of the main view screen giving way to an ugly brown face. Moist folds of skin surrounding a central lamprey mouth with little black eyes asymmetrically scattered to either side. The display flickered as the low-resolution recorder captured the Vautan's turbid countenance.

"You are the men from Earth, humans, yes?"

The computer didn't bother to translate this, he was speaking Kossovoldt Standard, a language seeded across the known galaxy and adopted by the Union Earth. No one knew why or how the Kossovoldt instilled their language across a thousand alien races, and if a starship captain survived an encounter with them long enough to ask, his or her priorities were generally elsewhere.

"Yes, I'm Captain Victoria Marin. We are not hostile, our intent is to—"

"Yes yes, I know what it is you do, just get us off this blasted wreck. The battle is lost. I have fourteen crew and I am the ranking officer."

There was another alert on her console. Her chief sensor officer's voice had picked up a note of alarm this time.

"Vick, we've got inbound, three contacts decreasing bearing rate. Thrust contrail suggests two fighter-type and a frigate. Must have picked up the active RF emission from the *Kreshna*. Designated Primary and Secondary One and Two."

Victoria swore. The *Condor* might bloody the nose of those fighters and escape before the frigate arrived, but it would be a close thing. She was in one of the most advanced ships the Union Earth could float, but the xenos were just so far ahead on the technological power curve. Her XO was already developing the warships' intercept solution, they would have time to grab the survivors or tear off part of the laser array, but not both. She knew which was more valuable to the UE government. But damned if she was going to have that blood on her hands. "Red, hold off on vacuum, we're taking on rescues."

"Aye, Vick," Major Red Calhoun replied. His marines would stand down, likely relieved, or maybe disappointed, at avoiding the inevitable firefight as they boarded the derelict vessel. The Vautan officer made a satisfied slurping sound that made Victoria's stomach want to crawl out her ears.

"I am pleased, Human Victoria, that in this the rumors

proved true. I look forward to the sights and scents of your ship."

"Passage ain't free, you know. I wanted to tear those laser charging coils off your hull. What's your hide worth to you?"

An annoyed series of chirps followed, which the computer was kind enough to translate as an expression of frustration. "Surely you realize I cannot authorize the release of any of my ship's weaponry. I would never hold command of my own vessel again!"

Soft shudders went through the *Condor* as the magnetic clamps energized, locking Victoria's Privateer onto the much larger vessel. At the same time, XO Carillo's intercept solution passed to Vick's terminal. Less than five minutes until the enemy ships were in firing range. She keyed the circuit for the marine channel again. "Hold off on that airlock, Red. The captain and I are still negotiating passage."

A nervous contraction of his mouth and throat muscles betrayed a hint of urgency in the ranking Vautan officer. Clearly, he too was aware of the approaching vessels and their intent, his distress call to the Vultures a calculated risk that he fell on the wrong side of. "Human Victoria—"

"*Captain* Victoria."

"Captain, time is of limited commodity in this venture, attempting to salvage parts in the midst of a battle is unwise."

"It is now that you're broadcasting our location to anyone with ears. Now if I don't get the parts we need, I get stranded at a neutral station and don't get to go home on time. But one of us gave away our position with that little radio stunt, and that bastard isn't going home at all without something to make up for it. So if you want to keep all the broken pieces of your dead-ass ship until it's blasted to atoms with you still inside? Well, I don't see your prospects for command looking too good if you're floating across the cosmos in a million pieces. What's it going to be?"

There was chatter from other *Kreshna* crewmembers offscreen, and a wave of static pushed across the transmission. Seconds passed. The ranging solution on the intercept fighters dwindled. Victoria waited.

The Vautan officer regained his post. "This is not the altruism I was told your kind possessed!"

"Altruism doesn't fill the cargo bay and fuel tanks. What's it going to be?"

"You're a scoundrel, Human Victoria, but I will do as I must, you will have your trophy. Terminate connection."

The section of the view screen winked out as the circuit was severed by the Vautan officer, replaced by the countdown until the frigate and fighters reached expected weapons range. Victoria's sensor team was still trying to identify their class and race of origin, but the derelict destroyer was blocking any view of the *Condor*'s sensors. She was cutting it awful god damned close.

"Major, get them off that fucking wreck, doubletime. Whether or not they manage to pry something loose, those crewmen don't deserve to die because of one asshole officer."

"Roger Vick, sounds like the crew of the *Kreshna* is already lining up to get off that tub."

Victoria looked over her command repeaters, the various ship's subsystems reporting their status. Engineering, tactical, sensors, and navigation all showed nominal. In the brief moment where every task was assigned and a captain found herself with no orders to give, the weight of the lives resting on her decisions seemed to grow even heavier. She looked at the back of Huian Wong's head, watching her run trajectory programs to double-check that their egress route back to the horizon jump was the fastest available. Victoria could find fault there if she looked hard enough. The impotence of waiting made her want to vent her frustration, but jumping down her pilot's throat would only undermine the girl's confidence in the midst of a crisis. She settled for calling up fire control instead.

"Carillo, prep countermeasures as primary response. If those interceptors were listening in then they have an idea who we are, and today isn't the day to make enemies by smearing more xenos across the stars if we don't have to."

"Aye, Vick, dummy loads, anti-fighter munitions in reserve."

Her executive officer, Cesar Carillo, preferred to lead the fire control team from their targeting room instead of his station on the conn. The Argentinian was busy plotting firing solutions on the three ships bearing down on the *Condor*.

The view on the main screen swiveled at a gesture from Victoria, superimposing a projection of the expected flight path of the fighters. They were Tallidox war birds, though the Tallidox manufactured and sold arms and equipment to many interstellar governments at prices Earth couldn't hope to afford. And unfortunately, they were always improving their export fighter designs.

Active sweeps began to bounce off the *Condor's* hull, and the iconography for the fighter craft jumped from the projected path to within line of sight.

"Shit," said Victoria. The engines on the fighters either received an upgrade since her last encounter with them, or they were running extra hot.

"Conn sensors. Targeting sweep just hit us. Fighters are 50KK and accelerating. Designating Primary and

Secondary target now."

"Seal the airlock, take what we've got and cast off."

The profile of the active sensors changed from a wide sweep to a focused cone as the fighters struggled to maintain a lock on the *Condor's* slick hull. The active radiation signature was similar to Earth radar, enough so that the surface of the privateer ship was conditioned to shrug it off. Xeno fighter craft by nature couldn't carry the advanced gravitic sensors that xenos in this stretch of space favored on their larger ships.

Victoria's pilot pushed the ship away from the *Kreshna*. And not a moment too soon, as visible-spectrum lasers began peppering the remaining active defenses of the derelict ship with quarter-second bursts of indigo light. At thirty-thousand kilometers the beams weren't focused enough to do much more than warm up the hull and melt off the remaining automatic defenses on the *Kreshna* just in case a few of them still had power, but as the distance closed, those indigo beams became more and more lethal. The fighters began carving off shards of red-hot composite hull off the *Kreshna* even as they maneuvered to keep the *Condor* in their active sensor overlap.

Something in the *Kreshna* took poorly to the lasers, and ignited plasma began to vent from the dorsal port-side. The force of the release sheared a fissure across the top of the ship that split the derelict in two. The aft section spun freely on the main view screen, the magnification level growing while the *Condor* accelerated away on a plume of ionized xenon with enough thrust to overcome her newly upgraded inertial dampeners. Victoria grunted against the g-forces pushing her back into her captain's couch. The frigate began to decelerate, launching missiles and more indigo lasers into the wrecked scrap of the *Kreshna*. The fighters kept on course, closing the distance with alarming speed even as their sensors struggled to find purchase on anything but her engine's heat signature.

"Tactical, deploy pursuit screen now."

Two small missiles fell back from the aft tubes of the *Condor*, deploying a reactive ceramic cloud between her and the Primary. With two fighters and only the waste heat of her engine, it was difficult for the xenos to determine the range to focus their weapons. The lasers on the craft could be configured for a range-finding mode, and the emitters on the Primary fighter began to flash in rapid succession. The energy alone from the ranging could potentially damage the *Condor*, but these new laser countermeasures seemed to do the trick. The ceramic particles reacted to the light-energy by transforming it to heat and expanding rapidly to block the distant fighters from view and offer nothing but garbage returns to their sensors. It forced the closer fighter to abandon the ideal ranging formation and waste energy adding lateral acceleration, giving the *Condor* precious seconds to accelerate to a safe Alcubierre vector. Huian Wong kept the ceramic countermeasure screen between the *Condor* and the fighters as best as the woman could without sacrificing acceleration.

Indigo light flashed within a dozen lengths of the *Condor* as the second fighter began taking wild stabs with his laser array using his limited knowledge of the *Condor's* position and path.

"Vick, ready to deploy anti-fighter defenses on your mark."

"Hold, tactical," said Victoria. The lasers were growing closer and more focused as the range shrank and the sensor returns improved, but firing the dummy missiles too soon would give the fighter too much time to react, and she

needed his response to be survival instinct, not the calculation of a hunter defeating a prey's defenses.

"Conn sensors, the sweep on the secondary just nar-
rowed. Zero bearing rate, waste heat increase from his engines. He's closing in."

The fighters could accelerate faster than a bad night of
drinking, and if the frigate stayed behind it spoke to their
confidence in the abilities of the pilots. Victoria glanced at
her repeaters. That second fighter, she could play to that
confidence. Let him think he had the kill.

"Engineering conn, vent heat portside."

Small alarms showed as hot coolant sprayed from the
port ventricles of the engine room, presenting an enormous thermal signature for the Secondary to see on his
thermal scope. The randomly firing lasers ceased as the
pilot squeezed every ounce of power into his engines, the
distance track closing at an alarming rate. To the fighter, it
looked like one of his blind shots got lucky and hit something critical, and now it was just a matter of finishing the
job. But he got careless too, and forgot to vary his bearing
as he closed.

"Tactical, fire the dummies," Victoria said. Her voice
was calm, despite her heart attempting to beat its way
through her chest as she felt the shuddering of the half-
dozen missiles launch from the aft tubes on the *Condor*.
Privateer ships had a variety of rear-facing weapons. They
tended to do a lot of running for their lives.

"Huian, take us about. Vector away from the Primary
and get us clear for transition."

"Aye skipper."

There was a brief moment of risk as the *Condor* presented a broadside to the Secondary, silhouetting itself against
the vented coolant. But in that moment all six missiles

screamed to life on a fume of solid propellant, blasting the fighter with a bevy of active radar in various lock-on profiles. Completely superfluous EM radiation, as they received all of their targeting information from the *Condor's* main computer. But the intended effect was simple, gut-wrenching, bowel-loosening horror. The sudden appearance of the seemingly deadly ordinance, stripped of their payload in favor of greater acceleration, took the fighter completely off guard. For a brief instant there was no reaction, as the pilot was caught between an ideal targeting solution and the certain death homing in on his craft.

"Conn sensors, secondary is reversing thrust, laser refraction pattern suggests a point-defense configuration. He's breaking off the attack," said Avery.

"Huian, get us out of here before he thinks to tell his wingman about our course change."

"Aye ma'am."

The tone of the engines softened to a dull roar as Huian Wong pulled the *Condor* back from emergency acceleration, and Victoria relaxed back into the conn. On the main screen, two of the missiles winked out when the fighter's point defense clipped them, and the other four sailed past as he desperately tried to change his vector. When the fighter's pilot found himself still alive, his thrust signature dulled. He abandoned the emergency evasive maneuvers and his laser banks stopped producing their defensive light-show. Victoria had no doubt that whoever was in that craft knew full-well she held the pilot's life in her hands and chose to be merciful. Most of these xenos weren't sure how to handle that. Some saw it as weakness, others as opportunity. Some, as her new Vautan shipmate demonstrated, saw it as convenience. The pilot at the controls of the fighter craft flashed his engines in two short bursts, an acknowledgement of her tactics. An interstellar tip of the hat.

Victoria snarled under her breath and thumbed the main circuit. "Stand down from battle stations," she said. The Vultures had almost no time to get the crew off that hulk, let alone pry loose any carrion. Goodwill didn't fill exotic matter tanks. She pushed herself up and stormed off the conn. She dropped down to the mid-level and was heading for the ancillary cargo bay when she was intercepted by Sergeant Aesop Cohen, her marine xenotech specialist, still in his vacuum suit.

"Captain, I was just coming to see you," the boy said, the distress clear in his eyes. Tears stained the corners.

"Christ, Cohen, what happened to you?"

The marine laughed, then coughed, and wiped his nose on the ceramic plate of his armored sleeve. "The Vautan, ma'am. Their skin reacts . . . poorly with oxygen. Secretes a cyanocarbon chemical that reminds me of chem-war training I had at Tel Aviv. At the end we had to take off our gas masks and sing Hatikvah in a room full of CS. Not harmful, but not pleasant."

"They're walking, talking tear gas grenades. Fuck me. Tell me you were on your way to deliver something other than that. Did we get anything?"

Cohen grinned. "That officer of theirs made a fuss, I think he was going to go back on whatever deal you made. The crew of the *Kreshna* almost left him over there, but settled for bringing him bound and gagged, which for them apparently means stuffing a big cork plug in that radial saw they've got for a mouth."

Cohen presented a small device to her, held as delicately as a newborn in his gloved hand. "One of their engineers was a quick thinker, pulled this off the ship's databanks before he scuttled them. Full schematics for their forward laser array, if we can find a system to interface with it. We don't know much about Vautan computers."

Schematics were, by and large, inferior to physical parts. Scientists jumped ahead years by analyzing and duplicating xenotech alloys and composites. And complex devices that eluded the top minds of the Union Earth still opened doors to new possibilities. Drawings and diagrams could go a long way toward putting the puzzle together once they had all the bits and bobs, and the Vautan ships the UE encountered were only a few hundred years ahead of Earth technologically. But such a divide was surmountable only with the proper application of reverse engineering, and for that Victoria needed physical parts. Union Earth had been after a shortcut to ship-borne lasers for some time now, especially following her experience with a Dirregaunt battleship almost cutting her ship in half at two hundred and fifty thousand kilometers the year previous, out of direct line of sight, by refracting the beam across the upper atmosphere of a planet. Hell, these schematics might finally be the key that let scientists crack the mystery of how the xenos could pump so much energy into their weapon systems without their ships exploding. But she doubted it.

With the hold smelling like the inside of a CS gas grenade, Vick headed for the foremost compartment, as far physically as she could get from the Vautan rescues. The tip of the spear was her Fire Control compartment, where her executive officer was squeezed into a console between two technicians and a midshipman learning the ropes before taking a post on another Privateer.

Even though the ship was standing down from general quarters, XO Cesar Carillo still had his nose to the screen, poring over potential firing solutions derived from a steady stream of sensor data. When it came time for the shooting,

Carillo was the hand that aimed the gun, and his grip was as steady as his midsection was thick. Which was to say, very. In fact, Victoria never determined how the man kept getting cleared for space duty with his physique. Maybe he ate the physicians. Or maybe you didn't kick out someone who stared down the barrel of hypersonic fighter craft without flinching. Victoria could see stains at the neck and armpits of the technicians, and you could have wrung out the midshipman's hair into a bucket. But Carillo's uniform was dry as a vacuum-sealed turd. He'd probably sleep through a firefight if she let him.

"Captain," he said beneath a wiggling gray mustache and bushy black brows. It wasn't a question or an invitation, simply an affirmation of her presence. It unnerved her, somewhat, that he seemed preternaturally aware of when she entered a room, and that typically he would make his egress moments prior. The two technicians turned, startled for a moment at her sudden appearance. Victoria jerked a thumb behind her. "Cobb, Mavis, out," she said. She pointed at the midshipman, a hint of a smile on the young woman's face. Probably thought she was getting included in the big-girl conversation. "What rig are you slotted for?"

"The UE *Artemis*, Ma'am."

"Shit, we'd better not get too chummy then. You'll probably be stardust within a year. Out."

Once the red-faced junior officer had left the fire control room Victoria leaned against the bulkhead.

"A fucking cabbie service, that's what we are, Cesar. Give us a ring and we'll come pull you out of a jam. No no, put that wallet away, your reactive charging coils are no good here. This one's on us."

"There are worse things than being harmless, Vick," said Carillo.

"I know. But what are we doing out here? Six months ago we were running Malagath princes through Dirregaunt blockades. The Big Three are barely even seen in this corridor now."

Carillo laughed, "And we've hauled more tech in these last six months than in the prior two tours combined. And we did it without the Dirregaunt breathing down our necks. Why let this xeno under your skin, Vick?"

"I have no goddamned idea. Maybe it was his expectations, maybe his lack of respect, or maybe how stupid he was to open a comms channel. Take your pick. But after we dump his ass off at Ersis, we're going to take a hard look at what we're doing out here. Humanity can't just be a free ride if we want to survive in this galaxy."

"You should leave that sort of talk to the politicians, Vick," said Carillo.

The dull roar of the ion engine cut abruptly as an oscillating whine crept up in its place. The Alcubierre drive pushed the *Condor* into superluminal transit. The mining station was off the beaten path, in a system whose star didn't support the properties ideal for a horizon jump. The trip to the nearest star that did would take them almost two weeks. Little happened during light speed transit, and so the ship would be put on Alcubierre stand-down with a minimal watch rotation. That was a long time for a captain to be alone with her thoughts, and Victoria did not particularly enjoy being alone with her thoughts. Paperwork and model spacecraft only kept her from the bottles that always seemed to find their way into her rack for so long.

"No sense putting it off any longer," said Victoria. "I suppose it's time to meet the new arrivals. Come on."

CHAPTER 2
SIMILAR STORIES

Edrus Vaan had spent the better part of a year stationed on Listening Post 121 of 142, nestled comfortably outside the sixth and outermost planet of the system. He was alone, or at least he would be if his partner, Kal, ever managed to annoy him to the point of murdering her. It had been a close thing on more than one occasion. She favored the shrill poetry beamed from the surface of the planet Pedres, when the receiver was in a position to catch it and when he or a rogue solar storm didn't manage to disable it. Unfortunately, his partner was an engineer, and the only thing that ever seemed to get repaired on the listening post was the multi-channeled acoustic receiver. It would be an easy thing, next time she took the skiff out, to rig the docking locks and leave her out there for the space walkers to come and collect.

Sometimes he questioned the Maeyar Fleet Ops' wisdom in sending husband and wife pairs to man long-term space postings.

Before he could come up with more ingenious methods of making his wife's untimely expiration appear accidental, a small alarm light flashed on his control panel. He looked at it, his lone eye swiveling as he pared the skin off the last of his preserved fruit. His attention moved to the small display in the wall, where numbers flashed in rapid succession, vectors and values which he was trained to interpret.

He swallowed. "Kal, jewel of my existence, are you doing maintenance on the superluminal sensor array?"

The high-pitched squeal of Kal Vaan's plasmic welder cut out, leaving only the high-pitched squeal of her poetry. Transmitted through sublight radio waves, the recorded verses were more than four hours old before they reached the station and mounted an assault on his ears. Kal appeared through the hatch, still wearing her protective mask. "No, light of my morning. The superluminal array is functioning as it should."

Edrus watched her perform the same scan he had just performed on the instrumentation.

"Impossible," she said, "not even Malagath ships have a darkspace profile like that. I don't know anything that does."

"Could it be that human freighter back with another shipment?" asked Edrus. The strange, primitive race setting up a trade depot on Pedres with the Maeyar had spacecraft with antiquated darkspace engines that suggested craft of a much larger size on the FTL sensors. He dialed the vector into the optics system, state-of-the-art lenses with a light amplification module to magnify what little of the core star's brilliance made it out this far. It would take a few seconds for that light to bounce off anything coming out of darkspace and return to the sensor, so he waited while his wife tapped away on a console, asking the neighboring station if their superluminal array also held the anomaly.

The nearest station was a few light-minutes away, and Edrus' quandary was answered through his optical sensors before the message ever reached them.

"Dark stars," he whispered, as spacecraft began to fill

his scope by the dozen. Nearly a hundred had transitioned into the system before he could pry himself away from the lenses. "Send a burst to Pedres, we're under attack."

Victoria stumbled off the ramp of the *Condor*'s airlock, gasping with relief. Ersis played host to a great many smells, few of them pleasant. But after the carnage the Vautan rescues wreaked on her nasal passages it was like being in the fresh spring air of northern Ireland. Thank Christ they were finally off her ship. Four days of shore leave for the crew while the *Condor* deodorized would help to raise spirits as well. Ersis was on a moon orbiting a gas giant so closely that it was completely shrouded by its nitrogen-rich upper atmosphere. The low gravity and an atmosphere dense enough to breathe made it an instant favorite for an interstellar harbor and for the businesses that grew to support the shipping and their crews. The Vautan survivors would have no issue finding passage here and soon their schematics would be on their way to Earth via secure FTL channels. Four days meant time enough for her to put the Vautan officer and his arrogance behind her. And maybe find some humans she hadn't seen every day for the last six months, and even more importantly, wouldn't ever have to see again.

As far as security was concerned, Ersis was about as safe as a xeno city could be if you avoided the rougher spots. Of course her Vultures were walking rough spots, and most of her marines would have to be hauled out of security lockup and stuffed back on the *Condor*. For personal protection, the sidearm on her hip and her Union Earth Privateer uniform jacket would suffice. Humanity was known to Ersis. Even so, she scowled as Major Calhoun caught the door of the magnetic train before she could get away. She ignored his self-satisfied smirk as he wedged into the seat between her and a xeno her retinal implants had difficulty identifying. Protocol dictated the captain have a security detail on xeno planets and neutral stations. It would be batteries or nothing for another six months.

The spaceport mooring the *Condor* accessed the city proper by automated trains traveling between free-standing magnetic relays. No visibly apparent force lifted the cars, but the ground smoothly fell away as Victoria lifted above the rooftops to her favorite part of the journey.

"Look Red, that's the *Apex*, one of the new class of light cruisers the Lereigh just put out. That forward ablative plate can shrug off almost anything short of a Malagath particle cannon. That at the next mooring over? That's a Jenursa boat. Diplomatic, must be an ambassador yacht."

Red, not normally interested in ships unless they were simulating boarding actions, leaned over and squinted.

"Two down from that, that's Maeyar, right? We pulled rescues off a smaller one."

The public car carried them higher and she could indeed see the dorsal point defense microwave emitters of a Maeyar frigate.

"Hell yeah, look, so is the one next to it. They've got those distinct flared fins back by the engines. Designed to dip into atmo, that's why they're so streamlined and have that reinforced ridge running down either shoulder. Those are vibration dampeners, those things can pull mach levels that would shake most ships apart. Love to get my hands on some of them."

"They're not alone," said Red, pointing out the opposite window.

Victoria pressed her hands to the glass, ignoring the

scandalized wheeze of the xeno whose personal space she'd doubtless violated. She whistled. "That's the *Twin Sister*, she's a carrier. Fighters, bombers, interceptors. We could park a dozen privateers in her hold. And she's got two more escorts, that frigate and that missile boat next to it. No way this is a coincidence, there's major fleet movement going on here."

The magnetic train car lifted them too far from the ships for her retinal implants to identify any further vessels. Newly upgraded after a brush with vacuum had damaged the old ones, this model had tighter text display and the color count upped from grayscale to 256 colors in the photo display, which was a first. Relevant data about the Maeyar scrolled across her screen, downloaded directly from the *Condor*'s computers. Most of it she already knew. Most of it was reports she wrote. By the time the train reached the city center Victoria was up to speed on the new entries drafted since she last encountered the xenos, up to and including an attack on Pedres. Though details were sketchy, Ersis' proximity to the Maeyar's second most populous world almost guaranteed that the battlegroup she saw was en route.

The Union Earth kept an embassy of sorts tucked away in the seventy-first level of a helical skyscraper just off the main concourse of the city. Slightly bigger than a broom closet, it was more of an officer's lounge for privateer crew, with an on-staff cook and access to FTL comms without having to resort to public terminals. There was no official ambassador attached to the embassy, and the sign in Kossovoldt Standard upon leaving the gravity lift simply read "Union Earth Office" in plain lettering. Sitting in front of it was a bored-looking local counting down the minutes until shift end. It perked up when it spotted Victoria, consulting

investigate the coffee. "An Earth animal, small, fat, and very tasty when fried. But they have a reputation for uncleanliness, so much so that a few human cultures refuse to eat them. They spend their days rolling in mud, snorting and snuffing and screeching at their own ugliness."

Sothcide's eye spun as he considered this. "To fuck one would then be loud, messy, and altogether impractical, I imagine. A colorful colloquialism. My culture has a similar one, though it requires some knowledge of Maeyar local dialects."

"We're practically cousins."

Sothcide took the seat opposite her, settling in as best he could to a chair never designed to accommodate his alien physiology. "It's not the only similarity our people share. I met with one of the human captains of your fleet, and upon my asking he offered, free of any cost, a paper version of your religious text. Though I am given to understand there are almost as many religions among the humans as there are stars in the galaxy, this one had a story that was of particular interest to me. Are you familiar with the parable of the Good Samaritan?"

"Intimately. Catholic school. The Maeyar have a similar story?"

The frills on the sides of his long, narrow face fluttered. Victoria knew it was ascent before her retinal implants chimed in. She remained quiet as he continued.

"The storms in Malvis, the northern reaches of my homeland, are said to have once been even more fierce than today. It was during such a storm that a woman became lost along the road to pilgrimage and sought shelter within a nearby community. Rather than offer aid, those of the village robbed her, and beat her terribly as they chased her back into the storm. For two days she wandered, filthy, starving, and ill from exposure. On the third day she collapsed upon the road, unable to move any further.

"Two textile merchants passed, and she begged them to let her ride their draft kanua. A beast similar in purpose to your ox, I believe. 'There will be no room for the cloth, and if you lay upon it you will soil it and we will not be able to sell it,' they said. And they left her in the road.

"Next she saw two men from her own village, and these too she begged for aid. 'Brothers,' she said, 'Help me along the path. I need only the strength of your arms.'

"But they felt great shame to look upon her, pretended they did not know her, and they left her in the road.

"Finally a beggar crossed her, dressed in rags and limping on a rod made from the stalk of a river frond. He lifted the woman, and leaning on her as much as she upon him, he brought her to a shack he made from discarded scraps, and returned her to health with a stew of wild roots. He asked nothing for his kindness. In time, her strength returned and she completed her pilgrimage. At the conclusion of her journey she returned and she married the beggar, for he had already acted as a husband to her."

Victoria cast a glance at Red as the parable hung in the air. "You're right," she said. "In a strange, endearingly misogynistic sort of way it is like the story of the Good Samaritan. This is about our last meeting, the time I pulled you off that burning frigate."

"Indeed it is, Captain Marin. But it is bigger than that. As the woman married the beggar, so too does this commonality of spirit marry my people to yours. There are few among the stars to show such compassion outside the bounds of their own peoples. When you found me I had been passed by twice by my own kind and left for dead, to be scuttled into stardust by one predator or another. Even the Maeyar seem to have lost this tenet of compassion, its warmth slipped away into the cold voids between the stars and the space behind space. Care and mercy have as little meaning there as time and distance."

Sothcide pulled a silk handkerchief from his uniform pocket to dab at the coffee dripping from his proboscis, flourishing the square of yellow cloth in his long fingers.

"Behold, Human Victoria, the fruit of our peoples' union. The softest of organic fibers, grown from worms I am told, though I believe it to be jests. The Maeyar cannot get enough of it to satisfy demand and fashion."

"Yeah, I've got some silk undies. Pretty great stuff."

"Your coffee, too, has become a luxury, a cup of this size worth more than its volume in engine coolant. And in return the Union Earth asks only alloys, silicas, and minerals widely available in asteroids across our holdings, safely away from trafficked darkspace lanes. But all trade with the Union Earth comes through Pedres. A planet which, as you likely surmised by our presence here, is under attack."

Vick leaned forward. "An attack that threatens any trade. But Scarves and dark roast are not a formal defense alliance. Union Earth won't want to be involved. If anything, they'll call a halt to excursions until it blows over." said Victoria as she accepted a mug from Red. How long had it been since she had spiked coffee? Bourbon woke her up better than caffeine. "Nor, and I don't divulge this information lightly, is our fleet in a position to fight an interstellar war. If you're looking for front-line allies, we're not in a position to help, despite whatever Jones tried to promise you."

Sothcide stood, holding a single slender finger before him, his lone eye fixed on her. It was black, speckled and dotted with luminous flecks like a star map. "One ship,

Victoria, the *right* ship, can make all the difference. I have seen how you can brush between the waves of radar, hide the heat of your engines and walk across space. Even our smallest fighters burn like stars in the infrared. Details are slim. We know who, and how many. But the *Condor* could discover the true nature of this invasion. The *why*."

Victoria sat back on the white leather and considered. Helping the Maeyar defend Pedres could cement their alliance. Or it could earn humanity a powerful enemy. In either event, it could get the Vultures killed and the wreckage of the *Condor* scattered to scrap above an alien planet.

But it could effect change in the landscape of the Orion Spur. Humanity tenuously clung to a half-dozen worlds with expeditionary colonies on a few more. The largest after Earth was a colony of just over a half-million. All were vulnerable. An ally like the Maeyar would ease defenses on a wide front, and open up at least two more scouted systems, and maybe even cohabitation. Few enough xenos needed oxygen atmospheres. And there would be xenotech. Where there was fighting, salvage always followed.

"South-Side, this isn't a call I can make on my own. My officers deserve a say in this kind of commitment. When do you leave?"

"Two standard days and nights."

Considering the possibility, Victoria stood to escort the Maeyar wing officer out through the airlock. The *Condor* was in fighting shape, and two days refit would patch up a few scars they'd earned in the months since they'd put human space in the rear view screen.

Once the rush of air died down enough to speak again, Sothcide turned to her, hands brushing the sides of her shoulders again.

"Thank you, Captain Marin. For the coffee and for

meeting with me. I hope you will see your way to joining our battlegroup as we leave for Pedres."

Victoria grinned. "I'll see you when I see you, Wing Officer Sothcide. And I won't tell your wife that you were putting the moves on me."

The frilly wisps at the sides of his head fluttered again. Laughter, this time, accompanied by a burbling whistle from his proboscis. "Captain, it was her idea to send me here. I may command the fighters in her bay, but the light of my horizon holds the reins of the *Twin Sister*."

CHAPTER 3
WHEELHOUSE

VICTORIA RELUCTANTLY turned away from the wardroom liquor cabinet to face her assembled senior officers. Carillo, Calhoun, Wong, Avery, Prescott, and Doc Whipple. She could count on one hand the number of times the seven of them had assembled in the wheelhouse, and truth be told she was surprised they all managed to fit at the same time. Poor Huian Wong looked crushed between the muscled arm of Red Calhoun and the tree-stump build of Davis Prescott.

Six officers, six tumblers, and one for herself. The magnets in the base snapped to the tabletop as she set them down and filled each with a small measure. Having explained the Maeyar request, the occupants of the wardroom displayed anything from unease to illness. Though that might be due to the lingering stink of the Vautan. She could hear the atmosphere cyclers running full-blast through the bulkhead behind her head.

"Don't everyone speak up at once," she said.

Avery was the first to reach for his glass, sighing as he looked at the geometric pattern etched into the shatterproof clear polymer. "This crew followed you to the Malagath Frontier, Vick. You know we'd follow you into hell."

"Huh uh. You think I jammed you in here like a pack of

sardines for a bunch of 'Aye Ma'ams'? You're Union Earth Privateer officers, not by luck or by accident, and before too long some of you will be sitting in my seat."

Victoria sat with a thump, as if to drive the point home. "This isn't some salvage run or unknowingly pulling a prince from the fire. This is declaring sides in an interstellar war. We came out here to lay low after we dragged the Dirregaunt through Taru and Pilum Forel. Too many eyes are on the *Condor*, and not just State and Colony's."

"It's not some random xeno bugger either," said Red. "I think he'd have done the same for us that you did for him, and that's not something you can say for most of the buggers out here. I don't think we owe it to him, but I figure he's one we want to owe us."

"I'm against it," said Huian Wong flatly. Victoria's navigation officer was the daughter of the Secretary of State and Colony. The girl showed iron guts for being a politician's daughter. Honesty was what Victoria had asked for, and honesty was something Huian had in ready supply.

"We don't have the right to speak for the Union Earth and decide which side of this war should win. That's an S&C directive, not a Privateer one. Plus, the Maeyar are vying to be vassals of the Malagath. Not knowing the nature of this invasion could mean a Dirregaunt or Kossovoldt proxy war is underway."

Assuming their itty bitty *Condor* was able to affect the outcome. A pretty big assumption. The Big Three angle was one Victoria hadn't considered.

"The right, maybe not. But the authority?" said Doc Whipple, "A privateer captain has almost unilateral authority beyond human space. Besides, we get a message to S&C and they'll fuss and bicker until the Maeyar are long gone. Vick is right, we need a decision now and only a privateer captain has the weight to swing."

Carillo shrugged. "Authority is granted to those who have the judgment to use it, as well as the judgment not to. No one in this room doubts your judgment, Vick. No other captain could have led us through the things you have. If you judge this intervention necessary, then I am behind you."

"Can we afford not to?" asked Avery, "No doubt this mission carries risk, but the potential for a formal defense alliance is clear. That means tech, trade, intel, protection, maybe even cohabitation. Opportunities like that don't come cheap. Or frequently. The Maeyar are hundreds of years ahead of us, if they shared surplus defense equipment that was two hundred years old it would still put almost anything in our fleet to shame."

One officer had yet to speak. Victoria looked at her new chief engineer, idly rolling his tumbler between sausage fingers and watching the amber liquid slosh within. Davis Prescott was the only officer at the table who did not yet call himself a Vulture, having stepped in to fill a hole in the roster left by the death of Yuri Denisov, a good friend to many of the faces in the room. Such an action was not easily forgiven by some, despite his playing no hand in Yuri's death.

"Davis?"

He looked up at her, small eyes deep beneath a heavy brow. His wide jaw offered a slight frown, canted as though only half his face held issue with her proposal. "I been over every inch of this vessel, Captain. She is many things. Strong, fast, and quiet as death in the night. But she ain't a warship, and saving for the Major's men, your crew ain't soldiers. You put this ship on the front line, one of those two is like to break. Now I don't know you like these folks do. Maybe that's why I can't bring myself to agree with your chosen course. But I will abide."

Victoria nodded. Five for, two against and with good reason. In all honesty, she had debated sending an FTL databurst to Earth to brief them on the situation. But Doc Whipple was right, they wouldn't receive an answer in time. It would take weeks just to determine who had the authority to declare war on the Maeyar's enemies on behalf of humanity. And the last time she'd deferred to the UE, they ordered her to hand the Malagath First Prince over to the Dirregaunt. An illegal order, as it turned out, all record of which was expunged. This was a Union Earth Privateer matter, the Vultures would be the ones putting their lives on the line.

"You're right, Davis. This isn't a warship, but none of our warships can play on the same field as the bastards out here. Not even close. We can, and the Orion Spur needs to see humanity as more than scavengers and cab drivers, or as soon as Earth or Ithaca or any of the other colonies get found, humanity is going to be scoured out of the galaxy because there's not a single xeno we know of that we could beat fleet to fleet."

Victoria glanced to her Navigator. "Huian, no disrespect to your mother, but State and Colony will talk themselves in goddamn circles while we wait to learn what happens at Pedres. The fact of the matter is that a xeno fleet officer sought us out. The *Condor*, by name. He came to us because he believes that we can make a difference in his fight. Whether or not we can I don't know. But this is why we were sent outside the 'protection' of the colonies. This is why Privateers have the backing of Union Earth. Not just so we can haul back junk for the eggheads to tinker with. Is that why any of you shipped yourselves a dozen horizon jumps from UE space?"

Resolution looked back at her from the faces of her officers. A body did not end up on a Privateer ship by accident. Whatever their reasons for being here, they did not extend only to picking the bones of dead xenos for trinkets. Victoria took a deep breath. "Let's give the Maeyar a call."

———

Sothcide looked at the command deck of the *Twin Sister*. Half a hundred Maeyar bustled about as Ersis dropped away in the main optical screen. His flight helmet was tucked beneath his arm, dress uniform packed away after his meeting with Human Victoria. The sleek bulk of *Twin Sister's* escorts lifted beside the carrier as well as the other four ships in the battlegroup, and the *Condor*, smallest of their entourage save for the fighter craft in his bay. His wife's bay, in truth, and the woman stood not far from him, fins wavering gently with the air circulation as she monitored reports from the system divisions across the vessel. As he watched her read the same report three times he approached.

"You are distracted, Jalith. What troubles my reason for being?"

She did not turn. "More vessels have entered Pedres, they continue to muster beyond Juna, and three more listening posts have been located and destroyed. At last count we identified almost a thousand vessels, all arriving from the vector of Gavisar."

Sothcide gently lowered her screen, bringing Jalith's attention to him. "Gavisar has never sought to expand. Not after . . ."

"They have never needed to," said Jalith, quickly cutting him off. "Not with a homeworld the size of a gas giant."

"Why now? And how did they amass a fleet of such size?"

"Questions that I hope your human captain is able to answer. Why the light of my morning puts such stock in the abilities of this primitive vessel I am eager to see," said Jalith.

"Are they in position?" she asked her contact tracker.

"Yes Matron, it's just . . . well, surely it's nothing."

Sothcide looked up to the tracking board. "Yes?"

"We are seeing a similar profile on the other side of the battlegroup, for moments at a time. I had thought at first they were out of alignment."

Sothcide shrugged. "Probably a glitch in the active radiation sensors. Reflection from the atmosphere of the planet. Who knows what kind of strange signatures Human Victoria's vessel gives off. Primitives really, these humans. Perform a service check on the array, we cannot afford errors when we arrive at Pedres. Contact the *Condor* and give them the necessary information on the *Twin Sister's* darkspace shroud so that she's close enough to enter the space tear with us."

"Aye, Wing Officer."

The *Twin Sister* had the tonnage and the reactor power to pull smaller ships with it into leaps between stars, or even in a ring of warped space to cheat the speed of light in more conventional ways. Ersis was too far for most of their battlegroup to make the jump to Pedres in a single bound, but riding on the back of the *Twin Sister* made it possible. The humans were unused to traveling by such a means, and required an explanation for the process. Spending time aboard the *Condor* had gifted Sothcide with a modicum of insight in the value such common knowledge might hold to the humans, and suspected that within the next few years he would see them employing the strategy to leave even messier holes in reality than they already did. More power added to a recording of poor poetry simply resulted in louder poor poetry. In the interim, the fighter wing needed inspecting. A sortie awaited his pilots on the other side. Jalith returned to her half-minded scan, thoughts on the distant star and the threat looming over the planet of her birth. So Sothcide descended to the deck alone, helmet a familiar weight beneath his slender arm.

CHAPTER 4
PEDRES

THE BLUE-BLACK WAVES of horizon space slipped past the *Condor*. Not really. Victoria knew they were only a digital artifact, a failure of the ship's sensors to discern the true nature of this pocket universe where time, speed, and distance seemed not to apply as thoroughly as the one she was more familiar with. Though if she was being fair, once you started fucking around with Alcubierre science and exotic matter, the universe at large started being a little less rigid. She wondered if humans would ever have broken the light speed barrier if they'd not found a vein of the stuff on Titan, setting off every radiological alarm the survey ships had.

"Battle stations, set general quarters throughout the ship."

Victoria had no way to communicate with the other ships in the battlegroup during the horizon jump. Thus far, humanity had not gleaned any hint such a technology existed, and some scientists argued that for all intents and purposes, no ships existed in horizon space other than the one you were in. It just further proved to Victoria that even scientists could be stupid fools, better off keeping their mouths closed and their noses buried in their obsolete books. Sciences and constants that had held for thousands of years were being challenged daily as the privateers brought back proof that more intelligent life had long since found workarounds to many expected physical impossibilities. Often before the theorizing physicists had been born.

Despite the lack of communication, a countdown timer superimposed on the main view screen ticked down the seconds in a way that reminded her a little too much of a descending range indication from the previous year. She swept it from the screen with a gesture.

"Huian, what do you want to bet we miss the star and just keep going into the great unknown?"

What little Victoria could see of her pilot's face paled visibly at the comment, eliciting a chuckle from her command couch. "Maybe we'll find the *Baron*. She went missing along this heading, right?"

Huian didn't answer. The steady heartbeat hum of horizon space started to falter, the view screen flashing as the sensors refocused and a band of stars appeared across the forward half of the conn. Pedres, they'd made it after all, and as her sensor repeater began to populate with little blue icons representing the *Twin Sister's* battleground it became evident that so did the rest of her escort. Victoria breathed a sigh she hadn't known she'd been holding.

"Conn sensors, no immediate hostile contacts, should take them a few seconds for reflected light."

Unless they had any kind of superluminal sensors, or had co-opted one of the Maeyar listening posts instead of destroying it. Even as she considered the possibility, her port-side sensor nodes picked up a spike in electromagnetic energy as the *Twin Sister* emitted a burst of active radiation. The active sweep propagated out into the system, returned reflection illuminating every contact within several thousand kilometers on her screen as bright as day.

Except one. One tiny signature on the other side of the battlegroup flared up for just a moment. Panning to the heading she looked at the spike in thermal emission that was gone in an instant. As quickly as she was able, she pulled up the optical sensors on the main view screen. Empty space greeted her. Empty space with a backdrop of stars. But as she watched, one winked out, then its neighbor as the first reappeared. And a brief glimmer that might have been the heat of an attenuator on an otherwise matte black hull. The hairs on the back of her neck raised.

Jones.

Her focus shifted as a score of fighters led by Sothcide cut across her screen on trails of scarlet exhaust, and when the residual heat cleared there was no sign of the other privateer. Jalith scrambled her fighters quickly, and as soon as her tactical display updated with fresh information from the *Twin Sister*, Victoria could see why.

They emerged from horizon space much more distant from the star than they'd planned, hoping to skip past the invasion fleet, but a formation of four ships blocked their way. The ship's computer identified one as a Gavisar light cruiser, almost two light-seconds away and already changing its trajectory to respond to the new threat of the *Twin Sister*.

The other three were human.

Alarms on her console lit up as active sensor pings swept over the *Condor*, dual emissions of radar and lidar that the coating and faceted surface on the *Condor's* stubby ablative wings deflected away.

"Avery, get word to the battlegroup, IFF paints the three in the rear as friendly. That must be the trade barge and its escorts. Make sure they don't fire on those rear three ships!"

"Aye Vick, I'm getting bursts of heat on the surface of that cruiser, missile launchers would be my best bet, tubes along its forward lateral faces."

As if to punctuate his point, the closest of the escort ships erupted in a pyre of burning plasma and composite hull. More heat bloomed off the flank of the cruiser as the last volley from the dying Union Earth Navy ship was cut down by point defenses. Not a single shot came within a hundred kilometers of its hull.

Victoria called for more acceleration, and felt the whine of the generators intensify through the decking of the ship. "Shit, we're falling behind the battlegroup. Huian, tightwave message to the other escort, let them know help is on the way."

———

Sothcide shook in the cockpit of his fighter, pushing his wing to max acceleration into the Gavisar vessel. The harsh explosion of one of the smaller contacts reflected off his helmet just before word filtered down that behind the light cruiser were three human ships, en route to Pedres and caught in the Gavisari web. Out here so far from the system's star, the glow was almost blinding in the dark of space.

"First Wing, disable the munition pods along the left side. Second Wing, look for the point defense and dust it. Third, go for the engine linkage. I want a kill shot."

The projected vectors of his other two fighter wings veered off on his tactical plot, tight turns compensated by the latest generation of vibration dampeners, which would let the Second and Third make their pass from angles the crew of the cruiser couldn't predict. Turn cost burn though, or so the saying went, and the First continued straight in on the most dangerous assignment with Sothcide directing the charge. Directional thrusters fired semi-randomly, an effort to deter any lucky shots, the repeating pattern of four hundred short bursts memorized by his gunner in order to compensate for their effects in his targeting.

The short radio of his gunner clicked in his ear. "Closing to target, have good range lock."

"Confirm," he called over the open channel, and was answered with the assertions of his other pilots as they deconflicted thermal targets. The cruiser was still beyond the range of optical targeting, even with the new vibration dampeners, but the missiles it continued to fire at the retreating humans painted every missile hatch on the vessel's starboard side as the broad front of the cruiser turned to face the new threat of Sothcide's fighter wings. The light cruiser was without escort or battlegroup. While his wing of interceptors lacked the raw firepower to destroy it, or in all likelihood even penetrate its armor, much of the Gavisar's fighting and defensive power was exposed.

The fighter weapons had one-tenth the range of the cruiser's anti-fighter defenses, but with their mounting velocity that range advantage would quickly evaporate. He could feel static dance across his skin as the capacitors charged for a single max-power barrage. "All pilots, target defensive range approaching, maintain thrust, we get one pass and one pass only."

His active sensors lit as the defensive laser arrays twisted to intercept his path. The wavelength emitted by the solid beams was too low for his visible spectrum, and too little matter existed to illuminate the deadly beams anyway. But a pinprick of light blossomed in his screen, one of the interceptors in the Second Wing had been struck from the stars.

No time to determine who it had been as their own range window approached. The point at which Sothcide's gunner had focused the six emitters came before the cruiser could recharge its capacitors, and all six pulsed in unison, the energy surge blasting static across his screens and sensors as his arrays launched a half-dozen coherent beams in less than a second.

When the view cleared he was greeted by a score of plasma jets erupting from the cruiser's starboard hull, visible for no more than an instant as his velocity carried him past the target and quickly closer to the two remaining human vessels, among several missiles still en route to their intended targets. Maeyar interceptors were designed with missile interdiction in mind. Several of their prominent enemies, the Gavisar included, employed directed nuclear, exotic matter warheads, or both. This was a chance to show Victoria he was serious about defending the trade pact.

"First Wing, wide dispersal, rapid beam configuration. Cut them down," Sothcide ordered.

Behind him he heard the reports of his other squadron successfully eliminating the point defenses on the cruiser, leaving it vulnerable to Maeyar missile fire even as he began systematically dismantling the few remaining warheads in pursuit of the human vessels. Then they were past the human vessels, carried away from the fight at breakneck acceleration. Sothcide flipped the interceptor around, beginning the long process of decelerating so that he could return to the *Twin Sister* and his wife. Third Wing hadn't managed to disable the drive linkage between the reactors and the engine, but the attack craft would be inbound shortly.

The *Condor* had better optical sensors than any xeno ship Victoria had encountered. Xeno ships had comparatively poor eyesight. When one looked at many of their neighbors in the Orion Spur, incredibly powerful active radiation and even some forms of gravitic sensor technology were readily apparent. But like kinetic weaponry and advanced computers, it seemed the local competition just hadn't bothered with electro-optic cameras. Xenos learned to employ the alternatives before refining primitive ideas. It was for this reason that only Victoria and Huian saw the state of the Gavisar cruiser as Sothcide led the first pass, extensive damage across the hull highlighted by the small explosions that peppered the starboard side of the ship. Warped and fractured metal exposed superstructure beneath the armored skin of the giant.

"No human ship did that kind of damage, and the fighters don't carry the weaponry to do the job either," said Victoria. She saved several still images to analyze—after the battle, but before the Maeyar left nothing to record. The battlegroup was closing with the wide, brutish cruiser, intent on destroying it before it could reach its comrades. In doing so, their commander dismissed the threat of the human ships, so primitive that their point defense systems could strike down any missile fired from a Union Earth Navy tube. Point defenses that the fighters had just disabled. Victoria opened a ship-to-ship channel.

"This is Captain Victoria Marin of the UE *Condor*. Primary target point defenses are minimal functionality and interior is exposed on the starboard flank. If you want to answer that fucker, now's your chance."

A small window opened on the main view screen, filled with a sweaty, rough-lined face above the collar of an underway officer's uniform. Eagles decorated both shoulders and lent their appearance somewhat to the stern, deep-set eyes of her counterpart, a full-bird Union Earth Naval captain. "Captain Bullock, ma'am, UEN *Hudson River*, and I'm damn glad you're here. Everything we tossed at him got knocked out, but I saved one last hurrah. Our optics are in a bad way, can you lend us your eyes?"

"My tactical team is transferring a solution now. Give 'em hell, *Hudson*."

Bullock left the channel open as he relayed orders to his own tactical team, parsing the targeting data into their system and ordering a volley of missiles. On the main portion of the screen, the *Hudson River* disappeared in a cloud of vapor and ice crystals as the calliope-style missiles fired in clusters of six on trails of solid rocket exhaust. Most were still struck down, even by weakened defenses, but sheer numbers overwhelmed the cruiser and a few began to strike home. Those that hit the hull boiled away ablated armor, doing little more damage than those destroyed enroute, but two or three of the hundred and twelve tracked missiles penetrated the weakened ship, and the starboard side of the ship expanded, venting gas and magenta flames.

"Conn sensors, reading a substantial decrease in the heat and light coming from the primary's engines, substantial drop in bearing rate increase."

"Nice shot, *Hudson*," said Victoria. "Suggest you make yourself scarce and let the Maeyar handle the rest."

"Don't need to tell me twice, damn thing dropped out of horizon right behind us. My magazines are empty and I'm glad to put him in my rear view screen. Hudson Actual out."

True to her prediction, Victoria watched as the Maeyar destroyers and missile boat closed with the larger cruiser, passing the 10,000 kilometer marker and opening up with tight-beam maser pulses that slugged into the crippled ship like the fists of an angry deity, releasing enough energy to rend the metal hull and set the Gavisar vessel rotating off course, even as her flight crew tried to right her and continue the acceleration on their escape vector.

The *Twin Sister's* missile boat escort, the *Slingray,* saw to it that escape was off the table. It launched a pair of missiles from its dorsal tubes that burned faster and hotter than even their fighters, armored and hardened against the weakened, laser-based point defenses. With nothing to stop the Maeyar artillery, exotic matter payloads detonated within a kilometer of the cruiser in a flat disc of violent blue-white light that sheared it nearly in half from stem to stern. The two halves of the ship separated, each continuing on a ballistic trajectory as secondary explosions tore and twisted through the ruined hulk. Victoria could hear the cheers of her crew.

"Huian, link us up with the rest of the battlegroup. We may be needed shortly."

CHAPTER 5
A CLOSER LOOK

"I'M CURIOUS, CAPTAIN Marin," said Jalith. Her bridge was abuzz with activity in the background of Victoria's main view screen, but the Maeyar commander herself was as still as stone. "How is it you were so certain that cruiser was in poor fighting condition before we arrived? My husband claims your optical sensors are beyond even that of the Dirregaunt. Lensing controlled and stabilized by computers, of all things. It sounds like perfect nonsense, to me."

Despite the cold regard on Jalith's onyx-black face, Sothcide's wife elected to use Vick's title instead of addressing her simply as 'Human Victoria'. That spoke either of respect, professional courtesy, or both. The xeno put a great deal of stock in the word of her husband while maintaining a healthy skepticism of her supposed abilities. That suited Victoria just fine, for the most part. The aspects of technology humanity uniquely excelled in was not common knowledge among the peoples of the Orion spur, and the Union Earth preferred to keep it thus.

"It's necessary, Ma'am. We don't have the power output for the types of active sensors you employ, nor the defenses to risk a standoff battle. You saw how poorly the *Clarke* fared, despite damage to that cruiser."

"Again, the damage. Not unusual for an isolated ship without escort or fighter wing."

"I agree, but Captain Bullock said the ship came out of horizon space right behind them. Wherever they got into a scrap, it wasn't Pedres."

The Maeyar wing commander considered this information, her eye spinning slowly in the center of her forehead, ticking along almost like the second hand of a watch. Humanity had no information on how Maeyar optometrics functioned, seeming to lack any of the familiar parts common to xeno eyes. Maeyar possessed none of the retina, iris, or pupil common to humans and even other xenos. Only a smooth black globe looked back at her, resembling a snapshot of the night sky as it spun slowly in its socket.

"The dawn of my day also speaks of your cunning and guile, and your ability to pass freely among enemies blind to your presence. If what you say is true, and we obtain proof, it may put us in a position to strike first. But we must know for certain before we endanger our fighting strength. Two of my interceptors were destroyed, and the loss of any craft jeopardizes our defense when facing such overwhelming numbers."

It was left unsaid that Jalith considered Victoria expendable, but she heard it loud and clear in any case. The *Condor* was not a battleship, a cruiser, a destroyer, or barely even a frigate by most spacefaring standards. When it came down to it, the Maeyar defense might not even notice her absence in terms of sheer strength.

"I am ordering the battlegroup closer to Pedres to establish a link with the Maeyar Fleet Operations. It appears nearly the entire strength of the Maeyar fleet is present, but most are arrayed around Pedres and the two closest planets. You will not accompany us, Captain Marin. Instead, you will use this guile and these optics and reconnoiter the Gavisar fleet. Discover how fractured and bruised this company is, and whether they can stand before the Maeyar's full strength."

That was a whole mess of xenos floating around the last planet, and it only took one lucky sensor operator to notice the *Condor*, even as slick-smooth as she was. Between Huian's sticks, Prescott's heat management, and Avery's near preternatural sensor analysis she had one of the best stealth teams in space. There were maybe two or three shit-hot ships she'd put ahead of the *Condor*. Unfortunately, she knew for a fact that one was floating around the system. Probably listening in on every communication between the battlegroup and Victoria. Maeyar communicative encryption was a joke for human computers to crack, and Jones was being treated to every strategic and tactical tidbit floating around the task force wavelengths. Victoria still wasn't sure what his endgame was, but the little bastard was no fan of hers. Would he resort to outright hostility? Unlikely. He was a pirate, first and foremost, not always patient enough to wait for a ship to need help before he set his sights on it. Even the Graylings seemed to leave him alone.

"We can do it. If they're all holed up near Juna we can get close enough without being seen to read names painted on hulls. Just give us time. Sneaking ain't a quick ordeal."

"Time is one thing I cannot give to you, there is no telling when the Gavisar will move for Pedres. The stream of their ships has slowed, and defense only mounts before them if they delay."

Victoria shrugged. "Maybe the delay is because they're not ready to fight. But then, that's what we're for, eh? Stay safe, Wing Commander Jalith."

"To you as well, Captain Marin. Stars' speed to the

Condor, and a safe return."

Ceremonious drivel. But brass always seemed to love the shit. Pride and pomp were universal. Victoria terminated the connection and the Maeyar's face disappeared from the forward monitor. She stood from the command couch, stretching the tightness out of her back and shoulders. Her mind immediately went to the wet stores in the wheelhouse. She tried to suppress the thought as well she could, which was not very.

"Huian, set a course for Juna. Sublight only, we know at least a couple of the heavy hitters out there are going to be packing FTL sensors."

"Aye Skipper."

The plating beneath Victoria's feet shuddered as the *Condor's* ion engine delivered a burst of acceleration. Worse than it should have, forward inertial dampeners must have needed work. But Victoria had a stop to make first. On the same deck as control, she made her way aft of the communication array to the tiny sensor shack. She slid into the dark room, illuminated only by the scrolling wash of passive sensor displays. Under Avery's instruction, one of the junior sensor operators was inputting commands using the virtual keyboard created by his retinal implants, synched to the computers on the *Condor*.

"Looks like photon doppler, but not as clean as mine," said Victoria.

"Good eye, Vick. You're right, the *Hudson River* sent this over. They happened to get the *Jackdaw's* old module before this patrol, and good thing too, since it gave them enough of a warning to get their missile countermeasures warmed up. The *Clarke* wasn't so fortunate. Captain Bullock thought we might be able to put it to use somehow."

The operator played back the event, showing a spike

where a superluminal wave compressed the photons moving past the *Hudson River*. Supposedly you could catch it on a view screen if you were lucky with the recording rate. For a few thousandths of a second, the stars toward the disturbance would be brighter, while the stars behind your ship would dim ever so slightly. The sensor module extrapolated the size and force of the wave to determine the origin and sometimes even the class of ship using it. It had been one of the earliest acquisitions of the privateer fleet, at a time when people remembered the age before first contact.

"Their cruisers have Alcubierre-type drives. Think they rode it all the way from Gavisar?" asked Victoria.

Avery glanced at her out of the corner of his eye. "No, they didn't. But you want to know how I know they didn't. Well I'll show you," he said, bringing up another display: the radiological sensors. "Coming out of horizon space isn't always clean, especially if you get bumped out a few million miles early, like by a solar flare or matter of sufficient size in your path. It creates a burst of light, heat, and radioactive waves. The light is easy enough to see, and xenos run hot enough that we barely notice the extra heat. But the radiation can get into the metal of the hull, seep in and hold fast, and with a half-life short enough to output measurable particles."

"More than usual?"

"That cruiser was practically bathing in it, once we got within fifty KK of the wreck it started setting off alarms." Avery crossed his arms. "Now how did you know?"

"You spend so much time looking at emissions and engine heat that you sometimes neglect the most important sensor onboard," said Victoria. She tapped out a command herself, bringing up the images of the cruiser before the Maeyar had closed to a killing range. It was at the edge of the *Condor*'s magnification, but Avery picked it up immediately.

"It was already in a fight," he said.

"That radiation could have just as easily come from weapons fire. Never trust anything you can't see with your eyes," said Victoria. "That cruiser was hurt bad, and whatever did it, did it before it got in this system. Trying to use an Alcubierre-type drive on a ship with a compromised hull risks compression shear."

"That ship was stranded, couldn't link up with his buddies, couldn't get past Pedres to make another horizon jump. Lashed out in fear at the closest thing, and it happened to be us."

"And how many of the bastards floating in circles around Juna are in the same shape? We're on our way to the lion's den here, Avery. Hell, our job is to pry open their mouths and get a close look at their teeth."

"Well, at least we know the Gavisari don't have many ships with gravitic sensors. If we go full dark they'll have to get pretty lucky to spot us."

Victoria shuddered. "They don't need much luck with a thousand of them rolling dice. I don't like this, but Commander Jalith has the right of it. They don't have a ship that could manage the kinds of missions we do daily."

"And we don't have a ship that can withstand the kind of punishment their warbirds can shrug off."

"Then we just have to make sure the Gavisari are really, *really* unlucky."

Avery nodded, and Victoria turned to leave.

"Vick, wait."

She stopped.

"What kind of weapon has a radiation profile identical to horizon space transference?"

"I don't know, but it chased over a thousand ships to the Maeyar's front door."

Juna had the distinction of being the sixth and last planet in the Pedres system. Despite the constant twilight its surface enjoyed, volcanic activity from active tectonics pumped greenhouse gasses across landscapes made mountainous by the shifting plates. Combined with the composition of its quickly rotating core, it retained the unusually high amount of heat that it generated while exerting an unusually strong magnetic field. Thick electrical storms were a near constant, roiling across its glowing surface. It was visible in the optics four hours after the *Condor* split from the battlegroup, but it wasn't until they were a couple million kilometers away that Victoria began to see flashes of continent-spanning lightning stretching into the upper reaches of the atmosphere.

"We're ballistic, ma'am. On our current course we'll get caught in Juna's gravity and slip into orbit," said Huian.

Victoria tapped her fingers on the arms of her command couch. As the *Condor* began its transition from the sunward side of Juna to the nightside, she began to see thin white snakes trailing across its upper atmosphere. Dozens of them traced their way across the night sky from sunset to sunrise.

"Conn sensors, sensors to the conn."

A moment later, Daniel Avery appeared through the hatch, floating in the microgravity as he examined the main view screen. Victoria didn't know that the Gavisar had gravitic sensors, but she also didn't know that they didn't, and so the replacement Gravitic Stealth Device was humming away in the back of the ship. She wished she still had the Malagath-enhanced version they'd rigged up while they were aboard, but tech-div had torn it out almost before they'd docked in human space.

"What's going on down there? Planetary electrical event?"

Avery scratched at his stubble. "I'm not sure what to make of it, but those are the Gavisari." With his virtual keyboard he pulled up their passive thermal sensors, highlighting the source of the anomalous lights. "Each one of those is a ship dragging a metal tether hot enough to melt steel. I'd say one in four have got one deployed. Never seen anything like it."

Victoria shook her head. Most xenos neglected the stealth elements of warfare, but not to the extent of towing ten kilometers of neon sign behind them. "Why would they do that?" she asked.

"Conn engineering," came Davis Prescott's voice over the open channel. "I just pulled up the main feed back here and I think I've got some notion of what they're about. It's a power generator. Dragging that line across the planet's magnetic field induces one hell of a current in a tether that long, enough to maintain some life support and maneuvering, but not much else."

A source of power, mooched directly from Juna's unusually strong magnetic field. "Any idea why they'd be running a setup like that?" she asked as Avery returned to the sensor shack just aft of her.

She could imagine the heavy Texan shrugging back in the engineering compartment, strapped down to the main station. "Damaged reactor? It's a constant supply of voltage, Skipper. Maybe your theory about them being in a fight was onto something if they ain't running their reactors."

"Huian, adjust course, three degrees starboard and two

positive on the azimuth. We need a closer look. Avery, what have we got for active sensors down there?"

"A lot of EM radiation pointed at Pedres," said Avery while Huian made the minor course correction, "So much that it's causing more interference than useful returns. I don't think they're as coordinated as they'd like us to think, lots of chatter but it's our first time breaking Gavisar's encryption. But down in middle orbit? If they're not running reactors they won't have the power for active sensors, and all that magnetic interference will be like gliding through white noise. We're losing some fidelity already on the *Condor*. We're ghosts here, Vick."

Victoria nodded. "Steady as she bears. Set for middle orbit, let's get into this formation and take a turn around the planet. Huian, how long will it take us for a full orbit?"

"One hundred and eighty minutes, Ma'am."

"Alright. One turn in the lion's den, then we break orbit and haul back to Pedres and the *Twin Sister*."

The light show of induction tethers grew as the *Condor* slipped beneath the majority of the Gavisari defensive scans, spreading as tiny streaks became vast luminescent scars trailing across the planet's night side. Small deceleration maneuvers brought the *Condor*'s relative speed closer to that of the orbiting ships, and within a quarter hour Victoria could see the inductive tethers above as well as below.

"Conn sensors, we've got a contact coming up bearing two zero zero, high bearing rate. They'll pass close in about thirty seconds. Another at zero four zero, low bearing rate but we're picking up strong horizon space radiation, I'd put them both within three thousand kilometers."

Close enough for a kill shot if either one saw her, but the matte black hull of the *Condor* shrugged off light as well as radar. Victoria brought up the first contact on the main screen, the ship streaking across the sky as the white-hot cord extended behind it. The ship was massive, larger even than the light cruiser they'd encountered before.

"Conn sensors, class identifiers suggest a bulk freighter. Spectral shows gas venting from heavy damage along her starboard side. I'm surprised she's still in one piece. Not seeing any substantial armaments. Reactor is definitely suspended but the ship is active. I'm getting radio transmitter signals from inside. Horizon radiation is strongest along the tear."

Victoria glared at the twisted and fractured metal striping the length of the freighter. An invasion fleet? This ship was barely holding together. The freighter didn't even have a conventional FTL engine, it was built to transit from horizon jump to jump on sublight propulsion.

"Avery, what about the second ship? Visual can't make it out past the light of the tether. Are we getting any comms chatter from them?"

There was a pause as Avery adjusted his sweep. "Negative, Vick. If there's anyone over there, they're not broadcasting with enough energy to reach us, and we're closer to them than any of the neighbors. It's small though, civil transport is my best guess."

"Huian, adjust course three degrees right. Bring us to four and a quarter miles per second."

There was an almost imperceptible shudder as the *Condor* fired her lateral thrusters. Just enough to induce a trend that would swing the ship on their starboard forequarter directly ahead, and match the speed as close as Victoria dared. The planet below completely eclipsed the sun now, lighting flashing periodically in its thick roiling storms beneath the trailing creepers of spaceships in low orbit around Juna. But that cover wouldn't last forever. They'd seen a lot, but not enough to bring back to Pedres. They needed more before the Maeyar Fleet could decide on a course.

"Passing the end of the tether now, Ma'am," Huian said from the pilot's chair.

Victoria panned the main viewscreen down, switching from the fore optical sensors to the belly-mounted modules. The tether itself was putting off incredible amounts of heat and light. The heat that mounted as the slack line dragged across the magnetic field of Juna had nowhere to go in a vacuum, and was somewhere between a vacuum forge and a rocket engine test. What she wouldn't give for a length of whatever material it was made of that could stand up to that kind of heat without melting. The ship's computer had to dim the display to compensate for the brightness, and the feed actually became grainy as Huian pulled the *Condor* even closer. The privateers ate up the kilometers of cable in only a few minutes, revealing the ship towing the line to in fact be a smaller, unarmed ship. Apparently without power despite the tether, its heading tumbled slowly, drifting independent of its orbital trajectory.

"Conn sensors, that wreck looks completely cold. Nothing on EM, spectral, infrared, or visual to suggest activity or any type of propulsion."

Looking at a dead ship was no uncommon sight to the Vultures, despite the circumstance being more likely in a long-finished battle than surrounded by close to a thousand hostile xeno vessels. Being fair, maybe this was the result of a finished battle. Something brought these Gavisari here, and expansionism seemed less and less likely with every passing hour. That ship might hold answers, or the key to finding them.

Victoria thumbed the main circuit.

"Prepare to board."

CHAPTER 6
TETHER

AESOP COHEN TIGHTENED the strap affixing the X-87 carbine to his chest. The vacuum suit gloves offered more dexterity than the previous generation, and had ingenious little hooks for getting underneath fasteners. The interior of the helmet smelled like a swamp sprayed down with copious industrial cleaner. The algae cultures in the oxygen pack were fresh, but over time the pond scum and ammonia odor would fade away, leaving behind fresh, clean oxygen. An escape, actually, from the desiccated air of the *Condor*.

A countdown cycled on his retinal implants, approaching zero as the hiss of air being pumped from the forward airlock dulled and went silent. Nothing but a soft shell of flexible composites stood between Aesop and vacuum now.

"Charge boots, set up the pulley," he said. His suit's microphones picked up the subtle buzz of the electromagnetic boots of his squad translating through the floor, and he reached to the bulkhead, swiping down the controls to isolate the airlock from the ship's artificial gravity field. Down vanished. Held in place only by energized pads on the bottom of his feet, he slid the hatch open, bathing the airlock in the artificial light of the tether.

"Target acquired, Sarge."

"Hold, Vega. We got a ship twenty-two hundred meters away and two thousand meters of cable to get to it. Let's keep it in our pants, eh?" said Aesop. He leaned against the upper edge of the hatch, gazing down the length of the radiant tether to the drifting ship almost two miles away. The *Condor* was catching up slowly. From the hatch he could see the underside of the nose, stubby and dotted with sensor modules. One offered a view of himself, the video repeated on a screen in the airlock. There wasn't much room to move around, but the marines were used to the cramped quarters. Every bit as efficient as any IDF unit he'd worked with planetside.

"Nineteen-hundred meters," Vega reported. Aesop tapped twice on the top of the airlock hatch with a gloved fist, and with that his marine fired the harpoon, carbon fiber coiling behind as the projectile passed near Aesop's armpit. It took only a handful of seconds before he confirmed the hit with the sensor shack. The reel buzzed as it drew the line taut, then clicked with finality. He could imagine the sounds it made as he sensed its vibration through his feet and his glove, having heard it a half-hundred times at the practice range.

"Alright boys and girls, let's go for a ride."

"Poor Cohen, can't wait to get over there and find another alien to fall in love with."

Aesop grinned inside his suit, eyes still fixed on the Gavisar ship through the translucent shell of his faceplate. "Mags, you're on the general circuit. I can hear you."

"Oh, look at that," she said, tone making it clear she knew exactly what channel she'd been on. She clipped her rider onto the line and threw a one-fingered salute as the device shot her out of the airlock. Vega and Singh followed close behind, then it was his turn to leave the *Condor* and enter the night sky of Juna.

It was impossible for view screens to ever truly represent the view offered by raw space. The curve of the planet and the luminous weather below dominated his field of vision. No matter how many times he performed spacewalks, each one was like the very first time. Wonder, excitement, and just a little fear. There was just so much *space*. Being on a planet, seeing a dozen miles in any given direction? Aesop would take the magnificence of orbit any day. The peace, too. Sure, the xenos squabbled as bad as Earth ever had, but here in the moment none of that mattered. Not even the thousand-strong fleet in orbit and between Pedres and Juna. Of those thousand ships, the old lady had elected to put him on one, ballsy move, that.

As he gazed at the Gavisari ship growing closer by the minute he felt a telltale shudder in his rider. "What's the tension on the line at right now?" he asked. Numbers flashed across his retinal implants as Vega sent him the information. Aesop reviewed it with a cursory glance. "Dial it back twenty percent, yes?"

"We're starting to introduce our own heading deviation," said Maggie. Another rumble translated through the cable as she spoke.

"Vega, what did you latch us on to?"

"What? The hull? The hell should I know, I look like a xenotech egghead to you?"

The *Condor* was running a full communications blackout, and Aesop's eyes weren't good enough to see what was going on. With one hand still on the cable rider, he loosened the straps on his X-87 and swung the rifle over his head, pushing the optics to their max magnification just in time to watch a sensor array pierced by the harpoon tear partly away from the hull with a shower of sparks and venting gas. The compartment on the other side must have still had some atmospheric pressure.

"*Harah!* Vega, cut the line!" said Aesop. Ahead of him the Gavisari ship began to rotate, less than a kilometer away now. The torsion pulled on the induction tether, and the whole ensemble began to swing closer. His eyes widened, and he frantically clawed at the release for his lanyard. He cut it loose just as the brilliant line of xeno alloy contacted the carbon fiber cable with an arcing flash, completing the circuit with the ship through the harpoon still wedged in its hull. The carbon fiber parted instantly from the heat of the contact. The tension on the line snapped back, whip-cord ribbon disappearing as it sprang back and struck the outer hull of the *Condor*.

Mags hadn't managed to release her own lanyard in time, and caught between the point of impact and the Gavisari ship, the voltage arced directly to the metallic components of her suit. She was maybe a hundred me-ters ahead of him, tumbling like a limp rag in the vacuum. All four of them retained their momentum, but now the rapid ride toward the derelict vessel became a high-speed free fall through the chaotic coils of molten-bright cable. Light assaulted Aesop from all sides as he engaged the EVA thrusters built into his heavy vacuum suit.

He passed Singh, who was using her thrusters to decel-erate even as he built speed. Ahead of her, Vega was busy trying to stop a wild spin, the cabling having snagged his lanyard as it snapped.

Maggie Chambers had been first through the airlock, as she was any time she could get away with it. She'd put on more speed than she should have, and details on the derelict were becoming alarmingly visible as Aesop raced to her vacuum suit, grabbing on and arresting her spin as best he could.

"Cohen, six o'clock!" came Singh's voice over his radio. He twisted, eyes widening as a searing loop of tether spread before him. Behind it, he noticed the *Condor*, visible only by the starlight it blocked, pulling away from the deathtrap. It had no way to get to them, and they'd just painted a huge target on the rest of the crew's back with their fuckup. Cohen put his feet against Maggie's armor, pushing enough to send them in opposite directions. The cable undulated between them, close enough for static to crackle through the radio in his helmet. Then it was gone, and too late to do anything to slow himself or Mags as they crashed into the hull of the Gavisari ship. His face struck the inside of the composite helmet. Everything went dark.

"Huian, get us in there for a pickup."

Victoria's navigator shook her head. "It's no good, Vick, computer can't determine a safe course, the model is too complex."

Despite her words, Huian Wong increased the shuttered thrust, only to be rebuffed as the end of the tether swung dangerously close to the prow of the *Condor*. Victoria clenched her fists, resisting the urge to throw her coffee cup through the main view screen. Four personnel alone, exposed, and she couldn't pull them out. Every maneuver with the ion engines increased the chance of detection, but that hardly seemed to matter now that they were waving a glowing, ten-kilometer banner across the upper atmosphere.

Victoria found herself in the worst position a captain can. She had no choice.

"Pull out," she said. The sound of the conn hatch closing

brought her around to the silhouette of a broad figure in a black vacuum suit.

"Oh, I think my ears must be stuffed, Vick. I've got four marines down there."

Just what she needed. "Major, this isn't up for discussion."

"Oh, I agree."

Victoria cupped a hand to her forehead. "Get the fuck off my conn, Red. Sensors, talk to me."

The open microphone crackled with Avery's voice. Even he sounded shaken at having witnessed the catastrophic boarding failure. "Got two xenos decreasing bearing rate, Vick. Someone's coming in for a closer look."

"And someone else, namely us, has a powerful reason to weigh anchor and be elsewhere. Huian, gain some distance."

"Victoria," started Red, but she wheeled on him.

"You think I want to leave four of my Vultures on that goddamned piece of shit scrap heap? Christ, Red, I'd throw you out the airlock after them if I thought you could make it without that cord cutting you in half. Now unless you have anything worth anything to spit out, get. The fuck. Off. My. Conn."

"Vick, please."

The Major's voice was soft. Softer than she'd ever heard it. Red Calhoun had been a soft-spoken man as long as she'd known him. In Victoria's experience, men his size said more with quiet confidence and hushed looks than with words. Victoria exhaled, the anger leaving her body as expended as the breath she'd been holding after her tirade.

"Break emissions control. Find out who you have left down there, Red. Don't make me regret this."

He looked past her at the Gavisari ship growing smaller on the main view screen. His eyes met hers, defeated eyes, but some measure of relief glimmered there. He strode to the executive officer's station without another word, helmet tossed on the seat. The Major was as well versed in the systems aboard the *Condor* as any of her officers, and it didn't take long for his fingers to open the tightbeam channel to the Gavisari derelict.

"This is Major Calhoun. Emcon suspended. Sitrep, marines."

The only thing on the line was static for several seconds, but eventually a South American accented Kosso came through the receiver. "Major, this is Vega. Cohen and Chambers are down but breathing, requesting egress sir."

Victoria bit back a curse. "Negative, Vega. No way for us to get to you. We're on track to break orbit in 20 minutes and regroup with the carrier."

"Hang tight, lad, we'll swing back. Till then, you've a job to do. That's not changed."

"You shitting me Major? "

Victoria closed the channel, cutting off whatever reply the major had been about to give. They'd broadcast enough, already risking detection. "Huian," she said, "time until we hit our return window?"

"We'll be on the sunward side of the planet in fourteen minutes, Skipper."

"Make the necessary course adjustments now. We're too close to the planet, I don't want bounced light giving away our maneuvering," said Victoria. She locked eyes with Red Calhoun. "We're coming back for them, Red. I swear to high heaven we're coming back."

CHAPTER 7
FALSE FLAGS

C APTAIN BULLOCK SCROLLED down a list of damage reports on his retinal implants as he ignored the lieutenant junior grade barraging him with the Union Earth Naval regulations concerning accommodations for rescued sailors. In truth he registered as little of one as the other, and sought only a distraction from the fact he'd just witnessed a fellow captain and crew snuffed out with little effort by a xeno ship that shrugged off everything he put down the barrel.

They were too far from home, escorts that couldn't even defend themselves, let alone the freighter carrying silk and coffee, of all things, to Pedres. Like they were some fourteenth century caravel. His ship was ill-equipped to confront any of the countless xenos, despite being thrice the tonnage of a Privateer. If that Maeyar fleet hadn't shown up when they did, he'd be as dust as the *Clarke*. Most of her personnel managed to make it off, but Captain Hill had gone down with the ship and his entire command team. Bullock looked at his own, packed into the CIC at half a dozen stations. He wasn't fool enough to stick around this system. They'd jumped into a war, and damned if he wasn't going to jump right back out again regardless of the freighter's full holds, and hightail it to the system's core.

Two fighters kept pace with his ship, a dozen kilometers off his starboard, according to his thermal sensors and active Lidar. The two little wasps probably matched his firepower, if not his armor. And their presence wasn't exactly reassuring.

"Open a channel to the lead fighter," he said.

The main screen clicked, a portion being taken by the low resolution camera on board the fighter.

"Wing Officer Sothcide. Go ahead, Human Hudson."

Bullock didn't bother to correct him. "Wing Officer, we're adjusting course to make best time for the core. It's a little too unfriendly in this neighborhood for us."

The communication feed was muted for a few moments before the wing officer replied. "Negative, Human Hudson. All traffic out of the system is suspended on the grounds of informational security. Proceed to Pedres approach as planned and wait for further instructions."

"Wing officer, we're staring down the barrel of a thousand-ship gun here. I can't keep my people in a system under active attack."

"I understand your reservations, Human Hudson, but my orders are clear. There is to be no traffic out of Pedres until further notice."

Bullock watched on his sensors repeater as one of the fighters crept ahead of the other and climbed in the azimuthal plane. It was a subtle movement, but the two craft were improving their ranging solution on the *Hudson River*. Not for the first time, he felt the cold dampness of his uniform collar against the back of his neck. The maneuver wasn't a threat, per se, but it was certainly less than a friendly gesture. At their current acceleration the formation was six hours from Pedres, or nine from the closest calculated jump point. But he also had the freighter to worry about. The freighter had no Alcubierre drive. It was too big. Though size didn't seem to be a problem for the xenos, humans were still limited by mass when it came to executing a horizon jump. Bullock terminated the communication, weighing his options.

"Skipper, we're picking up active targeting radiation," The words cut through his thoughts as his head snapped to the tactical officer's station. "Whose?"

The young officer looked at him, her eyes wide. "It's a Privateer profile, sir."

"Missile fire, missile fire! Port side, zero bearing rate!"

Captain Bullock got to his feet. "Battle stations!" he roared, "Point defense, target those missiles, get me a solution on the source!"

"Point defenses inactive, Captain. IFF paints missiles as friendly, I don't have time to override. Projected time to impact, eight seconds! *Seven, six,*"

"Evasive program," yelled Bullock, knowing that inertia would never let him move the bulky destroyer fast enough to evade the missiles. Had Victoria fired on him?

"Two, one!"

No explosion came. A half dozen missiles streaked past his ship, lancing out after the escort fighters.

"Incoming communication, textual only, human IFF code."

As the fighters reacted to the volley of missiles, words scrolled across the main view screen. *HUDSON RIVER – MAEYAR AMBUSH IMMINENT - MAKE BEST TIME TO JUMP - TIME NOW*

"Don't have to tell me twice," said Bullock. Helm, make the course adjustments to the nearest jump."

The view screen showed the icy contrails of the missiles as they streaked toward the fighters, and the warnings as the fighters fired back. A shriek of tearing hull pierced his ears as the lasers carved a channel through his starboard ablative armor. Not strong enough to penetrate at their max range without a cohesive saturation on a single spot, they still wiped out a half-dozen sensor modules, leaving a gap in his visual feed. He swore.

"Skipper, the secondary hit the *Yakima*. She's venting atmosphere."

The majority of the freighter was kept in vacuum during transit, outside the pressure hull of the inner compartments. If they struck atmo then the crew was almost certainly dead and the cargo boat dead in the water.

"What about those missiles?"

The tactical officer regarded her screen. "Impact on the secondary, no engine profile, no active radiation. The primary . . . Jesus, he just took out all three missiles. He's full burn sir, headed back to the picket fleet."

"Can we take him out?"

"Negative sir, our missiles can't catch up with a Maeyar fighter at full acceleration and a head start."

Bullock swiped the view screen displaying the *Yakima* to his primary repeater. At max magnification he could see the plumes of frozen atmosphere petering off as pressure in the inner hull equalized with the vacuum of space. The freighter had no hardening against directed energy weapons, the fighter had cut her apart like swiss cheese. There was no one left to escort. He'd failed his mission.

"Prep the Alcubierre, let's get out of here before the Wing Officer tells his friends what just happened." *Victoria, what did you do?*

The *Condor's* circuit carried it away from the boarded

Gavisari vessel and into the upper atmosphere where Victoria ordered her pilot to break orbit. Several hours of slow flight carried the Vultures far enough from the sensors of the Gavisari to risk acceleration, and from there Victoria watched her ship eat up the kilometers of space on the way to the rendezvous point, watching Juna shrink in the rear view screen. Long range passive sensors gave away the presence of a multitude of ships in the theater, the majority of the fleet in Pedres had moved to the staging point inside the last planet's orbit. By the time Victoria reached a distance she felt comfortable risking communications, the sensor team already identified upwards of fifty contacts at a destroyer profile or larger.

"Go ahead and growl up the Wing Commander," said Victoria, "Fleet Ops is going to want to act on what we saw. Guarantee they'll want to make a move when they find out half of those ships are without power."

"Even so, they can't field enough ships here without leaving Maeyar exposed. They're terribly outnumbered, Vick." said Huian.

"So are we." Victoria held up a hand to halt Huian's response as the communication channel connected. "Wing Commander Jalith, Captain Marin identifying, activating IFF transponder now."

Almost as soon as the transponder revealed their position, sensors warnings lit her command repeater with active radiation signatures as the Maeyar active sensor suites bathed the *Condor* with ranging and targeting radar.

"Christ, what a welcome," Victoria muttered, hopefully too low for the transmitter to pick up.

"*Condor*, do not deviate from present course. Reverse acceleration and stand down all active weapon systems. Prepare to dock. The *Twin Sister* will receive a delegation consisting of your captain and two additional personnel."

Victoria's retinal implants flashed with a message from the sensor shack. *Twin Sister scrambling fighters.* The Maeyar were pinning them in. Heat began to rise in her blood, and she fought back the urge to turn tail and disappear into the dark of space. The velocity game was not on their side, the fighters would overtake them before ever they reversed their momentum away from the battlegroup.

"Message received, *Twin Sister,* understand all. Reversing acceleration."

The channel closed from the other end and Victoria let her breath out. If they wanted her to dock then the Maeyar weren't on the verge of blowing her ship out of the stars. That cleared her for the next few minutes at least, but not much beyond that. She thumbed the general circuit.

"Attention all hands, this is the captain. Rig for docking. The XO has the ship."

Aesop Cohen opened his eyes, and almost immediately regretted the decision. The flashing glare of a nearby tungsten welding kit felt like needles jamming the front of his brain, but try as he might to fight it, the unfortunate reality of his surroundings continued to become more and more clear. Front and center was a pallid xeno face. As soon as the lizard part of his brain caught up with his vision center, panic seized him, and had him straining against a lanyard secured to the bulkhead before his rationality kicked in and told him the xeno was dead.

"Bout time you came round, Cohen."

A vacuum suit floated behind the lifeless alien, pushing it along the corridor. The voice in his helmet belonged to Singh. "Sorry about him. We moved most of them to the forecastle, but more keep floating out of hiding," she said as she unhooked his lanyard. His retinal implants received an alert that the woman was checking his vitals through the suit computer, and he instinctively looked to check on Maggie Chambers.

"Mags," he said, stomach dropping as his computer returned no vitals from her suit.

"She's fine, aside from a broken arm and some electrical burns. That tether fried all her radio gear, but your little stunt probably saved her life."

"Not that she'd ever admit it," said Aesop, looking around for the first time. The Gavisari still loomed, assumedly disfigured from the exposure to vacuum. An array of little horns ringed its round face like a sunflower, though the similarities to any Earth flora or fauna ended there. For one, the face seemed to be in the middle of its chest, with three fluted legs splayed out evenly around its core. Standing up on all three it probably could have stretched to ten or more feet high, explaining the ample leg room in the ship. Not much was known about the Gavisari, other than that they were oxygen tolerant, fiercely territorial, and non-expansionist, which meant the Union Earth had little cause to come in contact with them.

"Not that you'd ever ask her to," said Singh, following his gaze with her own opaque faceplate. Her oxygen cultures got cooked too, we've been bleeding our excess to her. And yours. But you'll need more now you're awake. We're going to be getting air-thin before—before too long."

Before the *Condor* came back. If it came back. "How many data bursts have we missed?"

"Three," said Singh. Their mission had been to ransack the onboard computers, then patch into the communication hub and report on activity at Juna. Every time the derelict came into line-of-sight with the *Condor* the marines would send an encrypted databurst, a highly directional packet of radio waves containing all gathered intel compressed into a half-second transmission. It was their only means of reminding the *Condor* that someone was still alive out here. "We've got the dish in place, but no one wants to be the one to try and integrate it with the ship's power."

Aesop nodded. Marines were excellent at slinging lead down range, but not so much at xenotechnology. "Smart. Last thing we need is Vega frying the transmitter. Do we at least know where their power bus is?"

Singh led the way through the inner compartments of the ship to the tether connection, where a soft hum began to translate through his gloves and boots where he contacted the textured tunnel walls. Before long they emerged into a low-ceilinged chamber snaked with various color cables and paneling. Vega was prying the lid off some sort of junction box when he noticed Cohen floating behind.

"'Oy, Cohen. You made it, looks like I owe Singh a beer."

"You bet against me?"

Vega shrugged. "I like beer. Help me out here, I think I found the artificial gravity."

"You think you found the artificial gravity in a sealed compartment marked secondary sublight alignment calibrator?"

Vega looked back at the panel, seemingly seeing the Kossovoldt standard scripting for the first time. Admittedly it was subtle, either faded or just a hair off the background color of the bulkhead and upside-down to his perspective. Maybe it was meant to be read by touch, or in a different spectrum of light. He just didn't know enough about the Gavisari. As he looked, Aesop could see similar markings on a variety of equipment crowding the small ship's engine room.

Instead of joining Vega, Aesop looked around until he spotted a small monitor embedded in the bulkhead. By some miracle it was receiving power from the magnetic tether, and before long Aesop had gained access. Xeno computers were so painfully primitive. A diagnostics page showing almost total failure of all ship's systems greeted him, and an automatic events log that detailed the jump into Pedres and the last moments of what he learned was called the *Blossom*. Not a warship at all, but a diplomatic envoy. Why bring a ship for missions of peace along on an invasion?

"Come on Cohen, can you get the gravity back on? We've been floating for hours, it's making me want to hurl."

"I don't think there is any gravity, at least not the way we're used to. I think they just have an acceleration dampening field, but they keep the ship in microgravity. Look how everything is designed to be in arm's reach for them. I bet they don't even have an up or down. But I do see a bus that the tether power is being routed to. We can hook the dish up to that."

Singh floated nearby, looking over his shoulder. "Does it say what did all this damage? We checked over the ship and there's at least a dozen compartments open to space."

Cohen shook his head. "This is just an engineering logger. We're not going to find any intel until we crack into whatever fleet broadcast codec they're running to coordinate the ships in orbit. It looks like they didn't have the voltage to power the array and the life support at the same time."

"What must that have been like?" asked Singh, "To choose between living a few more desperate minutes or to say goodbye to everyone you ever knew?"

"Who cares?" asked Vega, shrugging. "Neither helped them in the end. The pressure hull failed and those three-legged bastards don't do any better in vacuum than we do."

Despite Vega's callous remarks, Aesop stopped for a moment to reflect on it. He'd had the misfortune of losing two ships already, one to hostile xenos and one abandoned due to onboard fire. What he would have traded for a few minutes to say goodbye was not a short list.

"Let's get the power hooked up. I don't want to miss the next transmission window."

CHAPTER 8
A CHANGE OF HANDS

S OTHCIDE DID NOT ENJOY being away from Jalith and the *Twin Sister*. The Maeyar fleet granted her dispensation according to her rank of Wing Commander, but as a wing officer he was granted no such leeway and his loyalty had been called into question by the human vessel's attack on his fighter. His heart increased in flow as he recalled the wash of targeting radar painting his hull and the missile alarms painting the interior of his fighter in flashing ultraviolent tones.

"There is little cause to be nervous, Wing Officer."

The voice belonged to *Banner's* second wing lieutenant, records docket tucked beneath the arm of his flight suit. Now aboard the *Banner*, Sothcide would have to account for Victoria Marin before the Maeyar Fleet Operations commanders. And Victoria herself was being brought aboard. He had a few questions for her as well, such as why his wingman was scattered across the Oort Cloud by her comrade.

"I would say over a thousand Gavisar ships give plenty cause to be nervous." said Sothcide.

The lieutenant missed a step. "Ah, um, yes sir," he said. Only shy of two hundred Maeyar Warships and their assorted logistical and support craft had mustered in Pedres in response to the staging outside Juna. Fewer would leave the homeworld undefended. Outnumbered five to one, most of those had been pulled back to defend the planet itself. Even for the fleet near the skirmish line, attitudes seemed more of disbelief, as though the number of invading vessels was so high that it could not possibly be true. Desperation would have been more appropriate, but ever optimists were the Maeyar.

The corridor had been built with a vaulted arch reminiscent of Southern styles, the soft luxurious sweeps informative of their owner's station. The fleet commanders rose so from families just as soft and filled with luxury. Beyond the metal archways the ship widened, and Sothcide was led through a hatch to a room wherein a half-dozen Maeyar stood, three fleet commanders and their spouses. At their head was Senior Wing Admiral Yadus, also a former interceptor pilot long since risen to command the fleet at Pedres. Now he directed fleet movements from the *Banner*, his wife responding to runners while he reviewed information on an advanced screen built into his podium. The device could be controlled by touch, using a series of lasers in a grid array projected over the glass. Yadus looked up briefly and gave him a respectful nod as he came in, rocket jockey to jockey. Theirs was an elite club. Yadus' first duty was to the Maeyar fleet though, and his professional affectations would grant no leeway if his perception of the human betrayal extended to the *Condor* and her captain. The cockpit of an interceptor tended to hammer out the weak, and hardened onyx skin around the Senior Commander's features and fingers reflected a face used to grimace and a tight grip on the flight controls.

"Wing Officer Sothcide, enter and attend. You stand witness to a wartime betrayal and offensive action upon

Maeyar Fleet vessels by non-Maeyar military. Missiles from the Union Earth *Hudson River* tracked and destroyed a fellow squadron fighter craft. Is this an accurate recounting of the events?" asked Wing Commander Arda, a subtle breach of protocol from the mistress of the Third Battlegroup. Her silk uniform was crisp and glittered subtly as she shifted, reflecting in her eye as she glanced briefly at the hatch.

Sothcide placed his helmet on the desk before the small metal chair. "The stars of my night sky asks after your health, Wing Mistress."

"You may tell Jalith that I am fine, Wing Officer. Pl-"

"She will be overjoyed to hear it. She often speaks of your time at the command school together."

"Answer the question, Wing Officer," said Arda curtly. Before he could reply, the hatch opened and in sauntered Victoria Marin, captain of the Union Earth *Condor*. Her hip was empty of the heavy human slug-thrower she favored on the occasions he'd seen her away from her ship. At her side was a pair of security officers with handheld lasers to keep her in line, though both had tight eye motions that belayed their nerves. Though primitive their warships might have been, the reputation for deadliness the Privateer warriors had garnered was well in mind. Humans captured crews as often as ships.

The *Banner*'s second lieutenant leaned over. "The Fleet Wing Admiral brought the humans aboard? I hope he tightened the bolts on the laser arrays first."

"Captain Marin," said Yadus, not even lifting his eye from the display. "Please join us. I am given to understand that your culture also partakes in the practice of marriage. Is your husband well?"

Victoria scratched at the short stubble on the back of

her neck. "I never quite made it that far," she said. This caused some disturbance among the assembled captains and first officers, though Sothcide stepped in on her behalf.

"Humans have a phase that translates in Kossovoldt to 'married to the job' to describe those who eschew personal bonds in favor of advancing their field. I heard it used aboard the *Condor* to describe Captain Marin during my time aboard her vessel."

"Surely she could find a suitable male within her command structure," said Wing Commander Vehl, who thus far had been content to only open her ears. Her husband was looking over reports beside her, soft and light of skin. He too had a silk uniform. How quickly the Maeyar assimilated the textile, though the display of a full uniform was a statement of nearly obscene wealth. *These* were the defenders of Pedres?

"In fact," said Victoria, "Regulations strictly prohibit interpersonal relationships within a chain of command. Union Earth believes it creates unequal power dynamics and incentivizes special treatment of subordinates."

There was a pause. Vehl's eye spun slowly in its socket. "Yes? And?"

"We are straying from the subject at hand," Arda interjected, cleaving her hand through the air. "Wing officer, your report."

Victoria had taken a far-away look in her eyes that he'd noticed of the humans on more than one occasion when he cast her a sidelong glance, so he turned back to Arda and began. "It's true that I and my wingmate were fired upon by missiles along a bearing similar to that of the *Hudson River*, whereupon we engaged the human vessels before being forced to retreat. The *Hudson River* then engaged a faster-than-light engine and escaped to the interior of the

Pedres System."

Arda leaned forward in her chair. "Please clarify, Wing Officer. Was it a bearing similar to the *Hudson River* or was it the *Hudson River?*"

"Impossible to say, Ma'am, though spectral analysis does suggest aluminum oxide in the exhaust trails consistent with observed human weaponry," said Sothcide.

"So you agree that the trader and its escort fired upon you."

Sothcide's eye muscles constricted, and he let more frustration than he intended slip into his tone. "As I said, it is only evident that *someone—*"

"Thank you for your recounting, Wing Officer."

Victoria looked surprisingly nonplussed in her metal chair. Those soft pink faces typically showed so much foreign emotion, but her expression was as flat and level as he'd ever seen. "The *Hudson River*'s magazines were empty following the battle, Wing Commander. I'm forwarding the communication recording to your staff now. Unless Bullock managed to grow a few missiles between here and Pedres," she said, "Ones with enough acceleration to actually catch one of your interceptors." Her flippant tone suggested that she was used to explaining simple concepts to superior officers, probably on more than one occasion. "But if what you're saying is true, you murdered over a dozen crew on that freighter while I was off pledging humanity's support behind your war by dipping into Juna's upper atmosphere for intel."

Arda sputtered, her black eye focusing on Victoria. "As though your communication could not be doctored or faked. Need I remind you that your people opened fire without provocation?"

"Illegal detention isn't fucking provocation?" Victoria

interrupted. "Because on Earth we fight wars over that."

"Illegal according to whom? Mayar Fleet Operations is in command of this system's territory, and they ordered your people to stand down. You submit that the *Hudson River's* weapon banks were empty. But a dead pilot remains, and if a Union Earth Navy missile could not have done it, what did? Perhaps a Privateer variant? We cannot account for your whereabouts on your alleged intelligence gathering."

"Alleged?" asked Victoria. "Oh I was there alright, close enough to throw a god damned rock at a Gavisar envoy shuttle. But I didn't bring any rocks, so I had to settle for a squad of marines and some comms equipment. Turns out most of those incoming ships are beat all to hell. Something chased them out of Gavisar. Hell, nine in ten aren't even warships."

"The space walkers have been busy, Arda," mused Vehl. Her snout rested on her hand as she gave the other fleet commander a bored wave. "Perhaps your righteous indignation is misplaced."

Sothcide braced himself as he watched the anger build tension in Wing Commander Arda's shoulder muscles as the diaphanous membranes framing her face grew darker.

"Be that as it may," she snarled, "It still stands that the human fleet fired upon our ships of war, and here before us stands a human military captain. Until redress can be made, it is only appropriate that we hold her for questioning until after we defend Pedres."

Sothcide stood abruptly, in part before he realizing he had done so. Flying full burn at enemy battleships had never made him as nervous as standing before a panel of commanders, and now he had the attention of three of them.

"Pardon the interruption, Wing Commander, but it

appears you have been misinformed as to the nature of the Privateers. They are not part of the human military chain of command and Victoria holds no formal military rank. She is a civilian explorer granted certain privileges often extended to military vessels. Victoria is here at my express request, and by extension, Wing Commander Jalith's. If the *Condor* is to be considered a military asset, for all intents and purposes it is a *Maeyar* military asset, not a human one, and under the envelope of the *Twin Sister*. Any and all disciplinary action rests in the will of my sun and sky."

He glanced at Victoria, whose two eyes were both wide as they flitted between him and Arda.

"He has you there, Arda," said the Wing Admiral. Yadus lifted his gaze from the screen long enough to peer at Sothcide. "I don't know how much you've read up on the humans, but they're an odd cluster. The wing officer is technically correct; all disciplinary action should fall to my cousin."

Sothcide let out a breath. "Thank you sir," he said.

"Don't thank me yet. I agree with Arda's assessment. Beyond any doubt, and for whatever reason they held at the time, human warships bore arms against us in time of war and proceeded to flee the system, an action which by any metric is unacceptable. Now I don't necessarily believe them to be Gavisar spies, but this is not the action of an ally."

"Captain Marin, as it happens, I too believe something happened at Gavisar to drive the fleet here. And if whoever or whatever it was hurt them as badly as you say then time is now critical and we must push the attack to slow their advance while we shore up the defenses at Pedres. My strategists are analyzing the imagery you provided and we will determine the best way to execute an offensive."

Victoria stood, nodding her head. "If I could just gain access to the *Yakima*'s logs I could find out what really happened aboard those two ships."

"More space walker lies," said Arda, but a hand from Yadus stilled her.

"Perhaps," offered the admiral, "You can stop on your way to meet with the Malagath envoy. She asked for you by name. Well, by ship, if I am to be truthful."

The color drained from Victoria's face all at once, a vestigial camouflage mechanism. Sothcide had only ever seen it after poker bluffs were exposed.

"Come again?" she said.

The weathered frills on the side of the admiral's face fluttered with mirth. "Part of why I believe the Gavisar are not here willingly is that a Malagath delegation en route to Maeyar have decided to investigate an anomaly detected by their interstellar sensors. They are preparing to jump to Gavisar in a few hours' time, and as a Maeyar fleet asset, you will be joining them. I am sending the *Twin Sister* to join the defenses at Pedres, and you will accompany Jalith."

For once, the smart-mouthed human seemed to be at a loss for words. Sothcide could not blame her, to gain the attention of the Malagath was to invite death. He had not even been aware they were in the system, likely having jumped past the conflict all the way to Pedres. When she finally mustered enough of her senses, she offered a weak protestation. "Hold on now, this isn't what I signed up for when I agreed to come along."

Eru Vehl trilled a high note of laughter through her proboscis. "You came to perform reconnaissance, did you not, Captain Marin? It would seem to me that this is exactly what you signed up for. May the swift wind of the north be at your wings."

Yadus Turned to Sothcide. "You'll not be returning to Pedres just yet. Wing Commander Vehl's squadrons took substantial hits during the first wave of the invasion, and she needs an experienced wing officer leading her fighters for this counteroffensive. I'm temporarily reassigning you to the *Starscream*."

Victoria covered a cough beside him that sounded suspiciously like human laughter. "Wing Admiral, with all due respect—"

"All respect due to me would be not questioning my orders, Wing Officer. I know your place is with the *Twin Sister*. Once we cripple the key Gavisar ships you can rejoin her. As for you, Captain Marin," he said, his eye swiveling to the human. He shut down the monitor in his station and leaned back. "I know you're not here out of an altruistic desire to help the Maeyar, nor as a special favor to a friend. You're looking to solidify a formal defense pact. Wherever your planets are, it's safe to say you think we'd make strategically relevant partners, yes? Having fired on those interceptors sets that goal back, but do this for me and my weight will be behind your alliance."

Sothcide had been around humans long enough to recognize her scowl. But she would have to accept. She had no choice, the alternative was losing her ship and being forced to sit out the conflict entirely. And Victoria would never abandon the *Condor*. Humans proved a stubborn sort.

"If I may," he said, "I would like to escort Captain Marin back to the *Condor*."

"As you wish, but report to me aboard the *Starscream* within the hour. I think we're settled here, yes?" said Vehl.

Arda lifted her eye in submission. "It appears we are. But know this, Human Victoria: if I smell one whiff of treachery, I'll have your ship scrapped for parts and see you resigned to the void for the life of my pilot."

Before the human could say something flippant, Sothcide ushered her through the hatch and away from the fleet commanders. After a brief discussion with her security escorts he steered her back toward her ship with a light touch on her shoulder. Her boots could have left prints in the metal composite decking for how hard she stomped back to the docking facilities of the *Banner*, but by the time she approached the airlock tunnels she deflated somewhat.

"I'm sorry I got you wrapped up in this, Southside. That you were fired on, and that you lost a wingman."

He took his hand from her shoulder. For humans, interpersonal contact seemed a necessity to forming bonds, though it still made him uncomfortable.

"I lost two more when we first arrived, and perhaps would have been more were it not for your targeting data and the *Hudson River*'s final volley. This is not to marginalize the loss of Dat Un, but such an event draws the attention away from the full cost of this invasion. I do not think Wing Commander Arda wants to face the true cost. It's easier to fixate on a problem for which you can see a solution, even if it is not where your attention should be."

"You're going to be part of the counteroffensive." said Victoria.

Sothcide flourished his flight helmet. "I am, and for the first time in a long while, it will be someone other than my wife's voice in my radio."

Victoria nodded, then leaned in. "Be careful. I won't know for sure until I get a look at the Yakima's logs, but I think Jones may have piggybacked on our horizon jump. I maybe caught a whiff of him off that first active sweep Jalith did, but haven't seen sign of him since."

Sothcide thought back to his meeting with the man,

and to his encounter with the *Hudson River*. "When the missiles were launched, my bearing to the point of origination did not match my firing solution to the *Hudson River*. It was offset by a few degrees, though for the sensors of my wingmate it was correct. At first I dismissed it, but if the measurements were accurate then the missiles could have come from almost a hundred kilometers beyond your destroyer."

"He's dangerous, Southside. I don't know what his game here is, but you can bet it doesn't line up with ours. He's a prat, but he's the cold kind of vicious that leaves holes in your ships. Not all Privateers are interested in waiting for ships to be disabled."

"That is why I chose you instead, Human Victoria. Fly safe, and may your safe return mark the day of our victory."

Victoria extended a hand to him, a gesture he'd experienced several times aboard the *Condor*. He extended his own, slender fingers wrapping her comparatively small hand. "Good luck out there. If you can, make contact with my marines, they may be an asset during the counteroffensive."

Sothcide bowed his head. "I will try. What frequency are they broadcasting on?"

A corner of Victoria's mouth dropped, revealing white grit teeth. Ghastly things, teeth. He never understood how so many species were able to talk around a mouthful of them. "They haven't actually begun broadcasting yet. But I'm mostly sure they're still alive."

Sothcide blanched. "I, I see."

"Don't tell Arda," said Victoria, winking as she ducked through the docking ring and into the airlock.

CHAPTER 9
IN MOTION

"IS IT JUST ME OR ARE THE storms getting worse?"

Aesop looked up from mangled communications dish to Vega and Maggie floating near a small breach in the pressure hull of the ship. He'd seen IDF soldiers get shot exposing less surface area, but he stilled his nerves and looked past the marines.

"It's not just you. There're fewer tethered ships below us. Less light pollution so you're better able to see the surface storms."

"So why are there less ships below us?" asked Vega.

"I think we'd better get those damn communications patched through. How's it going up there, Singh?"

There was no answer, just soft static in his radio. Aesop tried again, looking at the deck above him. "Singh? Report, how's that comm array looking?"

Vega's hand shifted to his rifle as he glanced at the bottom of the deck above them. Unease had Aesop's hair on end where it wasn't flattened by the vacuum suit. A hand signal to Mags told her to stay put, and he pushed off the bulkhead, loosening the strap on his own X-87 carbine as he caught the lip of the hatch. Firing an assault rifle in microgravity resulted in interesting things happening to the trajectory of the shooter, even with the rifles designed for employment in space.

The chamber above was a mess of twisted cables and panels, dark screens and reams of translucent filament on spindles that would have printed sensor data. Everything was built into what he would have considered the floor and ceiling, creating the illusion of a canyon between high walls of equipment. Light from his helmet dispelled the shadows cast by dozens of tiny holes in the hull of the ship. Weapons fire had perforated the starboard side, and whatever had done it was spiking his suit's radiological sensor. Infrared wasn't helpful either, everything on the ship had cooled to a uniform temperature.

"Vega, cover me."

Two quick keys of the radio acknowledged and confirmed the order. Vega could be an arrogant condescending ass, but Aesop trusted no one to watch his back better than the Brazilian. With his rifle at the ready, Aesop floated forward to the plastic cloth separating the sensor shack from what remained of the radio room. It was further up the forecastle of the ship, and had avoided most of the damage concentrated near the stern. At least until their harpoon had pried it open like a tin can, exposing it to the vacuum of space. A wedge of the equipment packing the room was illuminated periodically by the bright flashes of storms below, and Aesop slowly swept his rifle across the rest. His back was tight, and sweat beaded on his upper lip as he revealed consoles of dead bulbs and magnetic tape deck storage where the *Condor* would have advanced computers. Some aspects of xenotechnology were incredibly complex, like power generation and chemical manipulation. But when it came to computers, it was better to look hundreds of years into the past to find their human equivalent.

It was in front of one of these banks that his beam swept

over the small frame of Singh, floating cross-legged and inverted to his perception. He lowered his rifle, releasing a breath. The panel in front of her was lighted, and black rubber human cables snaked among the silvery blue alloyed conduits of Gavisari design. A cord ran from Singh's suitboard computer to a patch panel, and then into the radio bank through means of soldered connections.

"Hold fast Vega, she's just got her pants down."

There was pressure behind him, and then the uncomfortable abrasion of two armored vacuum suits contacting as Vega forced his way in for a look. "Huh," he said, spotting her. "Hey, ask her if they can pick up the telecasts."

"At this distance? I think the earliest television broadcasts might have had time to reach us," said Aesop. Of course, the signals would have long since attenuated.

Aesop pushed Vega back and used the momentum to slide close to Singh, careful not to collide and potentially wreck her delicate work. He couldn't see through the opaque black shell of her helmet, but his lights flashing across it woke her from whatever reverie she'd found herself wrapped up in. She started, legs coming unraveled as her hand went to her hip for her sidearm before she relaxed and retuned her radio. Aesop could hear background chatter in Kossovoldt as she reconnected her squad radio channel. It was a much deeper and sibilant version of the language than he was used to hearing from his fellow crewmates. Humans had adopted it as the official Union Earth language after it became clear that so much of the Orion Spur used it. Aesop shared no human language with Singh, and only broken English with Vega. Maggie at least spoke some Spanish, and could understand a little of Vega's Portuguese by relation. Beyond that her only other language was English, like Captain Marin. The only language unifying the entire crew of the *Condor* was Kossovoldt.

"Sorry Sarge, I've been listening to some of their re-corded fleet broadcasts while I try and get the live coms working, but no luck there. The *Blessing* lost primary re-actor power shortly after jumping to Pedres and the auto-matic recorders shut off."

Aesop shined some light on her work, identifying a few potential issues with the wiring, which he pointed out. "The *Blessing*?" he asked.

"That's what we're on. It's not a diplomatic envoy, it's a ship for their priest caste. A lot of the recordings I've lis-tened to make reference to something they call the 'Great Exodus', but doesn't say what that is, only that it's arrived because the Old Ones have come back to reclaim the plan-et they loaned to the Gavisari, and that the 'Children of Gavisar' have begun it."

"A xeno Armageddon prophecy," said Aesop. "Not many species make it interstellar with religious dogma intact."

"'Cept us," Vega reminded him. Aesop waved him off and he left to give Mags the all-clear.

"Cohen, for all we know, the Gavisari here around this planet? They may be the only ones of their kind left. Any-where. Their whole surviving species might be packed into these thousand ships."

Which meant that the old lady signed them up for a genocide at the hands of the Maeyar. But even a hundred warships with orbital superiority was enough to scour Pedres clean of the Maeyar, and most of Gavisar's civil-ian ships could not make another horizon jump in such a damaged state. Hell, plenty enough of them couldn't make it to the star under their own power. Not only were most of them too damaged to risk engaging any kind of compression-based faster than light engines, several hundred were hauling around reactors too damaged to create electricity, and a few were probably leaking enough radioactive particles to slowly poison whatever survivors were on board.

But if this was the entire surviving population of the Gavisar homeworld, the whole of their planetary defense armada was here. And the non-expansionist society would have held a tight grip on their homeworld with a strong home fleet. What could have chased them off so easily? And why come *here*? Was it the only oxygenated planet within their horizon range? The local cluster of stars was fairly loose as far as horizon lanes went, only a few routes in and out. The *Condor* had needed help to make it in a single jump, and even the technique to accomplish such a jump was a treasure. The Gavisari had more highly developed interstellar plotting and equipment, but not by all that much.

"The captain may not know what she's up against here. Keep listening, Singh. But I want active comms to be your main priority. If there's a major fleet movement going on I want to know why."

All he had to do was fix the broadcast array while there was still someone left to hear his report.

"We're coming up on the remains of your *Yakima*, Captain Marin," said Jalith. Victoria winced.

Your Yakima. The message was clear, Jalith was separating the *Condor* from her command and lumping her in with the rest of the Union Earth fleet. Her reputation took a huge hit to shield Victoria the way she had, but the unofficial punishment would be ostracism from the Maeyar captain's battlegroup once she left to meet with the Malagath.

"Acknowledged, *Twin Sister.* We'll only need a few minutes." The Maeyar commander cut the transmission, and Victoria raised her voice to be heard over the open microphone. "Avery, see if the Yakima has auxiliary power for a remote protocol or if we're going to have to board her."

"Way ahead of you, Vick. Remote challenge was accepted and we're transferring the *Yakima's* logs now."

Victoria scanned the progress on one of her repeater screens. She opened a file at random to see an inventory manifest of the holds. Silk, coffee, preserved citrus fruits, and vegetables. It could have been the inventory list off a sloop coming home from the Indies. Union Earth men and women had died for *this?* Two ships lost in as many days, one to hostile xenos and another to friendlies. Victoria eyed her pilot, who had been unusually quiet since the initial skirmish. The *Hudson River's* sister ship had been the *Clarke,* Huian's original intended billet before Tech Div's director, Sampson, had put her on the *Condor* as leverage against the girl's mother. Had she not elected to remain aboard the *Condor,* there was a good chance she would have been on the control deck when those Gavisar missiles broke through the *Clarke's* defenses. Control was deep in the heart of a ship, away from the escape pods that carried crew away from a total loss. Many of the men aboard made it off the ship and had been picked up by Bullock and the *Hudson River,* but the pilots and captain? Unlikely.

"Hard, isn't it?" said Victoria.

Her pilot jumped a little, her eyes tearing away from the main view screen where the *Yakima* had been enlarged enough to see the rent metal where the Maeyar lasers had carved open her hull and exposed the crew to vacuum. A human could survive in vacuum for a few moments. Victoria managed it, and counted it a worse experience than waking up with a hangover, a migraine, and a jealous wife trying to cave in what was left of her head over forgotten carnal transgressions from the previous night. It had taken her weeks to fully recover. The crew of the *Yakima* never would.

"We're not ready for this, ma'am," said Huian. "How can we survive in this universe when we're not strong enough to play by their rules? Sometimes, sometimes it's easy to forget. Aboard the *Condor*. It's easy to forget just how savage and uncaring and *unfair* the odds are. And then you look at the rest of humanity, and our ships, and our weapons. And you realize that we don't have the advantages they have, and it kills us."

Huian upped the acceleration again to rejoin the battle-group. "But it's why we're out here. Why *they* were out here so far from Earth with nothing between them and the emptiness of space but a thin frame of composite hull and the trust that maybe these xenos wouldn't strip that protection away for some slight."

And now they were depending on the charity of the selfsame xenos. It maybe worked to some advantage that the Maeyar thought they were handing her over to death at the hands of the Malagath. Still, Sothcide and to some degree Jalith had stuck their strange membranous necks out for her. Whether it was out of a sense of honor or loyalty, as the two were very different things, she could not say and would not ask. Best Victoria set her mind to the task ahead. The Malagath and Gavisar awaited.

Sothcide inspected the *Starscream*'s launch mechanisms for her fighters. Six cylindrical magnetic rail systems with the fighters stacked inside ready to be rotated into position and launched at speeds that pushed the limits of their inertial dampeners. As flippant as Vehl outwardly appeared, the pristine condition of the flight deck revealed her competency as a commander and her husband's diligence as her chief maintenance engineer. Every contact was greased or polished, every electrical connection secure, and each magnetic coil buffed of the inevitable burn scuffs from the intense heat the system generated. The *Starscream* could launch a full squadron of fighters every four seconds, emptying her total complement of fifty-two interceptors and bombers in just under a minute. The *Twin Sister* had a larger complement, but could not match the speed of deployment.

"Call to bearing!"

Sothcide wasn't sure who shouted the order, but every crewmate and officer on the flight deck snapped straight as an arrow, right hand across belly and left across the small of the back in the traditional salute. Wing Commander Vehl Ku had entered the deck through the magnetic lift as it hummed gently down to seal with the gravity plating beneath. She had switched her formal uniform for one of war, with a long silk shawl buckled about her shoulders patterned after the southern reefs of Maeyar.

"Stand at ease," she said, eye on Sothcide. She nodded to her husband on top of one of the launch coil capacitors before handing Sothcide a docket of paperwork. "Your orders and stratagem. Long-range sensors have identified a displacement of several ships outside of their line. Yadus wants Arda to push up toward Juna, draw them into a fight while we drift outside the moon and wait to join battle at a full burn run. As soon as we strike, her forces will withdraw in the confusion to avoid being drawn in by the main body of their defense fleet."

Sothcide looked at the diagrams, committing the timing, positioning, and astrogational distances to memory. "A quick strike to blunt the tip of their spear when it comes. Do we know the nature of the target?"

"Juna tends to throw off sensors, but the gravitic distortions suggest three light cruisers and a battleship. Gavisar vessels are heavily armed and armored, but sluggish. And if the report of your human captain is to be believed, they should be damaged to some degree already. They have no logistics train here, we are targeting engine linkages, propulsion shrouding, anything that cannot be fixed without the aid of a shipyard."

"What of the ships trailing the magnetic tethers that Victoria reported? A dozen fighters could make quick work of many of them."

Vehl Ku's proboscis wagged at him. "Greedy. They are not our priority. Stick to what the Wing Admiral ordered. Are you ready, Wing Officer?"

Dipping down into orbit would have given him an opportunity to locate the human warriors, though he did not know which ship they had landed upon and by all accounts the number had grown to nearly 1400 vessels. Still, he had their communication protocol and an opportunity might yet yield itself. Sothcide saluted once more. "I stand ready, Wing Commander."

Vehl returned the salute, if lazily. "Good. Allow me to introduce your second."

She gestured, and a younger pilot nearby jogged up in his flight suit. He had the lightest skin Sothcide had ever seen, likely a Pedres native.

"Wing Officer Allid. With the Senior Wing Officer's unfortunate fall, seniority now falls to him. But he lacks experience against the Homeworld Defense Fleet, which is why I requested you. Allid will lead the second wing, four additional squadrons to apply pressure where you see fit."

Allid offered his hand, and Sothcide clasped his wrist in greeting, meeting his nebula-patterned eye.

"The reputation of this battlegroup's pilots precedes it. You require little from me." said Sothcide.

"Just an exhaust trail to follow, wingboss. From what I hear of you, we'll have to keep up full burn just to see it."

Having the *Yakima*'s logs and deciphering them were two separate beasts. Despite their human origin, the encryption on the data would take some time for the *Condor* to crack. That gave her plenty of time during the horizon jump to Gavisar to ponder over the possibilities with no way to validate her hunches. It was just another form of stealth and subterfuge the rest of the galaxy seemed to have left behind. Even the Big Three tended to use open-air communications with encryption being reserved for distress calls and position reports.

The *Condor* had been brought aboard the Malagath imperial yacht for the jump so that the Duchess could meet humanity, this new curiosity of the Malagath Empire. The zero-gravity cargo bay in which the *Condor* floated was almost the size of the Maeyar fighter decks. Victoria would just as soon have avoided contact all together, but couldn't deny that she was curious if the minor noble was anything like the First Prince, Tavram. Her notion was dispelled as she was swept into an ostentatious throne room draped with Malagath tapestries that hung in the air without apparent suspension or power source. Her retinal implants were going crazy, marking and cataloguing bits and bobs throughout the ship.

How many humans had been aboard a Malagath vessel? A better question might be, how many left again? Several Privateer ships exploring systems near the Perseus
Arm remained unaccounted for, captains on the doorstep
of the Malagath Empire where Victoria had delivered the
First Prince of their empire. Hope that Tavram put his brief
contact with humanity to the back of his mind while he
pursued peace with the Dirregaunt was quickly fading.
Staring down indecisive flag officers was one thing, being in the crosshairs of one of the biggest empires to ever
spread across the cosmos was another.

The duchess herself preened at the top of the throne,
an array of crystals casting vibrant patterns of light across
her skin as they drifted through the air near her seat. They
followed her as she turned to the new arrival, as if somehow surprised by the presence of the human she herself
had commanded. The blue face regarded her at the end of a
long, slender neck wrapped in an intricate lattice of jeweled
chains. The rest of her extremities were similarly bedecked,
and unlike Tavram, who had worn the uniform of his crew,
the duchess wore a shimmering dress of shifting colors.

"The human captain, Grace Tora," announced a member of her retinue as the hatch behind Victoria rolled shut.
This was no combat center. The whole of the space had
been designed and arrayed to meet the aesthetic demands
of a single person, to display a measure of wealth and arrogance befitting Malagath imperials. Her retinal implants
informed Victoria that it was not appropriate to offer a pla-
cating gesture in the presence of the duchess, which suited
her fine since she seemed to be having difficulty taking her
eyes from liquid crystals that formed into a faceted fluted glass in the duchess' hand before a younger Malagath
scaled the substantial height of the throne to fill it from a

sealed flask.

"So you are the lesser empire captain that helped dear Tavram defeat Best Wishes. It is a shame his body could not be recovered; it would have looked a fine thing hanging from the imperial palace at Malagan. I must say, you are not as frightening as I would have expected from such a *scourge* of the Dirregaunt Praetory."

The corners of the duchess' eyes tilted in a way that Victoria did not need the aid of the retinal implants' explanation to know she was being teased. And not in a kind way.

The Duchess continued between sips of whatever liquor she was sampling. The noble was obviously exempt from the Malagath prohibition of intoxicants while serving in the fleet. Perhaps it was the fleet that was serving *her*. "When I heard the rumor that a human ship was among the defenders of Pedres it offered a curiosity, but when I learned it was the illustrious Victoria of Human I knew I simply must have you for myself."

As an ally or a favored pet? Neither was where Victoria would have liked to find herself. She'd come to this part of the Orion Spur specifically to avoid further engagement with the Malagath Empire and the Dirregaunt Praetory. What was Duchess Tora even doing this far from the frontier?

"Clearly the creature is confused into silence," the Duchess said to her crew in Malagath. Chittering singsong laughter floated up to answer her.

"I was wondering," Victoria said, responding in Malagath rather than Kossovoldt, "What brought you to Pedres."

That cut the laughter fast enough. The duchess nearly dropped her glass, leaning forward. The crystals floating about her began to cast a deep scarlet light. "Those words are for we above your station. You will not profane them with your voice aboard my ship again if you wish to leave it," she hissed. She settled back, obviously agitated, and looked away from Victoria.

"The Maeyar are a curiosity of mine these few years past. I thought to offer them vassalship if they can prove their martial skill by repelling this invasion and so came to witness. But when I arrived, sensor signatures from the system you call Gavisar require my more immediate attention. Tavram spoke of the quality of your ship's optics, and so you will be my eyes and alert me to danger."

More like her canary.

"I understand, Duchess. I will make ready my ship for a jump to Gavisar."

Again, the birdsong laughter from the duchess and her hangers on. "Oh I cannot leave to you such a delicate calculation. I'm told you use *computers* to plot your interstellar events. How barbaric. No, human, we have already made the jump. You need only rejoin your crew."

CHAPTER 10
THE ENEMY'S FACE

"I'M TELLING YOU COHEN, it was a human external comms frequency."

"Well it's not there now. If the old lady were here she'd have signaled us as soon as she got a fix."

Aesop looked at the transceiver readout again. He'd managed to fix the equipment, or at least thought he fixed it. But if it was picking up human shipboard radios there was a chance it had gone into some sort of operational test mode using known frequencies, and if that test mode included wideband broadcasts it could potentially give away their position. He pulled up the manual on his retinal implants, but no obvious troubleshooting directive presented itself. Besides, if he could fix an alien power module he could fix a damn radio. Sometimes the world had seemed simpler when all he had to worry about were his rifle and his squad mates.

"Look," said Vega, "there it is again."

This time Aesop caught it, that faint VHF signal with singularly human encryption. On and off again, several more times and then nothing. He waited, but it didn't return.

"Next broadcast window is coming up, what do you want to do?" asked Vega.

"Hold off," said Aesop. "This doesn't feel right, let's not announce ourselves if we don't know who all is listening." He switched channels to the squad-wide. "Singh, any xeno chatter in the last few minutes?"

"Barely any, just one broadcast on and off and it was fleet wide."

Aesop went to scratch his chin before remembering that it was behind a quarter-inch of one-way see-thru polymer. Vacuum suits were designed to be worn for a few days in the long term, but that wasn't exactly with the user's comfort at the forefront of the engineering. There were a few things he would have done differently if he'd been on the project team for the latest generation. Maybe if he survived being a privateer he'd go to the Earth-side factory and have a say in the next model.

"Do they match up with these timestamps?"

There was a pause as Singh compared them to the *Blessing's* newly repaired onboard communications receiver. The tether couldn't generate enough juice to jump start the main engines or maintain life support, but several of the smaller, tertiary systems drew little enough voltage to run off the roughshod electrical patch.

"Negative, they're staggered."

Maggie Chambers floated in from where she'd been watching the fleet movements. She found a workaround to her fried radio by having the rest of the squad run a speech-to-text program in the background of their suit computers that synced via laser whenever she was in line of sight with one of the others. She caught up quickly to his line of thinking, and her ideas appearing on his retinal implants echoed his own.

A Privateer is giving fleet-wide instructions to the Gavisari.

Only one it could be. "The major warned me about this. Jones piggybacked on the horizon jump and he's two-timing us with the invasion fleet. Singh, is the recording equipment up and running again? Playback the xeno half of that broadcast if you can, please."

"Aye, give me a moment to patch it through the box," she said. A handful of seconds later, the deep grinding Kosso Standard that the Gavisar vocal cords produced began playing back over the squad channel.

"Brothers and sisters, last Children of Gavisar, this is Fleet Admiral Raksava. A dark shadow over Gavisar ushered us here as we knew one day it must. In times past we sought to make safe this day, and were punished by betrayal so that we would not stray from the true path. Now it is known that we were not worthy to claim our promised land, and only by persevering through this trial can we begin the Second Era.

"So few of us escaped the cataclysm, we have all lost everything we had, everything we remember. But we have gained a guiding star in an unexpected place, this Man of Earth and his primitive vessel and access to knowledge of the betrayers' plans. I invite him now to share his wisdom with us, and together we shall retake Pedres and make for ourselves a new home. Please listen as vessel assignments are delivered."

Following that were pauses as the Fleet Admiral listed ships and captains, and periods of dead air as Jones delivered instructions that Aesop could not hear without the encryption key. Finally, Raksava's personal chaplain was given leave to say a brief prayer for their success, which Singh interrupted before it could finish.

"It ends after the invocation."

Vega pounded a fist into the bulkhead. "That mother fucking traitor. He knew we were backing Pedres and he went and joined up with the tripods anyway."

Aesop considered. "It makes a certain sort of fatalistic sense. The Gavisari don't know the old lady is helping Jalith, and the Maeyar don't have a clue that Jones is sidled up to the invasion fleet. Earth backs both horses, so Earth has a claim to whoever wins."

"But it still makes it more dangerous for us and the Captain." said Singh.

Aesop nodded, even though the marine couldn't see it two decks up in the radio room. "What I want to know is what Jones said to convince them that he should be dictating strategy to their fleet admiral. We're only here because we had an in with Sothcide. What's his angle with Gavisar?"

"What did they mean when they said 'Retake Pedres'?" asked Mags

Good question. Aesop had read up on the known history of Pedres and Maeyar during the horizon jump. Horizon space affected everyone a little differently, and for Aesop it manifested in anxiety unless he could find a task to manage his nerves. Usually that meant maintenance, but in this case he decided to be one of the few marines that did the required reading.

Pedres had been pegged as a Maeyar planet for as long as humans had been in the know. Which to be fair, was only a few decades. But Pedres had a population of several million, which even in galactic terms wasn't something that popped up overnight. It was their biggest colony with significant infrastructure and over half the Maeyar fleet had showed up to defend it. So why did the Gavisari want it so bad? They had a stake here, and it wasn't that Pedres was the only oxygen-rich planet within their horizon, because Privateers had scouted at least two others. Was this their land of milk and honey?

"Singh, I've got a new job for you. Go back through the recordings. See if you can get that encryption codec Jones is using to direct fleet movement. The old lady might not be answering the phone, but If we can feed that back to the *Twin Sister* maybe we can give the Maeyar a leg up on whatever the invasion fleet is planning."

Captain Marin where are you?

———

"Vick, the Malagath evacuated the compartment. We're go as soon as they drop us."

"Thank you, Avery. Davis, prime the ion engine and make sure the goddamned attenuator is secured."

Victoria knew they had left the horizon jump before her command repeater displayed the indication, by the way the familiar chill she had at first taken for the Malagath's indifference drifted from her skin. She reached up, flipping the main view screen display from ship's diagnostics to adaptive visual sensors. Slowly, the panels of the curved forward bulkhead were replaced by a view of the Malagath receiving bay, where the *Condor* was held in a lattice of gravitic projectors matching her mass. A flick of Victoria's eyes brought the monitor to the sensors on the bell of the ship where she watched the belly of the ship slide open despite the lack of any obvious seams or retraction mechanism. Instead of the black of space there was a green glow and a spike on the thermal and gamma radiation sensors facing the opening.

"Christ, they jumped us right next to the core star. Any closer and we'd have sensors melting off the belly."

"Skipper, I'm getting some internal comms chatter from the Malagath. Apparently the Duchess Tora missed our target coordinates by almost two million kilometers.

They don't sound happy."

"Happier than if she had missed by three and put us in the fucking corona. Still, not like the Malagath Nobles to be so far off on a jump calculation. Are you getting anything else?" Victoria asked. One way the Malagath Imperials kept control of their interstellar feudal empire was by trusting the formulas and calculations for long-distance jumps only among those of noble standing. Ships without a member of the royal family were limited only to a distance many times that of humanity. Hell, thought Victoria, they probably taught horizon jump calculations in their version of grade school. Most of their children put Earth's advanced computers to shame.

Huian listened to the chatter on her headset for a moment. "It sounds like an unexpected mass that their drive couldn't overcome from deeper in the—"

Whatever she'd been about to say was interrupted as Victoria's stomach tried to jump up into her mouth. The gravitic lattice expelled the *Condor* with almost spiteful force, enough to overcome the freshly spooled up inertial dampeners. They had gone from a relative velocity of zero to several hundred kilometers an hour in the span of a few breaths, and if the dampeners hadn't been active, she and Huian would be dripping off the ceiling.

"Bastards got tired of us listening. They can tell which of our systems are active while we're aboard. No secrets from the Malagath. Avery, get them on the horn."

As she spoke, the computer oriented itself to the local stellar plane and then began the process of adjusting known constellations of stars to determine their location. Not that it mattered much, humans had never jumped to this system before. They knew very little of Gavisar, only secondhand knowledge from Sothcide that it was a vast planet, incredibly dense and unsuited to most non-native life. Freshwater oceans on the surface, but the crust and mantle were honeycombed with caverns and the background radiation was unusually high. It took a few moments for the computer to spot three likely planetoids from reflected light, but only one was her best bet for Gavisar. She adjusted the computer entry manually before the Malagath video signal bulled over her comms channels and the severe face of the duchess filled all of her screens.

"*Condor* Actual. Go for course correction," said Victoria. She had to resist the urge to grin. The duchess' perfect jewelry had been knocked out of alignment and rather than surrounding her like a rich tapestry, the crystals now seemed to buzz about her head like angry hornets. The vents on her neck were pulsing in time with her breath, cooling her blood. Tight muscles stretched across her forehead as she regarded Victoria.

"*Condor*," said Duchess Tora, rolling the unfamiliar word around in her mouth. "Our proximity to the star's gravity lessens the chance of gravitic detection and presents an opportunity to come from a perfect vector to mask our thermal signature."

Good cover. But Malagath weren't as practiced at deception as humans.

"You will investigate and transmit your findings back to me," the Duchess continued.

Any desire to grin drained from Victoria. "I think I might be misunderstanding."

"Quite possible," said Duchess Tora. Now it was her turn to grin, or rather, their equivalent. Victoria didn't need her retinal implants to provide the translation of the Malagath noble's pupils dilating practically to the full width of her eyes. The First Prince had never shown her that particular expression, and it wasn't one she cared to see ever again. Christ, it was probably a view most xenos only ever saw at the end of their life. "I am better equipped than most to study the idiosyncrasies of the lesser empires. Sometimes I wonder how creatures such as yourself function. There is so much you do not understand."

Victoria felt a 'but' coming.

"But some have the potential for more. I saw this in the Maeyar as I did in others, in their discipline and their ingenuity. I saw the potential for them to serve the Empire. When Tavram looked upon you he saw little of either quality, but the First Prince saw merit in your sense of sacrifice, and usefulness in your guile and wrath. However, I expect I am more likely to find merit in your guile and usefulness in your sacrifice."

Victoria bared her teeth, unsure whether the duchess was watching commandeered cameras or just listening to her through some other means, as she had never actually opened a communication link between them. If she could barge her way onto her viewscreens, what else could the duchess do? Tora had Victoria in her little xeno pocket, shunned by the Maeyar and far from friendly skies. And now the bitch was sending her, alone, to investigate the origin of a fleet over a thousand ships strong that had arrived with the singular purpose of scouring Pedres clean of humanity's most lucrative interstellar trading partners.

"Well fuck me. I'll write you a postcard when we get there."

"A tightbeam communication will do. I'm told by the Maeyar your ship manages encryption for you. I expect details within six hours by secure channel. I shall maintain my current position. Approach as close as you are able."

Her current position, within jump distance of Gavisar's

blue dwarf star, what a reassuring thought. Still, the fighting weight of a Malagath Star-runner was nothing to scoff at. It was a match for any ten of the heaviest ships buzzing around Pedres right now, Maeyar or Gavisar. And it wouldn't even be considered a warship, more like a glorified yacht. Not to say the duchess would bring those arms to bear in order to bail Victoria out, but a girl could hope.

"Understand all, Duchess Tora. *Condor* out."

Victoria reached out the cut the circuit before she remembered that she had never established it in the first place. One did not hang up on the Malagath.

The duchess reclined in her throne, tall glass goblet held lazily between slender blue fingers. "Do not fail me, human. There will not be another opportunity to prove your worth to the Empire."

The launch rails always put Sothcide in the mind of carnival attractions, in the way the enormous pitch black cylinders rotated through their warm-ups while he conducted his final pre-takeoff checklist. In the corner of his onscreen display a small timer counted down the seconds until the *Starscream* reached its launch position. The carrier group was drifting without power, preparing to use the moon's gravity to adjust course. Once behind it, it would mask the heat of the launch systems and the fighters would drift into an attack run position before circling the planet.

Seventeen ships making a bulwark ahead of the Gavisar fleet screened the invasion against an attack from Pedres, but had left themselves exposed.

"Two minutes, Riz," He signaled in his radio. The gunner in the seat behind him clicked back an assent. His fingers would be on the firing controls, but Sothcide cycled through the configurations for the laser arrays, performing a last minute verification that the delicate apertures and mechanisms functioned as expected. Riz responded by cycling through a set of targeting simulations and off-the-cuff solutions that had margins of error that impressed even Sothcide with his high standard. While the discipline of the crew aboard the *Starscream* left something to be desired, he had never found reason to question their unerring intelligence. They were a clever set of scoundrels, and they knew the qualities that Wing Commander Vehl desired.

One minute.

Sothcide disabled the final safeties on the launch mechanisms, releasing the mechanical clamps and energizing the magnetic rails. Snow crept across his display from the electromagnetic interference. When active, the sets of launch rails accounted for roughly forty percent of the ship's total voltage consumption, an even higher load than the engines. He could hear the whine of the power translating through the hull of his fighter, even as the polarity of the rails pushed it back against the wall of the launch chamber. His primary screen switched to the forward optical display, offering no useful tactical information but demanded by many of the pilots out of tradition and the sheer rush of riding the vacuum of space closer than any other.

Except the humans, of course. Somewhere above Juna were humans separated from the cruel pull of space by little more than plastic, climbing through cored ships like bugs on driftwood. He had their communication channel loaded into one of his radio backups, but Arda had insisted on radio silence. Still, his receiver was tuned, and if they were still down there and spoke up, he would hear.

"Fighters, launch by squadron, mark in ten seconds."

Sothcide closed his eyes for a moment, trying to

imagine that Vehl's voice had a soft enough canter for him to convince himself it was Jalith. Then the three second alarm sounded, and he felt the aperture shudder as the fighter before him was launched and his chamber rotated into position with a hiss of escaping gas. The white cloud of nitrogen had barely faded before the array of magnetic coils switched polarity, and he was pressed into his seat as the intense force of the huge magnets chased him out the launch tube on a shimmer of nitrogen heated by the pressure of his interceptor's nosecone.

"Launch, launch, launch!" came the automatic recording. Several seconds late, as ever.

It took only a fraction of a second to be clear of the long magnetic aperture, and the *Starscream* dwindled in his rear view screen as he assumed manual control over the fighter and polled his squadron for position reports.

The wide arc of Juna's dark moon dominated his view, blocking out the stars from two thirds of the sky beneath its ribbon of light. Soon the fighter began to push past, and then Sothcide and his squadron were greeted to Juna in all her storm-covered glory, and to the fight that had erupted in her upper orbit.

Ahead, his passive sensors already indicated Arda's battlegroup appearing to attack with a diminished force, drawing out the overextended members of the screen with exchanged standoff fire as they struggled to climb out of Juna's gravity at an unfavorable angle. Yadus had been right; their flank was horribly exposed as the majority of the Gavisar fleet was orbiting the planet in the opposite direction and would have to reverse acceleration and climb to offer resistance. Even with the naked eye, Sothcide could see the induction streamers hanging off the backs of the ships, generating enough emergency power to keep their crews alive and little else. So many streamers. . . .

One by one his squadron checked in, and after that it took only seconds for Sothcide to interface with the leaders of the other fighter and bomber squadrons even now coming onto the proper trajectory thanks to the dual gravity wells of Juna and her moon tugging him into alignment.

This would be the day Pedres held.

CHAPTER 11
FORWARD VITACUUS

THE FIGHTING HAD intensified above Juna. Aesop could see the small explosions from missiles and lasers as the Maeyar fleet made contact and exchanged fire with standoff armaments. Without the ship's sensors operational, his knowledge of the scope of the battle was severely limited. But the communications array had begun to pick up some snippets of the Maeyar fleet chatter, and from what he could tell, another wave of the Pedres Defense Fleet was about to cripple an over-exposed picket. It was a ballsy move on the part of Pedres if they could pull it off.

The only problem was that Gavisar fleet comms had ordered the bulk of the fighting ships to pull back, so what were the Maeyar engaging up there? Had a few warships missed the order? The wing admirals were assaulting a superior force, but every Gavisari ship destroyed carried with it a non-insignificant percentage of their entire population. It was hard to imagine they would leave any out of position.

"Singh, tell me you found Jones' key. *Ben-zona*, Singh?"

There was no answer. Probably plugged into the banks of recordings again, lost to the dead Gavisar communication recordings. Growling, Aesop swung around and nearly raised his rifle to the figure of Vega in the hatch, hands squeezing the rim. Mags floated behind him.

"Sarge, you need to see this."

It took him a few moments to realize why Vega sounded odd. The grunt had only ever used his rank a handful of times, when shit was really hitting the fan. "Where's Singh?"

"Trying to raise someone on the dish. Anyone, but no one in the Maeyar fleet is listening. They've shut out external comms."

"What?"

Aesop launched himself through the hatch. Broadcasting communications other than the discrete databursts carried an entirely unacceptable level of detection risk. The isolation couldn't have gotten to her in only a day, so what was that girl thinking?

"Sarge, come on," Vega protested as Aesop pushed past him. He could see Singh at the breach in the *Blessing*'s pressure hull where he'd clamped the portable communication array to the deck. Sure enough, his marine had patched into the unit and was issuing plain-voice radio signals on Maeyar bands. Hands grabbed him from behind as he made to push toward her and he found himself spinning through the compartment with Vega slapping the side of his faceplate.

"Vega, let me go!" said Aesop, trying to pry the marine off him.

"Not until you look down below, you dense mother fucker."

Aesop calmed himself and released the grip he hadn't noticed wrapped around his knife, still sheathed, thank God. Vega was a Privateer marine, and a hell of a fighter. But Aesop had seen the worst of the fighting in Gaza and Tehran and it didn't take much to slip back into those days.

Mags and Singh were both staring at them, having bounced off enough walls for their scuffle to translate through the metal and composite bulkheads.

Maggie motioned for him, and after he and Vega untangled themselves he drifted over to the hole in the hull that faced the space-ward side of Pedres. He watched for a second, then two, and then raised his rifle to use the magnification built into his sights to be sure of what he was seeing.

One after another, Gavisari ships were coming to life. Running lights, engines, and active EM emissions as scanners swept the sky. There were bursts of light, and ship after ship sped up their orbit with the terrifying acceleration only possible with warship-grade inertial dampeners, leaving behind thin tethers of white-hot metal.

"Keep at it, Singh. Get the old lady, or the Maeyar fleet, or whoever you goddamned can."

The Gavisar Home Defense Fleet hadn't been overextended, they'd been lying in wait disguised as refugee ships barely capable of emitting power. Aesop swore. That was the fleet movement they'd witnessed before they could get comms running, when so many of the ships had pushed into upper orbit on their last legs. They'd swapped the induction tethers to their fighting vessels and trusted the storms to disguise their nature.

And it had worked. It was human deception, and Aesop should have spotted it. Somewhere up there Jones was watching through the view screen on the *Howard Phillips* as humanity's would-be allies fell into his trap. And Aesop was helpless to stop it.

But there was something he could do. . . .

"Contact bearing zero zero four, up nine on the positive azimuth. Designated Gavisar heavy cruiser. No active emissions."

Victoria looked at the sensor repeater on her captain's console, lips pursed. So far there had been zero active emissions from deeper in the system. No radio waves, microwaves, collect calls, bird calls, just . . . nothing. For a planet of thirty-six *billion* and a habitable moon they didn't seem to be the talking type. If there are any of them left.

Victoria shuddered, and watched as Huian swung them to keep the railguns trained on the contact. As if they would do serious damage to a heavy cruiser. By all accounts the Gavisari knew how to build a beastly cruiser, and they'd used their fleet to repel all would-be conquerors.

"Avery, give me lidar on that cruiser."

"Aye Vick," her sensor officer replied with a tad more hesitation than usual.

"Fire Control, get me a solution on him just in case."

Typically used for mapping planetary surfaces and terrain features through low visibility, the *Condor's* lidar could also be used to construct a millimeter-detailed model of any surface, including derelict ships, in just a few seconds. The only problem is that shining a thousand lasers at your target was a good way to get their attention, but Victoria didn't expect that to be an issue as she watched the computer reconstruct the heavy cruiser on the main view screen. Or rather, three quarters of the cruiser. The rest had been shorn off by some cataclysmic ordinance. It almost looked as though some celestial giant had gripped the ship at stem and stern and pulled as hard as it could until the thing parted. Debris floated along the same vector, scattered across dozens of kilometers, and Huian maneuvered the *Condor* to remove any risk of collision. At these relative speeds, being unlucky enough to hit a sizable chunk of the cruiser would result in the *Condor* being spread across a similar distance.

The scan continued as the *Condor* sailed past, filling in the holes of the surface model. It didn't take long for Avery to paint another contact on her screen, and more after that. Eventually her scope had gotten so full that her sensor operator had given up labeling designations on individual ships and instead had his sensor techs group them in groups of five or ten.

"They're all trying to crawl to the star for a jump. Every fucking one," said Victoria. Hundreds of warships and thousands of civilian vessels floated in a moving graveyard toward their eventual stellar cremation. If even a third of the wreckage had cleared the star as viable fighters they'd have rolled over Pedres like a three-legged tide.

Huian entered another course correction that carried them close enough to a broken transport to trip the radiological sensors on the starboard side of the *Condor*. The torn hull still glowed where the rest of the ship cast it in shadow, the same assortment of gamma and beta rays that infiltrated horizon space. Meanwhile Victoria continued to monitor on all open frequencies for even a single sign of life in the ghost fleet and the growing orb of Gavisar beyond.

"How many do you think this fleet carried?" asked Huian. "Millions? Perhaps a billion Gavisari?"

"How many never made it off the surface?" Vick retorted.

The closer the *Condor* approached Gavisar, the slower the main force of the Homeworld Defense Fleet drifted, many still venting burning plasma from breached reactors. All the while the planet continued to grow in the sensors, revealing the vast swaths of deserts and mountains across the surface.

"Huian, start the deceleration."

"I already have, Skipper."

Victoria frowned, eyeing the astral distances winding down at a slower rate than she'd have expected. "Avery, anything in orbit yet?"

"I've got a dozen more infrared radiation signatures, Vick, zero bearing. And we're about to lose it over the planet. Fire aboard orbital defense platforms. No radio waves, no active emissions. Dead quiet out there."

It was a new sensation for Victoria, a new kind of chill creeping down her spine as she approached a planet in broad daylight. The light didn't concern her, the surface of the *Condor* absorbed ninety-six percent of all light all the way up into the ultraviolet spectrum. Even if you shined a flashlight at the hull you'd miss a Privateer. No, she'd flown through hundreds of uninhabited systems and never experienced such an errant and oppressive stillness, as if the entire planet were becalmed. Forty billion souls and not a single one was talking. Not only were the air waves quiet, but whoever had silenced them left no sign. An entire fleet torn apart, and not a single confirmed kill on whoever had done it. Victoria's hair began to raise as the distance to Gavisar crept down. Whoever had done it could still be out there, and the list of possible culprits was growing worryingly thin.

———

Sothcide's impressive combat record included fleet action against a race called the Pfelt in contestation of a mineral-rich moon in an independent system, in which he claimed four confirmed kills on enemy fighters and disabling shots on two light frigates. His second combat patrol he'd met the light of his horizon, Jalith, and offered himself for marriage to the young bridge officer less than a year later. By then, Sothcide had proved his merit and been given an assistant squadron leader position on a nimble support carrier, smaller than the *Twin Sister* by over half. In that position he completed four successful combat sorties against the Grah'lihn, or Graylings as the humans called them. His third tour, his squadron's carrier was shot out from under him and he was picked up by Victoria and her Vultures.

Now, drifting about the sunward side of Juna, he led a full wing of able pilots at the controls of deadly fighter craft. The snow of the magnetic rails was gone from his screen, and he could see clearly ahead the pinpricks of light as Wing Commander Arda threw punch after punch at the hardened Gavisar line with missiles and tightbeam masers. In his rear view screen he could see that the *Starscream* and her sister ships had come out of hiding, piling on the acceleration with a brilliant flare on his thermal scopes.

"All craft, full burn. Maintain designated targets and soften those anti-missile defenses."

As soon as he gave the order, the thirty-two fighters and twelve bombers of the *Starscream* flared to life in a new constellation brightening the sky so far from Pedres. The whine in his own ship increased tenfold, manual controls bucking under his grip as Juna grew and his ship began to feel the pull of her gravity. His targeting systems began to pick up the profiles of the hulking Gavisar ships.

"*Starscream* fighter wing, this is Commander Arda. Enemy response has underperformed expectations and fighter presence is minimal. Perhaps there was something to your human's report after all. I'm ordering the *Trepid* and the *Vitacuus* forward to cover your initial run with our point defense."

Arda was pushing her own cruiser closer to the front. The *Vitacuus* was one of the heaviest ships in the system, and once committed it could stand toe to toe with anything short of a Gatekeeper ship. Or Big Three, as the humans were wont to call the Malagath, Dirregaunt, and Kossovoldt.

"Understand all, Wing Matron. Our attack run will commence in thirty seconds, followed by an atmospheric braking maneuver around Juna. We'll cover your withdrawal after the *Starscream* hits the picket. All fighters, report firing solution status."

Entering orbit at full acceleration the fighters would need the aid of Juna's thick upper atmosphere to slow down enough to rejoin the fight. The relative speeds would make it almost impossible for Gavisar ships in orbit to react quickly enough to return fire, and the pressure wave from dipping into atmo would make targeting almost impossible. The fighter wings would be *under* the majority of the invasion fleet ships. The maneuver would take only a few minutes, compared to the hour a full orbit would waste.

"Twenty seconds to firing range. Report solutions." Sothcide said for a second time. The radio clicked in his cockpit as his other interceptors reported, almost reluctant with their status.

"Poor solution, Wing Officer."

"Poor solution, thermal can't identify armament pods."

"Poor solution, active sensors show target is unstable."

Even his own gunner was struggling in the seat behind him. Sothcide could see the laser arrays adjusting their angle on his side monitor as the targeting solution tried to locate the anti-missile defenses on the ship ahead. But there was no time left, and no changing course.

"All wings, fire when in range, solution agnostic. Trust your eyes."

Visually targeting at this speed would leave only a fraction of a second to identify something to shoot at, and gunners would be firing wastefully on redundant targets. But anything was better than nothing. The ship began to buck as they began the evasion program, the point defense from the *Vitacuus* slapping down the sparse anti-fighter missiles that his display warned him of almost before his gunner could identify them.

Steady . . . steady . . . here it comes.

His displays dimmed as the power draw on the tiny fusion reactor drained to the capacitors and the lasers burned away at the Gavisar ships ahead of him. They cut through something volatile, and the resulting explosion left Sothcide wide-eyed and shaken. Not because it had been close or unexpected, but because in that brief moment before the interceptor passed the picket he had discovered why the firing solutions had failed. Gavisar civilian ships had no armament pods for the thermal sensors to track, and lashed together to mimic the size and mass of warships presented no solid silhouette for the radar to return. Certainly there were warships among the defenders—someone had to be offering return fire to draw the Maeyar fleet into the jaws of the trap. Arda had pushed in, and Vehl wasn't far behind.

"Pedres fleet, abort abort! Picket is a scam, repeat, picket is a scam, majority non-combat vessels, abort ab-"

But his arc carried him across the horizon of the planet, cutting off communication. As it did, dozens of contacts began to appear above his altitude on the thermal scopes.

"Evade, evade! Damn it!" he called, and fire began to erupt in his formation. Then the fighters and the Gavisar warships passed within a few hundred miles of each other, too close for coincidence in the vast sea of space. The invasion ships had built up enough momentum across the starward side of Juna to intercept and crush both Arda and Vehl before either could escape.

Reports began to fill his screen of losses within the wing. Nearly two-thirds of the fighters and all but two bombers had been destroyed. Sothcide had been spared by virtue of leading the charge, riding past the anti-fighter defenses too quickly for the warships to gain a solution. The rest of his wing was not as fortunate. In solemn silence they dipped into the atmosphere to chip away their incredible velocity. It would take them four minutes to complete the maneuver. Would there still be a battle to join when it was over?

Ahead of the *Condor,* Gavisar loomed. There was no other word to describe it. "Two-fifty KK, Vick. Do you want me to take her around the planet?" Huian asked from the pilot's station. The same distance between the Earth and the moon, but Gavisar filled the entire view screen.

Victoria shook her head, her attention pulling away from Jones' last communication to the *Yakima* before opening fire. Her suspicions had been confirmed, and they'd left the slimy bastard back in Pedres to play havoc with the Maeyar. Stupid, stupid, stupid. "Not yet Huian, hold thrust and let's growl the duchess. Avery, get me a tightbeam."

"Conn sensors, aye Vick. Sending the communication package and imagery."

"She won't see it for another sixteen minutes, unless the Malagath can read radio waves before they arrive. You know what? I wouldn't even be fucking surprised. But all she's going to say is to bury our noses in the dirt. Let's take a closer look at one of those orbital defense stations. Match our orbit, Huian. Low power, if any living xenos are listening out there we don't need to paint a bullseye on our ass."

As the *Condor* descended toward the thermal signature of an orbital defense platform, Victoria eyed the readout for their relative velocity.

"Coming in a bit hot, Huian. Not like you to not factor in the increased gravity of a large planet."

Huian glanced back from the pilot's station, a mixture of confusion and annoyance on her narrow face. "I did, Ma'am. Gavisar is pulling more than its size should suggest, even corrected for a nickel-rich composition," she said. As if to illustrate her point, she gestured to the orbital defense platform growing on the main screen. "The platform's orbit is decaying too."

She was right, the orbital defense platform was falling, if slowly, into the planet's surface. In a day or two the thing would either begin to break up in atmo or would crash into a cliffside down below. There was a certain sort of finality to that idea, Victoria decided. The scene would not be so dissimilar from Earth if the xenos managed to spot it. Not if, *when*. They would have to be better prepared than Gavisar, and as it stood even the battered and bruised remnants of the fleet above Juna could wipe out the entire Union Earth Navy ten times over.

"Conn sensors, heavy radiation off that platform, recommend we don't get much closer."

No one down below was going to fire back, but she had other reasons to slow down and so she leaned over and gave her pilot the order. Someone nuked the space platform, but the precise radiation profile didn't match any nuclear device or particle cannon that humans had yet documented. It was closer to a horizon space transference.

"Alright, Huian, keep your distance from the platform."

"It's not the platform, Vick. It's the planet, the whole thing is irradiated. Not just the high background radiation we were expecting, it's almost like it just left a horizon jump."

Victoria brought up the display on the main view screen, showing radiation hotspots across the valleys and deserts of Gavisar. For enough radiation to be reaching the *Condor's* sensors at this distance, standing on the surface would be like taking a naked spacewalk near Sol, and would turn a human body to jerky in just a few minutes.

Between the density and the radiation, the people of Gavisar must have been damned near impossible to uproot once they settled into the tunnels and caverns of a planet. If they had been aggressively expanding, they'd be a force to reckon with in the local neighborhood. And Earth would have been one of their potential habitats. There were only a few oxygen-tolerant species around, but just as few oxygen rich planets that the UE had surveyed. Even with advanced human optics and remote study, the only thing that could give accurate compositional detail was an atmospheric probe, and to deploy those you had to be in-system. Ithaca had been the first. And between the growing human population and infrastructure, and the utter inequity of the defenses arrayed around the planet, by some metrics, in more danger than Earth.

The orbital platform spun as it continued its orbit, a lazy derelict hulk of metal and rock. The light of the system's star revealed the enormous laser arrays capable of cutting down capital ships that strayed within almost a hundred thousand kilometers by their estimation of Gavisari advancement. Impressive, though less than half the range she'd personally witnessed the Dirregaunt capable of reaching. Crystallized coolant from the platform's reactor left a frozen trail of vapor behind it in a gentle, expanding spiral. The power required to operate such a weapon could have lit half of Europe for a year. Or burned London in an instant. The silent display was almost serene, were it not for the fact that someone had struck down those awesome arrays without leaving a trace.

"Perhaps it was civil war, Skipper," said Huian, mirroring Victoria's own thoughts on the absence of perpetrators.

Victoria shook her head. "That would account for only seeing Gavisari ships, but not that conga line of hulks all trying to claw their way to the jump. Besides, thinking they get all rowdy, nuke the surface of their planet 'til it glows, and then decide to go find a new one? I don't fucking buy it. Spacefaring cultures don't nuke themselves," she said. She eyed Huian, who might have grown up far enough west in China to have had family in the fallout zone from the nuclear exchange in north India. "With some notable exceptions."

"Xenos don't nuke themselves and *survive*," Huian pointed out. "The Gavisari haven't survived yet, they're still barely holding on."

"Shit, that's a fair point. Still, smart money isn't on civil war. Whatever happened here happened quick, and it happened *to* Gavisar. This stinks. Let's finish the recon and let the Duchess know we found fuck-all."

The investigation of the orbital defense platform wasn't revealing anything beyond the gaping holes torn into the side of the structure. But as it carried them over from day to night, her thoughts were interrupted by her sensor officer.

"Conn sensors, superluminal contact. Photon doppler coming from the star."

Before he could even finish the report, sirens blared on the conn as the hulk of the Duchess' yacht appeared only a few thousand kilometers away, and her face once again commandeered the majority of Vick's screens, though her command repeater remained on the exterior visual feed of the planet's dusk band.

"Shit," said Victoria, as much in surprise at the Malagath countenance forcing its way onto all her monitors as at the light speed maneuver that had announced their presence to anyone with sensors capable of detecting the approach of a superluminal vessel. "Duchess Tora, hello, hi, a pleasure as always."

"Be silent, fool, and attend. I thought these images you sent were in jest, or you had found your way in ignorance to the wrong planet. But this is Gavisar and something is terribly, terribly wrong."

Victoria looked at the images of Gavisar, the deep valleys and high mountains that marked its barren surface. But it wasn't supposed to be barren, was it? Victoria mentally recited the brief description the young Maeyar wing officer had left her. *Large, dense, fresh . . . Shit!*

Sothcide mentioned Gavisar to be the home of vast freshwater oceans that were in no way apparent in any of the imagery. The entire rock was bone dry. But how? Entire oceans didn't just disappear. Where the fuck had they gone? It was like someone had pulled the plug on a planet-sized bath.

The *Condor* fell into shadow as it crossed the sunset below, and there on the starward side of Gavisar was the cosmic drain valve.

CHAPTER 12
RAKSAVA MOVES

S OTHCIDE HEARD THE screams on the radio before he finished the full circuit of the planet. Even with his screen completely washed out by the hypersonic pressure wave riding his bow, the signal bounce from the moon revealed the fate of Vehl's battlegroup with crystal clarity. The battleships who had disguised themselves as derelict drifters were the heaviest hitters of the Gavisari fleet. Sothcide had seen Raksava, the Gavisar Home Defense Fleet's admiral. Or at least his flagship, the *Bulwark*, in a state of disrepair. It still towed the induction tether, a banner to all those still stranded in Juna's orbit. The same gunners aboard the *Bulwark* poised to intercept Sothcide's wing of fighters had delivered firing solutions that crippled the *Starscream* and destroyed several of her escorts. A second wave of Gavisar frigates and destroyers had followed and finished Wing Admiral Vehl before Sothcide could even rejoin the battle. There was barely a battle left to join. The loss of a heavy carrier, two light cruisers, four destroyers, and two artillery cruisers with accompanying light frigates and fighter wings had crippled the forward line and would leave open the shortest route to Pedres.

Now the admiral was leading the detachment around the moon to use its gravity to double back and catch the second battlegroup, even as the remainder of the fleet closed in from the starward side of Juna. Vehl pressed the attack, and was now in a poor position to retreat. Momentum and gravity both pushed against her escape. Gavisar fighters dotted the battlegroup, climbing and using the gravity of Juna for maneuvering.

"Wing Commander, this is Sothcide of the *Starscream*, we're coming to cover your retreat."

Arda's harsh voice clicked over his fighter's radio as he accelerated to engage the wing of enemy fighters. His gunner offered solutions on a few of them, and wing assignments filtered down through his squadron. "Vehl's gone. The *Starscream* is a total loss. We've only got a few minutes before the *Bulwark* catches up."

There was a flash on his side monitor as one of the Gavisar fighters took out the external propulsion couplings on a heavy frigate. Sothcide swiveled his interceptor and put on a burst of acceleration, lining his gunner up for a barrage of laser fire as the larger craft emerged across the bow of the frigate. The lasers sheared off a section of wing, but the ablative coating on the belly of the fuselage absorbed most of the weapon's energy. Tough ships, they could take a lot of punishment. Even with Sothcide's pilots among them, the Homeworld Defense Fleet's fighters were focused on the engines and propulsion components of Arda's ships, to the exclusion of the enemy fighters or even the exposed anti-fighter defenses that hammered away at the HDF's ships.

Tough as they were, the Gavisar fleet was losing fighters at an alarming rate. But if they held Arda's battlegroup long enough for Raksava to swing back around, then the tradeoff of a few fighters for a battlegroup's worth of frigates and light cruisers would be incredible for the invasion fleet.

Not to mention the *Vitacuus,* and two of the Maeyar's experienced wing commanders in the span of a few minutes.

Arda's battlegroup boasted an impressive sixteen warships, with half again as many frigates. If she died here at Juna with the majority of her strength, Pedres would not hold. Her survival was paramount. But he could not see a way for her to escape Juna.

A light on his communications panel got his attention, the channel he assigned to the Privateer frequency winked at him, and having received the codec from Victoria, the familiar voice of Human Aesop filled his cockpit as he switched the channel to active. He listened as he climbed out of Juna's gravity for another attack run on a fighter harassing the *Vitacuus.*

"Attention all Maeyar forces, communication may be compromised, reply on encrypted frequency only, Gavisari Fleet is hiding among civilian derelicts," it said.

Regrettably late, unfortunately. Warnings blared in his cockpit as an indirect Gavisar laser scored a sizzling white cut across his portside ablative plating. A missile took the heavy fighter before he could finish the job on Sothcide. His eye scanned the frequency modulator, the message was coming from closer to the planet, one of the tethered ships passing below. The signal quickly faded as the orbit carried the humans away from the battle and the ships falling into the thick atmosphere of Juna.

What followed in its absence was a fleet-wide broadcast from Wing Commander Arda.

"All craft, dive dive, make best speed for Juna low orbit, Break line-of-sight in the storms and maintain close proximity. Repeat, all craft dive."

Sothcide relayed the orders to his own squadron, "All craft, disengage and dive. Break break break, make for the cloud tops, make altitude sixty thousand meters and maintain spacing. Repeat, Wing Six is diving."

One by one the engines flared to life on the Maeyar ships still able to move under their own power. The *First Flight, Kel Vehru,* and the missile boat *Longbow* were left to drift. There was nothing that could save them from the brunt of Gavisar's next strike. Noses spun toward Juna and the warships began to push forward directly into the planet's welcoming gravity. The pressure and heat of the atmosphere began to mount, stressing the limits of the sleek Maeyar vessels. Several Gavisar fighters with more bravery than brains attempted to follow, but without the Maeyar dampeners they were quickly torn apart. Even equipped with the systems, Sothcide's skull rattled inside his helmet, eye blurred as the cockpit warmed from the intense pressure of the mounting atmosphere.

"Battlegroup *Vitacuus,* brace for broadside," Arda ordered over the fleet-wide channel.

On the side and rear view screens Sothcide could see the massive spearheads of Arda's battlegroup thrusting through the cover of the rolling anvil tops of the thunderclouds below, massive pressure waves building around the ships and fighting against their intrusion into atmosphere. The light cruiser, *Maeyis Canal,* began shedding components, and finally erupted into a burning ball of plasma before the Gavisar fired a shot.

The battlegroup was far beyond the range of the fighter detachment, but the Gavisar cruisers and destroyers suffered no such handicap, and as the ships passed above, invisible through the plumes of burning gasses in his rear monitor, their fire began to lance down from thousands of kilometers away. Dulled and refracted by the atmosphere of Juna, the scattered laser fire's deadliness had been blunted, but two more frigates vented plasma and erupted, and the main engines on a destroyer near the *Vitacuus* winked out. The destroyer began to twist and spin, flinging hull fragments far and wide. The propulsion and guidance failure pointed to an emergency scram of the main reactor, depended upon also by that class of ship's artificial gravity generator and inertial dampeners. Sothcide harbored no doubt that the G-forces of the spin had already crushed out the life of all hands aboard against the bulkheads. Sothcide looked away, and the opposite side of his cockpit was lit by the flash of the destroyer's conflagration.

Ahead and below, Juna's lightning reached up to embrace them, blinding flashes seeking a way inside. Sothcide pushed his interceptor to the breaking point. Now encased in atmosphere, his ship howled as though caught in the worst the northern storms could throw at him, screaming and tearing at the stubby wings of the barely-aerodynamic interceptor. At two hundred thousand meters the proximity alarm began the blare in his ear, and he pulled up on the controls. Still plummeting at hypersonic speeds, even Maeyar inertial dampeners couldn't keep the blood in his head and the dark hexagonal cells at the corners of his eye became visible as he neared unconsciousness. How many of his wing mates would succumb and miss the maneuver?

All excess power from his meager reactor was being pumped into the overheated anti-gravity system to slow their fall, and Sothcide prayed there were no mountains scraping the edge of the sky below. The thick gray and red blanket carved by jetstreams was becoming more and more detailed in his monitors.

Then the clouds swallowed him.

"Avery, get me a fucking read on that thing," ordered Victoria.

Hanging in space like a tear in some gaudy pinstripe suit was what could only be described as a look at the blue-black bloomers of the universe. The foundation of horizon space research rested on the theory that the universal truths of gravity and light speed were different on the other side. Therefore, the two could not coexist, but could be breached for a time in areas of extreme space-time distortions caused by large amounts of mass, like a star, and by using large amounts of energy and an exotic matter catalyst, like the *Condor*'s micro thorium reactor. But the amount of mass and the amount of energy were largely mathematical limitations, as evidenced by the Malagath's incredible dominion driven by the range of their horizon drives and particle cannons.

The problem of coexistence had evidently been solved by someone else, because even without gravitic sensor technology Victoria knew the anomaly was the cause of their early exit from horizon space just as it was the reason for the utter lack of Gavisar's many oceans. These blue-black tendrils of horizon space licking from the wound in the planet's orbital path chased an entire civilization from their home planet and into the territory of the Maeyar.

Or left them to die in their tunnels with no water or air.

"It's like there's nothing there, Vick. Electromagnetic, radio, all quiet. Electro-optical is getting the same artifacting interference consistent with horizon space travel, but unless someone looks out the front airlock I have no idea what it actually looks like. Radiological is off the charts with horizon radiation and spectral is showing gas and water crystals being sucked into that thing at thousands of cubic tons per second."

"Carillo, warm up the rails."

Someone whispered something to the Malagath duchess and she disappeared from Victoria's screens. Instants later the imperial vessel triggered an active sensor pulse that briefly washed out the monitors as the energy passed over and through the composite hull of the *Condor*. Warnings flashed across not only her command repeaters, but her retinal implants and the main view screen.

"Conn sensors, active return on the Malagath sounding, two contacts bearing one two eight and one three seven, both down six on the negative azimuth near the anomaly. Silhouette suggests—Captain, it's the Kossovoldt!"

Huian spoke up from her pilot's station. "Ma'am, the duchess is moving to engage," she said. She was pointing to the view screen where the imperial ship's engines had flared to life, pushing toward the distant specks which her fire control team had already labeled as the primary and secondary.

"Follow her in, Huian."

Huian hesitated at the controls.

"We can't escape them, Huian. Our only chance is supporting Duchess Tora. Fuck if I want to take up arms against the Kossovoldt," said Victoria. Though there was little enough the *Condor* could do. Of the Big Three, the least was known about the Kossovoldt, even how their language became seeded across so many worlds. All Victoria knew was what she could see, that the two ships dwarfed the largest heavy cruisers of the lesser empires, that their profiles were jagged, wicked things, and that they were shunting forward a few hundred miles at a time as the Malagath bathed them with active targeting sensors.

Warnings beeped on Victoria's screen as the Duchess began discharging particle projectors and laser banks at the two ships. Only the Malagath and the Dirregaunt could stand in the same arena as the Kossovoldt, but she'd never been near one of the titanic battles that had left the remains of fleets scattered across so many systems. Nor did she want to be.

"Huian, drop us down at twenty degrees and line up the rails. We don't want to get caught in whatever the Kosso throw back at the duchess. Split the bearing on her active sensors so Carillo can get a better ranging solution."

Something on the Malagath starboard side exploded in a shower of sparks and venting atmo. Though no weapons alerts had triggered, another spike in that horizon transference radiation washed over the *Condor*.

"Avery!" she shouted.

"I know, Vick! Whatever they're hitting the Imperial with, it's something we can't track!"

In the distance, Malagath weaponry struck home on one of the Kossovoldt ships, and it began to shunt away, as if the universe was a pond and the ship was a rock skipping across it. The other pressed forward and struck again at the Malagath, scoring close enough that the flash briefly whited out the forward sensors. Thermal on the Malagath vessel began to escalate without explanation, radiation levels on the hull rising in lock-step with the surface temperature. At their range it would take the railgun rounds over a minute to reach the Kossovoldt's position, their missiles even longer. With the Kossovoldt hulks jumping around like spastic space monkeys, her tactical team would never be able to lock down a solution that would penetrate their point defense, let alone land. Hell, even if it landed, it was a coin toss whether the Kossovoldt would even notice.

The sheer arms race between the Big Three had become a matter of attrition and armor as titans tossed enough directed energy at each other to level cities. Victoria had never been present for a true battle between such forces, and witnessing removed any ambition to help the Malagath. Even her nuclear-tipped missiles weren't a match for any of the six particle lancers the Duchess was bringing to bear.

"Huian, turn us around."

There was no hesitation this time. The engines groaned as Huian Wong pulled into a high-g turn more appropriate to a fighter than a Privateer sloop. With a gesture Victoria kept the main screen focused on the battle behind the *Condor*, confused as the range indications continued to drop.

"Huian, increase thrust."

"I am, ma'am, antigravity dampeners are at maximum load, any more acceleration and we'll be feeling the flight forces."

The ranging solution to Duchess Tora's imperial star runner began to decrease by dozens of meters per second, then hundreds. Huian hadn't been wrong about the dampeners being pushed to their limits. Her command consoles were vibrating under her hands even as the deck rumbled beneath her feet. They hadn't been accelerating hard enough to be fighting this much to reverse it. Unless. . . .

"Conn sensors. Massive power spike on the Imperial, heat building on the bow like crazy."

"Shit! Davis, cut down the engine, run up those dampeners with as much juice as you can give them," said Victoria. She thumbed the main circuit, "All hands brace, we're in for a hell of a bumpy ride."

The range was ticking down more than six kilometers per second now, the *Condor* was hurtling down range almost as fast as the railgun slugs would have, and accelerating *backwards* while Victoria's teeth tried to rattle out of her skull. What little light reached the dark side of the planet began to twist and bend as the immense mass at the bow of Duchess Tora's ship took shape. For a moment the star runner seemed to warp itself as if stretched along the edge of a soap bubble, then it vanished, leaving the *Condor* hurtling directly toward the anomaly and the two Kossovoldt hulks at a velocity she couldn't hope to control, let alone reverse. The final ignition of the Duchess' emergency engine had sent the *Condor* into an erratic tumble, and it was all Huian could do to keep the ship from being pulled apart at the seams from the sheer force of the singularity the Malagath had forced into existence for a fraction of a second. She'd seen that force rip the front third off a Dirregaunt dreadnaught, and now it was throwing them at the tear in horizon space, if the antigravity generators didn't burn out first.

But the Kossovoldt didn't seem content to wait for her to come to them. Off the sunward side of the *Condor* there was nothing but the night-darkened landscape of Gavisar, until the visual sensors on that side were filled with the mass of a Kossovoldt hulk, a jagged wedge-shaped body with faceted protrusions snaking into a metal and composite superstructure. The entire ship seemed lit from within by a suffuse red glow, looking less like the metal she knew it to be and more like a living thing. Her command repeater lit up with a positive firing solution for the railguns.

"Hold fucking fire!" she almost screamed. No human had ever come this close to a Kossovoldt ship and lived to tell the tale.

Might still be true after today, she thought. A sobering thought for Victoria, and she very much wished she was not sober for this. That last bottle of scotch stashed in the outboards of the wheelhouse wasn't doing her much good now. The red glow intensified, silhouetting the Kossovoldt hulk against the planet, and then focused into a beam that washed out the *Condor*'s sensors with a deep crimson. It came from no apparent emitter on the hull of the ship

"Huian, get us level," Victoria heard herself say, but her own voice sounded far-off and muffled as a whine built up within the hull of the ship. Huian Wong seemed to be struggling with her control inputs. She was claiming something, that she'd been locked out of access to the ship's maneuvering but Victoria had stopped paying attention. Ahead on the main view screen, the sensor artifacting caused by the horizon space tear loomed closer and closer. That great blue-black maw opened above Gavisar dominated the night sky now. It must have been five, no, *ten* thousand kilometers across. Big enough to swallow her itty bitty *Condor*. Hell, big enough to swallow a whole damn planet.

Or spit one out.

Victoria stepped down from the conn, approaching the main view screen as the Kosso hulk drew closer. It was matching the momentum of the *Condor* perfectly, and it almost seemed as though she could see shapes moving beneath the metal surface, as if the hull was a sheet of thick ice. She walked past the empty XO's chair and the pilot's bench, approaching the flickering screen. She was oddly calm, she thought. The Malagath resigned them to death as soon as they engaged that emergency engine that sucked the *Condor* into the anomaly. Even at full acceleration she couldn't have overcome the momentum that instants-long singularity demanded of her ship.

Why were they just watching her sail into it? Not worth whatever space-boiling weapon they'd unleashed on the Malagath? And just what had *that* been anyway? Victoria couldn't venture. Despite having seeded the language used across the known galaxy across countless fledgling worlds, humanity knew next to nothing about the Kossovoldt. And they weren't alone in their ignorance. All anyone knew was that they zealously guarded the Sagittarius arm from the Dirregaunt Praetory and the Malagath Empire, warring with them across the core-side of the Orion Spur. They never claimed worlds, never interacted with the lesser empires beyond outright destruction, and *never* were seen this deep in the Orion Spur. The galactic drain valve was practically a stone's throw from Earth.

And now they studied Victoria as her Privateer ship tumbled into the waiting teeth of the horizon space tear, following her across the event horizon into the nebulous tangles of horizon space. Victoria watched the red light of the Kossovoldt spotlight intensify, and then every light on the conn blew out at once, leaving her in darkness.

No wait, thought Victoria, *It's just me.*

The *Bulwark* had been built to repel and defend, making safe the skies of Gavisar from any who would claim her. Now it served as vanguard to the Exodus fleet and the Last Children of Gavisar, and would guide the children back to their new home. Originally the design had lacked an interstellar engine, as a symbolic gesture the vessel's architects had placed a shrine in its place. Now it held a subspace penetrator, and the installation had finished only days before the Gods finally returned to take back what had been gifted so long ago.

Admiral Raksava had fought at first, in an effort to afford the children of Gavisar more time to escape the surface. Some might have called it vain, others simply blasphemous. The Homeworld Defense Fleet had been positioned as soon as the new gravitational displacement sensors

aboard the *Bulwark* had detected the foretold tear forming above the night sky. And for a time it worked, until the
Kossovoldt took notice and began to boil the metal from
his captains' hulls. It took only hours to dismantle the majority of the fleet and drain the seas and skies of Gavisar,
leaving billions dead or dying.

He had left Gavisar before, of course. But never here,
never to Pedres. Pedres had been his people's temptation to
stray. Now he rested upon his knuckles, forelegs wrapped
around protruding coils of cabling that ran across the view
screen. He watched, as below him the storms of Juna swallowed up the Maeyar survivors. The human's aid had been
invaluable in spotting their maneuvering and timing the
counter-attack that had crushed Eru Vehl and her spoiled,
faithless crew. The lightning that stretched up into the
vacuum of space caused interference on his screen, so he
turned away from it to find his personal chaplain, Jessad,
floating nearby.

"Admiral, the human has initiated contact once more.
He wishes to know our next move."

"Have the signal routed here."

"Yes Admiral. Is there anything else?"

Raksava paused. On the screen, gentle flashes represented his fighters destroying the last of the Maeyar flanking fleet above Juna, though leaving the remainder at his
back could seriously jeopardize the noncombatant ships
orbiting the planet. Those noncombatants and their broods
were the future of the Gavisar, if they could pass this final
trial.

He considered, briefly.

"Why did the Kossovoldt give us Gavisar only to later
reclaim it?"

Jessad was silent for a moment. "A chaplain offers

spiritual guidance, admiral, not insight into the mind of the divine. I cannot presume to know the minds of the Kossovoldt."

"Then guide me."

"The Kossovoldt have returned as they promised in ancient times. Their gift to us was not Gavisar, but the written and spoken word, and with it the opportunity to forge our destiny in exchange for stewardship over the planet. So that we would no longer *need* Gavisar."

"And are we ready to forge our own destiny?" asked Raksava.

"That will depend on your leadership, Admiral," said Jessad, and with that he passed through the iris hatch, leaving Raksava alone with the silent display, until it was replaced with the image of the Human captain, Jones. It was an ugly little thing, long narrow face with hair on one half, and more surrounding a thin-slit mouth. Humans possessed the bifold symmetry favored so often by spacefarers.

"I must commend you, Human Jones. Your timing was exquisite, truly an ambush worthy of those who bested the Dirregaunt. Now the path to Pedres lay open and the scales swing in our favor."

The human called Jones showed Raksava the top of his furry head. "Thank you, Admiral. It is my sincerest hope that this victory signifies the beginning of a friendship between our people."

"This war is not over yet. The greatest challenge lies ahead, and with the *Vitacuus* behind us Arda will be nipping at our backsides. Pursuing her on the surface without the *Bulwark*'s gravitic sensors is suicide, and if she is left to threaten the brood ships any siege of Pedres will prove a pyrrhic victory."

The human considered for a moment. "If I may, leave

me a detachment of ten ships. Your vessels may not be able to detect and outmaneuver the Maeyar in Juna's storms but the *Howard Phillips* can be your eyes and ears. I can get close enough to transmit ranging information and navigation adjustments."

The humans must be desperate for friends indeed if they were willing to brave the thunder of Juna. "You will be nearly blind. It will be like fighting underwater."

Jones just smiled, an expression involving the corners of his mouth exposing tiny white teeth and the reddish tissue that made up the insides of humans. The expression was meant to convey warmth, but it held nothing of the sort.

"Very well," said Raksava, "You will have your spacecraft. Destroy Arda on the surface or force her out of hiding and destroy her in space."

———

"It looks like the majority of the fleet is moving out, they're headed to Pedres. We counted eight warships heading down on a shallow approach to the northern hemisphere, but Raksava's transmission promised ten so be on the lookout. That was some stunt you pulled with the dive. It will take them a while to follow you."

Aesop listened as the scratchy reply came over the communication array. Sothcide had to climb dangerously clear of the storms to make their broadcasts. He risked detection, but Aesop had access to the Gavisari communication network, and hopefully soon limited sensor operation as well depending on how he routed power.

"Heavy losses in the planetary dive, two ships never checked in."

Sothcide didn't recognize the voice making the report.

Down four ships in total then. That put them at or below force parity with the detachment Jones was leading, but he'd have to find them first. Down there the murky black of electrical storm clouds would offer no visibility and practically blind any advanced sensors outside a few thousand kilometers. Jones wouldn't be as hampered as the Gavisari, he could navigate the treacherous peaks and canyons with lidar that would keep him above obstructions and able to hunt the Maeyar. He'd been a blue-water navy submarine officer before being accepted into the Union Earth Privateer program. He experienced tracking and outmaneuvering the quietest Chinese ships in the world through hundreds of miles of open ocean. This was his calling, and it appeared that he could no longer remain in a recon role. This is what Red Calhoun had warned Aesop about. Jones was taking up arms directly against the Maeyar in a visible show of support for the invasion fleet, and whatever happened, Aesop couldn't reveal information that would put another Privateer ship at risk, even one at odds with the goals of the old lady. But he could still follow orders to the best of his ability.

"You're outgunned, but they're still reporting their communications from the ionosphere through a compromised network. I can help you stay ahead of them, but without sensors we're limited to optics."

"Do as you can, but we cannot afford to sit idle. Wing Commander Arda has positioned us to meet their strikes. I must go, human Aesop. The clouds here are thinning, and my risk of detection increases. I will relay your words. Good luck, and I hope your captain returns soon."

Yeah, well, it wouldn't be the first time the old lady had left marines on station when the situation demanded it. "Copy Sothcide, see you on the next pass," he said. Aesop

Cohen cut the transmission, returning the recording equipment to the general Gavisari bands. When he turned away from the dish he found Singh waiting for him, floating halfway through the hatch down to the sensor compartment.

"We have a problem, Sarge."

Singh's North Indian accent carried a harder edge than usual. Aesop had been about to have her switch the power bus back over to the sensors so he could continue working on them, but that could wait. Without further explanation, the marine swung back through the hatch and Aesop pushed himself after her. In the deck below he found Vega, hard connected to Maggie Chambers' vacuum suit via a fiber optic line. His black faceplate lifted up as Aesop drifted into the room.

"Her arm showing sepsis symptoms?"

"Her arm's fine. She lied, and it's real bad, Cohen. Something punctured her suit when you guys hit the hull, and it self-sealed but whatever it was tore a damn hole through Mags. That's why she been self-dosing with painkillers, but now she's almost out. And the bleeding never fully stopped."

"How bad's the bleeding?"

Vega put his hand on Maggie's shoulder, as much in admonishment as compassion from the way he squeezed the composite plating. "Her back teeth are floating," he said.

"And of course she didn't see fit to tell us. Didn't want to be a bother, eh Chambers? Christ, girl, you could have died."

Maggie shrugged silently inside her suit, which quickly turned into a spasm. Aesop shook his head. "Vega, could you patch her up?"

"Shit Cohen, I don't know. I don't even know what's in her. Maybe if I got a look, and maybe if I had my field-dress kit or a battle surgery kit, but you can't swing sutures in a vacuum. She needs atmo."

"I know," said Aesop, the palm of his hand pressed against the translucent faceplate of his helmet. "She's lucky to be alive at all, but damn if I'm losing her just because she was too stubborn to admit she got hurt. I'll think of something."

Vega squeezed her shoulder again as Maggie Chambers twitched in pain. Whatever she was feeling in that suit must have been hell if she'd been pumping herself full of painkillers. "Better think quick."

CHAPTER 13
THE FATE OF GAVISAR

VICTORIA AWOKE somewhere other than her rack. Naked.

Not an altogether unfamiliar circumstance, though it lacked the characteristic screaming of a jealous wife. Also the characteristic light source of any kind whatsoever. And if she was being completely honest, the characteristic not-being-sucked-through-a-tear-in-horizonspace that she'd thus far enjoyed in her life. The things one took for granted.

Before long her eyes began to adjust to the gloom, and instead of the perfect pitch black she'd initially took herself to be in, there was in fact a subtle glow in the floor, defining an elevated ring. *The conn.*

"Huian? Are you there?"

No answer. Slowly more of the *Condor*'s control room began to take shape around her: the command couch, her repeaters, and lower down, the navigator's station, having lost the majority of its Chinese population in just a few short minutes. Not that Victoria had any idea how long she'd been out.

"Avery? Carillo? Red?"

Not even the hum of the engines answered her, nor the reverberation of the metal and composite hull. Hell, the air didn't even taste like desiccate. Whatever this was, it wasn't the *Condor*.

"Davis? Doc Whipple?"

Nothing. No sailors, no marines, none of her officers or crew. She'd been separated and isolated from the one thing she couldn't manage without. Humans.

"Alright enough, the jig is up. Who's pulling the strings here?"

A shadow passed over the dim luminescence of the conn. Victoria looked up. There was no upper bulkhead. Instead there was only the vague, distant, blue-black artifacting of horizon space, and a black silhouette drifting across it. The hair all over Victoria's body began to prickle. She was a bottom feeder, looking up at the underbelly of a great white shark. This place, this thing, this *not Condor* was a creation for her benefit, fabricated from what? Had they torn apart her ship already? Had they plucked it directly from her brain? No one knew what the Kossovoldt were capable of. Rather, no one knew the extent of their capabilities.

Down it floated, swimming against some unseen current as tendrils snaked out behind it, like something between a squid and a deadly man of war. Its flesh had the same red patterns as the hull of the hulk, and Victoria could see the back of the thing was ridged with undulating vertebrae. The Kossovoldt spiraled down, its enormous streaming length suspended in the air, until it could regard Victoria at eye level. Not that the xeno had eyes, just a slick sensory band wrapping around the foremost protuberance, wherein perhaps it had what one might recognize as a brain. It passed directly over her, smelling like a truck full of dead fish, and she could see multiple openings underneath crossed by a lattice of small triangular teeth. The bulk of it was the size of a van, and tentacles and streamers that snapped and sparked with static in the air extended another forty or fifty feet. Hard to judge while the thing was in constant motion, waves rippling through its trail while she tried not to vomit. In part because of the smell, in part because watching the thing was making her seasick.

"So here we are," said Victoria. "Middle of fucking nowhere, my ship falls into the hole you tore in the ass-end of space, and now what? I hope you don't plan on just killing me after all this song and dance."

A tendril reached down, causing Victoria to recoil. The Kossovoldt retracted it, almost startled.

"Wayward child, I have no intention of killing you."

It was strange hearing Kossovoldt spoken by its namesake species. Every xeno had their own unique spin on it, Earthlings included. But coming from the multiple mouths on the underside of the Kossovoldt it sounded . . . right. Almost enough to lull her. It was a siren song. Ultimately, the Kosso were predators, all the apex xenos were. You didn't get this far ahead in the stars without a carnivore's mindset, and those teeth Victoria had seen weren't for shredding veggies.

"No? Well then why am I here?"

"I brought you here."

No shit. Who would have thought that her first time meeting a Kossovoldt, Victoria's biggest concern would be minding her own belligerent temper? She grit her teeth.

"Alright, then why are you here?"

The Kossovoldt performed a slow roll that translated down through its myriad appendages. "To speak with you, wayward child."

"Why do you keep calling me that?" Victoria asked.

The hues on the Kossovoldt shifted from red to a deep

blue, its pattern mimicking the horizon space artifacting. "It is what you are called. You who has turned the atom upon yourself, and yet made it to the stars. You whose world is ravaged still by war, and yet made it to the stars. You who have shunned our gifts and yet made it to the stars. You are truly our most wayward child, and now have found yourself embroiled in a conflict older than your written word."

Victoria shook her head. The Kossovoldt spoke like it had a personal interest in humanity. "Gifts? What gifts? I think if you'd been to my neighborhood there would have been some record."

The Kossovoldt stopped its swimming, and in doing so took on a new motion. Its skin became a deep brass hue specked by eye-like markings. Its tendrils curled into enormous rings that spun and undulated slowly about each other as it tread the air before Victoria. It had stopped directly above the main viewscreen, which flickered and displayed a blue marble hanging in space.

Earth.

"We gave you the first gift, our spoken and written word. But that tribe like so many others was swallowed, and so it remained only in your past until you rediscovered it from your neighbors. Ever you would be satisfied only with what you stole or built for yourself, never with what you are given. There has been contention, whether it was worth the journey at all. Your flame burned so dim it was argued that it would never be bright enough to pierce the wall of light. It was argued that you were best left forgotten. But yet again the wayward children found another unlikely path. Through this."

The blue orb of Earth was replaced with the small insectoid shape of a microchip. Humanity's secret weapon in a universe of tape and punch cards.

So contrary to popular opinion, the Kosso language had been given to early humanity. Which meant that a Big Three xeno knew the location of Earth, and if that were the case then likely they knew of Ithaca, Eden, and Kepler. The Kossovoldt could snuff out their entire species in an afternoon, and judging by the Kosso Standard's uncanny similarity to Ancient Sumerian, Victoria surmised that they could have done so anytime in the last seven thousand years or more. But they wouldn't even need to do it themselves, all it would take would be a few hints dropped to the right xenos, and the enemies of humanity would set aflame the skies of Earth. Not exactly the Kossovoldt's typical M.O., but then Gavisar had changed all that, hadn't it? Victoria burned to ask the question, but not wanting to give the floating fish any ideas, refrained. But the question of Gavisar still remained.

"Why did you destroy Gavisar?"

The Kossovoldt resumed its circuit, as the main view screen now displayed Gavisar as it had been before their arrival. Lush blue and green oceans covered the planet, while thick white clouds twirled overhead. An aurora crested the northern reaches, and but for the unfamiliar continents, and the size which Victoria knew to be closer to Jupiter's, it might have looked like home. Or at least as much as Earth had ever felt like home. Victoria had been on space assignments longer than she'd been planetary.

"You know why."

"Do I? You're the one who brought me here, rebuilt my conn, told me that you visited Earth and I still don't know why. Shit, I don't even know why you stripped me naked. If it was to try and intimidate me, you should know I've been naked in more compromising circumstances."

There was a hesitation in the forward momentum of

the xeno, causing the trailing streamers to bunch up briefly, as if the Kossovoldt was noticing something for the first time.

"Your nudity was not of my doing, wayward child. The Kossovoldt do not share your need for garments, but I did not take them from you," it said, with some measure of incredulity. It pointed a barbed tentacle tip at Victoria as it drifted overhead. "You left them behind."

Victoria looked down at the stocky frame of her body, marred by the chronic bruises of life in space. Shit. That actually was more plausible than some tentacle-on-tushie back shelf pulp fiction. She had spent near on fifty years in the thing, and would likely spend another seventy if the job or the drinking didn't kill her first. She was more comfortable in her skin than in any uniform.

"You, wayward child, have found yourself not only centered in a thousand-year war, but to be one of the driving forces at the helm of it. Now your intervention demands a more immediate response on our part."

"The truce talks between the Dirregaunt and the Malagath."

"Just so."

Victoria considered as the xeno shifted to hues of blue and green. "Dirregaunt halted Malagath expansionism into the Orion Spur with their war near the Perseus Arm. That expansionism was pressing into systems defended by the Kossovoldt on the side of the Sagittarius arm. The Duchess' interest in the Maeyar is an indication that things with the Praetory have becalmed enough for the nobles to resume their favorite pastime of empire building."

"Now follow the chain to its logical conclusion."

"The Kossovoldt can keep the Malagath and the Dirregaunt from pressing into the galactic core, but only so long as they are also at war with each other. A unified Empire and Praetory could jointly be a threat to the Sagittarius bottleneck, so your presence this deep in the Orion Spur is meant to provoke one or the other into diverting their attention to you, leaving them too vulnerable for the other to pass up."

Victoria's unearthly companion turned a slow circle in the air. "I am pleased that our most wayward children have not lost the spark of guile for which I sought to elevate you. It is amazing how leaving a body behind can free ones perceptions in this place."

"This place?" asked Victoria.

The blue-black lines of horizon space pulsed for a moment, and Victoria noticed the familiar chill creeping up her skin. For the first time she realized that her retinal implants had not picked up anything the entire time. Did she even still have them?

"My home."

Victoria shuddered. The Kossovoldt was casually gifting her knowledge stretching back a thousand years before civilization.

"Well you still murdered an entire planet just to get the Malagath's attention. Likely two, if we can't keep the Gavisari from scouring Pedres. Can't see as you give much of a shit what happens to the Orion Spur or us Lesser Empires."

If it were possible for a color to be somber, the Kosso managed it with a dark shade of red speckled with shifting sprays of dark blue that reminded Victoria of rainfall on a terrestrial cockpit.

"Nothing could be further from the truth, wayward child. The Unveiled are our pride as much as any other. Our coming gave them what they always wanted: A second chance at their place among the stars, a place so callously stolen once before that their only way to cope as a species was to rationalize a collective falsehood of dogmatic inequity. May you someday forgive us, for we removed the only thing holding back the Gavisari, as you call them."

"And what was that?" asked Victoria.

"Themselves. We do not lightly intervene to elevate a mature culture. In this it was necessary. Gavisar had certain physical properties unique and necessary if we are to keep the Malagath and the Dirregaunt and all other challengers from the . . . Sagittarius Arm, you call it? Yes."

"What's down there that's so great it's worth all this fuss?"

Jet black shot through the Kossovoldt. Electricity snapped and arced in its tendrils as it lifted an admonishing coil at Victoria. "That," it said, "is not for you to know." It drew back, coiling on itself again, the soft streamers spreading out like a sunburst. "The time is coming, wayward child. You are not a chosen one, but you are the *choosing* one and you must decide. Will you return to your war under the watching eyes of the Malagath, and by proxy their Praetory wardens? Will you continue helping the Maeyar and the Gavisari to kill each other? Or will you leave, and draw yourself away from this conflict? I can deliver you to your world of wayward children, or anywhere you desire. But I will not make this choice for you."

There it was. No matter how hard and fast she ran from the choices she'd made with the First Prince aboard her ship. Humanity was visible now, and having an impact disproportionate to their standing in the Orion Spur. If the war across the thin stretch of stars connecting the Perseus and Sagittarius arms ignited in earnest then no world was safe, no party neutral, and billions, perhaps trillions of lives across countless worlds would be snuffed out as the Big

Three seized strategic systems and resources to better position themselves. The Kossovoldt began already, whatever they were doing at Gavisar was not a peaceful act and the Malagath were not likely to see it as such. Through their watchful eyes they had known just how to stimulate the invasion of Pedres, and it seemed not even the secrets humanity harbored so closely were safe from their reach.

Victoria had to do what she could to safeguard Earth.

"Take me back to Pedres."

Sothcide grimaced as he listened to the squadrons report in. The Gavisari had grounded another ship from outside their own estimated engagement range. The four high-altitude destroyers were able to engage with relative impunity, and the return missile fire of the *Vitacuus* and Arda's other ships having to climb against gravity to deliver their deadly payloads robbed them of their killing power. But the handful of light cruisers that Raksava had left with them had elected to brave the storms of Juna to bring their heaviest arms to bear. Even with the interceptors scouting, the Maeyar ships were being given almost no warning of the impending attacks. Something wasn't right, and more and more Sothcide was suspecting the interference of Human Jones as Victoria had warned.

Sensors within the electrical storms of Juna were limited at best, though the hot and bulky Gavisari ships burned like candle blossoms on six different sensors. But by the time the *Vitacuus* or the fighter wing were able to filter the noise into a workable ranging solution the Gavisari were already lined up for an attack run at speed. If not for Victoria's marines listening in to the strategic communications and risking themselves with periodic broadcasts as their orbit allowed, Sothcide would likely be escorting an empty fleet.

"They're maneuvering again. North, arrayed like an arrowhead. I think they caught wind of your last course change. Recommend bringing your lead ships to two-two-zero and descending another six thousand feet. That'll give you a better range and they should cross in front of your bow on their next run."

The human radio was surprisingly clear and crisp through the murk of the storms, much more so than his own fleet internal communications. "Acknowledged, Human Aesop, I'll pass your recommendation along. How is your gun fighter doing?"

"Poorly. We don't have any way to patch her up without depressurizing her suit."

Space walkers. Sothcide shuddered at the thought of a thin layer of composite between himself and the void. Many of the cultures they encountered had been mistrustful of the Maeyar's appearance—the shadowy onyx physique was the subject of many a stellar legend. But the humans wrapped themselves in it, thought nothing of traversing the great black vacuum in little more than silk swaddling. But they were just as frail as any other when it came down to the true horrors of space. "If not for the light cruisers, it is possible one of the frigates might have climbed up to accommodate you. All of our vessels have functioning medical facilities."

"Hell, the *Blessing* has a fully stocked medbay, we just have no way to pressurize it. We're passing out of range up here. Good luck Sothcide, and I'll see you on the next pass."

A quick flip of his radio severed the connection between his interceptor and the marine communication array. Angling the nose of his interceptor down, he dove back into the clouds and pushed west as the tiny fighter descended through the storm. Lightning licked at his hull, as if curious of the battle damage that marred his left wing, but without a ground it was harmless. His altitude plummeted and the clouds began to break as he entered the eye of a Storm where the *Vitacuus* skimmed the mountaintops of Juna's northern hemisphere. Arda's flagship showed damage along its port hull where it had taken laser hits and more than a few concussions from anti-cruiser nuclear missiles exploding within a dozen miles or less.

Sothcide's radio crackled as he addressed the *Vitacuus'* communication hub. "This is primary wing officer seeking *Vitacuus* wing commander."

"Affirmed, wing officer. Patching you through now."

A brief pause followed, in which Sothcide spotted Jalith's last missile destroyer, the *Slingray*, temporarily assigned to Arda's battlegroup same as himself. It was unusually bulky for a Maeyar vessel with its payload of long-range missiles. Stuck as they were in the storms of Juna, the battlegroup had no way of providing the artillery vessel with the means to accurately target its nuclear and exotic matter weapons.

"Battlegroup commander," said Arda over his radio. He could hear the background chatter of her bridge crew as her face filled his comms monitor. It was clear her attention was focused elsewhere. "Go ahead wing officer."

"Victoria's marines report the Gavisar moving north across the plains. They recommend turning south southwest to cross behind them."

"Do they now? Ral, did you get all that?" Arda asked, raising her voice to her husband and first officer behind her. Sothcide's close range sensors showed a spike in EM as the starboard antigravity generators forced the hulking ship to lean into a port turn. The other visible ships followed suit, and Sothcide heard the orders filter down through his fleet-wide circuit.

"All fighters be advised, fleet coming to two-seven-zero, altitude two-seven thousand feet. Prepare for engagement."

Arda was ordering the battlegroup due west, on a track to intercept and engage, rather than to evade. Sothcide hesitated. "Wing commander?"

"Interesting how your human friends seem to give us just enough to evade, but nothing that furthers our goal of returning to Pedres. Vehl was convinced of their intentions, and now she is dead. Your wingmate trusted them and now he is dead. I do not trust them, and I am alive. Perhaps they are earnest, or perhaps their efforts serve to delay our return to the defense of the planet. Regardless, this finally offers us an opportunity to strike back and swing the numerical advantage to our favor."

Sothcide wanted to argue, but the wing commander was right. Every moment the battlegroup squandered in evasion, Admiral Raksava drew closer to his wife in Pedres' orbit. "Where would you have my wings, Commander?"

Arda glanced at the monitor, her eye cold and hard, but twitching with excitement. "I need your fighters at the front. Targeting data is going to make or break this maneuver, and we can't chance the active sensors. I need you close enough to the strike force to develop a solution for the *Slingray*. This plan is not without risk. Do not make me explain to Jalith why I made a widow of her. Understand?"

It was a risky move, but a bold one. Arda's career had been hallmarked by fighting from a poor position and emerging successfully. "We will be going in blind," said Sothcide. "Without the humans to alert us, we may miss any changes in the Gavisari attack profile."

"The lapse of the human overwatch is why we're

attacking now, Sothcide. Besides, I'm sure the marines are capable warriors, by the stars I've heard the rumors too. But I've spent the last ten years coordinating fleet movements. I think I might know better than a gunfighter who can't perform a targeting calculation without the aid of a computer, don't you?"

"Yes, wing commander. I'll rally the wing immediately," said Sothcide. He didn't add that the human's deficiency in math and the physical sciences did not equate to a lack of strategic and tactical competence. But again, Arda was right. His own fondness was clouding his judgment, creating a desire to defend the humans from criticism and perhaps ascribing more merit to their skills than was warranted. And to their loyalty. But for the immediate future, the humans were nonfactorial.

Arda was on the hunt.

CHAPTER 14
ALTERNATIVES

"I'VE BEEN DOING SOME thinking, and the way I see it we have a few options."

Aesop counted off on the fingers of his vacuum suit glove as their stolen Gavisari ship passed over the storms of Juna. The small laser on his shoulder blinked out his words to Maggie Chambers, who leaned against the bulkhead trying not to look like she was in crippling pain. "One, we wait for the old lady and hope she gets back to Pedres in time to stop Mags from bleeding out."

"You ever rely on hope in the Mossad?" asked Singh. "Marine Commandos didn't. We can't wait, we need to take action."

"Two," said Aesop, "we radio Jones for an emergency pickup. Whatever else, he's still a Privateer. Chances are he'd come get us."

"Fuck no," said Vega, slapping a hand against the bulkhead. "He'd probably blast us instead of pulling us out. He's too far up the ass of the tripods. In any case, I'd rather eat a box of broken glass than call on that guy for anything. We may got bullshit orders out here, but I ain't bailing on Marin's orders and shacking up with that asshole."

Aesop looked at Maggie. "You're the one hurt. If you say we call, then we call."

Mags shook her head. She'd never ask for help from anyone, let alone Captain Jones of the *Howard Phillips*. That left one other choice.

"I guess that leaves option three. We take a ship with a functioning medbay and perform the surgery there."

Vega bit back an excited laugh, but Singh was more skeptical. "Take a ship with a functioning medical bay? How exactly do you propose we accomplish that?" she asked.

Vega held out two fingers like a pistol. "We pull up alongside one and knock on the door. Then when they answer it? Boom boom, our ship now. Easy."

"I've already checked the *Blessing*'s doc office. It's fully stocked with surgical tools and equipment. The Gavisari may not look much like us, but physiologically speaking I don't think they're all that dissimilar. Brain, heart, lungs, liver. They're oxygen breathing and they have an arterial circulatory system. Vega, I think they'll have whatever you need, including a pressurized suite. There's a thousand ships floating around this planet, take your pick."

Maggie's light pulsed. "You Israelis are nuts. I'm in."

Aesop turned to Singh, who was already shaking her head. "I can spoof their comms, send a phony distress call on a narrowband, but this is crazy. You want to board a hostile vessel with three marines? Sorry Mags, but you're in no condition to fight."

Aesop shrugged. "I've taken more with less. This plan involves direct action against xenos though, including against civilians. All their fighting ships have left. We have to hit them hard and fast, before they can get their own distress call out. If anyone here has an issue killing a non-combatant, this is the time to speak up."

"Hell Sarge, there ain't no noncombatants anymore. A

xeno is a xeno, and I just want to blow some shit up." Vega checked his X-87 and cycled a round into the chamber. "Just say the word."

Aesop didn't bother asking again for Singh. She would kill a thousand xenos to save the life of a marine. A thousand xenos with families, spouses, children, who knew? Her quiet demeanor belied the fact that she'd been in the Indian Marine Commandos during the Indian Exchange, the only nuclear event between major powers since World War II. The aftermath had been some of the grisliest fighting of the last century across burning and irradiated territory between India and Pakistan. Whatever she'd seen, a few dead aliens were a drop in the bucket.

"Alright Singh, get on the horn. Vega, prep whatever we have. I need to talk to Mags."

"Aye bossman. I'll be ready," said Vega. He tossed an unnecessary salute as he drifted through the broken airlock. Singh launched herself in the opposite direction, headed to the communications deck where she could patch into the fleet comms through the portable transceiver. Once they were gone, Aesop turned to Maggie Chambers.

"How you holding up? Honest truth, Mags."

The light on her shoulder began to tap out a message. "I can still fight, Sarge."

"The hell you can. You can barely move, and don't think I haven't spotted you holding the puncture site when you think I'm not looking. You're going to sit this one out. You can't be first in this time, Chambers. It'd kill you."

"I won't have anyone else dying for me instead."

"Then say you want me to call Jones. I can't order you to flip hulls, but damn it Maggie, that's the only way I see you realistically walking away from this."

Maggie Chambers' composite helmet swung back and

forth. "No."

Aesop sighed. He didn't want to call Jones any more than she did, but he wanted to lose a marine even less. Still, regs were clear. Marines calling for rescue effectively abandoned their previous billet to whichever ship picked them up. Their days on the *Condor* would be numbered, and until the next port they'd be taking orders from the captain working to directly undermine Victoria Marin's efforts to solidify a formal defense agreement. The Maeyar were a culture within the boundary of advancement. Their technology was close enough to directly reverse engineer for practical applications, not just theoretical ones. Victoria Marin had gone to Gavisar in attempt to secure that technology for Earth, at great risk to herself. Jones had just latched on like a stomach worm to suck on the anticipated success of the invasion fleet, but had no real stake. The old lady knew the easy road and the right road were rarely the same, and her crew always willingly followed her.

Looking around at the battle-worn remnants of the *Blessing*, Aesop shrugged. "Guess it's time to trade up to the newer model. I've had about enough of this dusty old hulk anyway."

Maggie hesitated before blinking out a reply.

"Thanks."

"Yeah, well, it will all be for nothing if you bleed to death before we hook a drifter. Try and get some rest if you can. I know it's tough in L-grav."

Maggie nodded, and Aesop left her to check on Singh. The comms room was as cramped as any of the others, ceiling and floor only about four feet apart. Two Gavisari had been viciously stuffed into a tight crevice to make room and Aesop had to drift past them to reach Singh. The callous brutality was not a trait Aesop admired in his fellow humans, but without it humanity didn't have much of a future in the stars.

"Give me some good news, Singh."

His marine held up a finger, and Aesop arrested his approach. Singh's other hand was wiggling in the air, typing on her suit computer's virtual keyboard. Aesop called up his own computer, using his command circuit to listen in on the text-based communication between the *Blessing* and an ECW scout frigate in too poor a shape to fight, but not quite bad enough to need a tether.

"This was easier than expected," said Singh. "Even in the midst of invasion, it doesn't occur to them to be suspicious."

"No concept of opsec for a lot of the xenos."

"No concept of 'repel boarders' either. They'll be in range to dock in a little under an hour."

And the frigate would have clean air and a medical suite. Vega was no surgeon, but he could maybe keep Maggie alive until Doc Whipple could fix her up. Only a dozen dead xenos stood between him and taking his helmet off. His curly stubble itched like hell. A thousand tiny annoyances could drive a vacuum jockey nuts after a day in the deep, and they were pushing hour seventy-two. Aesop had been awake for almost the entirety of them. He'd be relying on stimulants to keep him alert through the boarding acting.

Better stimulants than opiates. He thought of Mags. She wouldn't be first in this time.

———

"Positive bearing migration, Wing Officer. Ahead at three-nine thousand meters."

Sothcide checked his own gunner's ranging solution

before transmitting the information back to the *Vitacuus*. He hesitated as his interceptor vibrated under the turbulence of the storm. It must have been furious for him to be feeling it. His fighter wing spread across an embedded thunderstorm, both to hide their individual signatures and to form a picket that could use shared sensor data to provide a rough estimate as to enemy ranges when the signatures weren't being masked by Juna's magnetic interference. They were close enough to the Gavisari formation to distinguish individual ships, or at least tightly packed clusters to within a few kilometers based on passive sensors alone. Not good enough for a kill shot from one of the *Slingray's* planetary missiles, and lasers wouldn't penetrate more than a few kilometers of storm cloud before refraction robbed their strength.

The light for Sothcide's intercom winked on for the first time since they left the mountain passes through which the *Vitacuus* maneuvered. His gunner Riz, nominally silent as she performed her targeting and weapons calculations, piped up from the rear cockpit of the interceptor. "Wing officer, engine signature for the invasion fleet is decreasing, the formation appears to be slowing."

Slowing. Perhaps. Such a maneuver would allow Arda's ships to rake across the underbellies of the formation, an inviting prospect that could tip force parity in favor of the Maeyar remnant fleet if Sothcide was quick to signal the battlegroup. But the overextended Gavisar line had been an inviting temptation too. "Ranging solution?"

"Unchanged, wing officer."

Sothcide's eye spun to an inverted position, examining the different perspective offered on his tactical display as he puzzled over the Gavisari actions. Thus far the commander of the cruiser leading the formation had been both proactive and reactionary, and the question was whether the decrease in engine signature was an effort to pen in the Maeyar fleet or a reaction to new information. And if it was a response to new intelligence, where had that come from? Sothcide switched to his squad-wide circuit.

"Transmit a cautionary to Wing Commander Arda. Hold on the attack, Gavisari fleet is realigning, battlegroup position may be compromised. Attack risks approaching a defensive formation."

As he was speaking, the bearing rate of the Homeworld Defense Fleet abruptly dropped, and the engine signatures all but disappeared even as active sensor alarms blared across his consoles. The Gavisari were initiating a rapid course change, and it was only thanks to their sturdy design that half of them didn't fall out of the sky at the stress on their hulls from the maneuver.

"All ships, brace! Position is compromised, incoming HDF attack!"

Sothcide didn't wait for the response before he signaled his own squad into action. "All wings, climb, climb, clear the interim zone and prepare to engage!"

The powerful engines on the interceptor, kept barely at a level to maintain flight, roared to life, unrestricted by the vanishing need for stealth. Active sensor radiation from the direction of Arda's battlegroup washed over his squadron, and IFF weapon warnings followed behind as the *Vitacuus* and her sister ships began launching weapons. Even without a complete targeting solution, exotic matter warheads had killing power of more than a dozen kilometers, and Sothcide wanted to be well clear before they arrived. At the same time, active heat emissions from the vectors bearing the Gavisari contacts increased tenfold, as their own initial salvo streaked into the space Sothcide's wing of fighters had just occupied. Even in the thick murk of Juna's clouds he could see the streaks of light pass below him on his climbing ship's rear facing cameras, shockwaves trailing behind the bursts of the missile propellant.

Only instants passed before the answering salvo returned in the opposite direction, and then the thunderclouds of Juna were shown what a real storm looked like.

———————

Light washed over the *Blessing*, columns of white brilliance that slid over her hull as the Gavisari scout frigate examined what was left of the temple ship. Not much, to be told. The frigate was an ECW boat called the *Oracle*, armed with sophisticated electronic counter-warfare equipment, and Aesop hoped that whatever scan they were performing didn't extend to the realization that no life-support systems were receiving power, and no compartments on board were pressurized. He pulled his head back from the hull breach as the lights swept over the opening, casting harsh rays on the interior of the ship, where Vega and Singh were pressed to the bulkheads, short rifles tightened in slings across their chests. They were silent, EM emissions, even internal suit-to-suit comms, ran the risk of detection here, and any giveaway would rob their tactical advantage.

Or at least increase their already severe handicap.

The light passed, and the beams coalesced on the open airlock of the *Blessing*, leaving the hull breach in shadow. With an archaic hand signal, Vega swung through the hull breach, followed by Singh with the comms package. Aesop followed behind, Maggie's unconscious form under one arm. The last of her carefully rationed painkillers were spent, and she had succumbed to the agony of her untreated injury. Small vents of super-cooled vapor allowed the marines to control their flight, aiming for the open gasket of the airlock on the approaching scout frigate. A halo of light winked in and out on the other side of the frigate, careful adjustments in thrust as they closed the distance. This version of a boarding was never drilled, but then no fleet intel office had ever expected marines to be jumping from one crippled enemy ship to another.

Singh still offered text communications even as they floated across the exterior hull of the scout frigate. They could enter through one of the Gavisari ship's own hull breaches, but they would have to go compartment by compartment, vacating the atmosphere as they went with no way to reseal it. It would clear the ship, but ruin the medical facilities. No, the humans had to knock on the front door and be let in.

As the gap began to tighten between the two airlocks, the privateer marines slipped inside and clamped down with magnetic boots on the sides of the squat tunnel. The light from Pedres' distant star began to wane, and as the gasket closed around the battered airlock of the *Blessing*, Aesop uttered his own prayer, far from any god that might have heard it. Total darkness engulfed him as he laid Maggie Chambers against the curve of the bulkhead. Artificial blue light flooded the interior of the evacuated airlock. Vega and Singh had already knelt against the surface of the scout frigate hull, rifles unslung and pointed down at the metal doors between them. Aesop joined them, his heart beginning to beat the steady cadence of combat.

White gas flooded the airlock and Aesop suppressed his nerves, reminding himself that it was just air, not VX, as the Gavisar ECW frigate refilled the space with oxygenated atmosphere. Slowly, a hiss began to build, and behind it the sounds of the thrusters on the frigate continuing to make small corrections in course and speed. Sound, heard through his ears instead of translated through his boots for the first time in days. It grew louder as the pressure mounted, and he could feel the space in his vacuum suit pressing against him as his retinal implants registered Earth normal atmospheric pressure, and then continued to mount.

The exterior airlock on the small frigate was the same iris-type hatch the Gavisari favored for separating their interior compartments, and it had no window or porthole. Nothing to warn the xenos within of the death that lay on the other side of the thin metal veneer. Spaced around it at equal intervals, Aesop and his marines raised their rifles. Each would maintain nearly full cover as he or she fired down at threats from all angles. It was a textbook microgravity breach maneuver Aesop had hoped to never have to employ.

A thin thread of light appeared at the center of the iris, expanding as the metal slid back to reveal the harshly lit interior. As soon as the door swept aside, Aesop saw the clinging legs of a Gavisari maneuvering itself through the airlock. He took aim, and began to fire as Singh and Vega did the same.

The harsh, rapid bark of the stubby assault rifles preceded high screams from inhuman mouths, and was unexpectedly answered by a spike in Aesop's radiation sensors. The air crackled, and a shower of sparks erupted from the bulkhead behind him. He ducked as the free-floating slag of the docking ring spar spun through the airlock, and leaned over to finish off the xeno he'd wounded in his first volley. It had some sort of armature around its flat head that shattered as Aesop's rounds tore through it. Even without his xenotechnology degree he would have recognized a weapon-type emitter for an excited particle gun.

"The bastards are armed," announced Vega as he swung in through the airlock. "Jones must have warned them, has them expecting us. Where are the others?"

"Retreated, I know I hit one," said Singh.

"As did I," said Aesop. "They don't die easy, tough xenos."

Aesop followed after Vega, taking the communication array that was now being used to jam outbound transmissions. Vega covered the hatch, and they watched as Singh pushed Maggie through the iris last and closed the airlock door in case the Gavisari tried to evacuate the air. Aesop jammed the interior hatch open for good measure, if they tried it they'd be spacing the forward half of their ship. They had to have heard those shots, and even if they didn't know exactly what they were, the tripods had to know they shouldn't have been aboard the Gavisar ship. Once the iris was closed he pushed off the wall past Vega. "I'll take comms. Singh, you get to the pilot. Vega, make sure they can't sneak up on us."

Vega cleared his magazine, swapping it with a fresh one as he nodded. He took position as Singh followed after Aesop, bracing his leg against the narrow door to maintain control over the rifle. Aesop reached the corner of the passageway and barely dodged another blast of the Gavisar small arms, warned only by his radiation alarms. His retinal implants were trying to classify the device as a directed nuclear projector, something that probably wouldn't penetrate the pressure hull or kill their own kind but would certainly cook any marine caught in the blast.

If communications was in a similar location to the *Blessing*, Aesop would need to get past the two xenos covering the passageway, and they had it locked down. He took several shots at them, succeeding only in slowing his approach

enough to hook a hand hold on the bulkhead and maneuver
out of sight behind a junction. Singh took that path, rifle at
the ready as she floated down the passageway leading to
the nose of the small vessel. He pushed his rifle out of cover
to look through its camera and didn't like the long, narrow
passageway between him and the communication center,
which offered little in the way of cover or concealment. The
staff on this frigate were trained in electronic warfare, even
if their knowledge didn't extend to advanced computing.
Spacefaring xenos typically had minds as impressive as any
computer. Soon they would overcome Singh's jamming,
and then they'd call down reinforcements. Maybe even the
fleet left behind to mop up Arda's battlegroup.

More sparks slagged the corner of the bulkhead junction, the blast hot enough for Aesop to feel even through
his vacuum suit as the projected particles slammed into the
paneling. He could hear the panicked calls from the other
end of the passage.

"Space walker!"

Good, let them fear. Let the Gavisari think that the humans slipped in from the dead of space to haunt their ship.
For all the good that did him. He risked another look down
the passageway. The recess the two tripods were firing from
was shallow enough that he'd never nail it with a grenade.

The communications compartment was critical. The
longer he took to secure it, the higher the chance of failure
for this mission became. And a compromise of their position in orbit compromised the fleet below as well, blinding
their eyes in the sky above Juna.

Aesop looked out again, almost losing his head in the
Gavisari's weapon discharge. It was a clear line of sight, no
twists or winds to storm with the clever tactics he'd learned
in Pakistani tunnels.

The vacuum suit's radio crackled, and Vega's voice came over, competing with the sound of sporadic gunfire. "Sarge, They're trying to push around this junction, I can hold them here but you're going to be cut off if you don't hurry up."

All of their lives depended on him getting down the hallway. He took two deep breaths, steeling himself against the odds of being charbroiled by Gavisari radiation if he failed.

As he made to swing around the corner, he felt a pressure on his waist holding him back, and looked down to see the armored legs of Maggie Chambers wrapped around him. Her arm wrapped around a pipe to arrest his momentum, and her other hand held something small up to his faceplate. It was a loose rail-mag grenade. She must have pulled it out of the underslung launcher on her X-87.

Humans had never fully adapted to L-grav combat. It was too foreign to the lizard parts of the brain that still controlled fear and response. Firing the grenade wouldn't work, but it didn't need to be fired. It just needed to be encouraged, and Newtons laws would take care of the rest.

Two more blasts from the Gavisari emitters made molten scrap of the bulkhead behind him as he moved aside and Maggie Chambers pushed the grenade around the corner with just enough momentum to send it tumbling in the direction of the opposite end of the tunnel. He held his rifle scope out next, viewing the feed through his retinal implants. The newer models had color transmission, but he had to settle for black and white as the 30 millimeter shell drifted abreast of the guarding Gavisari. Almost . . . almost . . . there.

The suit computer automatically muted his sound feed as he squeezed the trigger with the grenade just outside the sensor shack. The scope feed on his retinal implants whited out completely, causing him to curse and shut his eyes tight. The impact of the shockwave hit him in the gut from almost 10 meters away, even around the bend in the passageway. A churning cloud of dust followed the blast. No hiss of air or vicious wind betrayed a hull breach, but an explosion alarm now blared in a prerecorded Kosso Standard. Coughing despite the composite face mask, Aesop pushed into the cloud at the opening.

"Nice one, Chambers," he said. She offered a sardonic salute in response. Aesop supposed it was foolish to assume she'd follow orders if it meant staying out of the fight.

Once in the passageway, he engaged his magnetic boots against the bulkheads and began to pace down. He could feel the vibration of Maggie doing the same behind him. She must have saved the last of her painkillers to prove she could still fight, true to her word she wasn't letting anyone else do the dying for her. The bulkheads had been peppered with shrapnel, and twisted metal reached for him in jagged shards as he traversed the length in a low crouch. A fire suppression system was adding to the dust as it sprayed from a nozzle, so Aesop raised his rifle and used the infrared companion sight. Hotspots abounded wherever his grenade had damaged, and as he watched, a hot mass emerged from the sensor shack. Aesop squeezed off two rounds and the thing went limp, drifting near the rear of the chamber. He couldn't tell if that was one of the xenos that had been trying to fry his face. The delicate nuclear projectors were no match for the carefully crafted and honed X-87 assault rifles, built for L-grav combat with downward shell ejection and vectored exhaust to counteract the rifle's recoil.

"Cohen, vibration sensors are going nuts, did something blow up?" Vega asked.

"Yeah I ran into a slight roadblock up here, but it's nothing a half-stick couldn't clear. I'm coming up on the sensor shack now. Singh?"

"Control is secure, Sarge. The frigate is under our control. I'm moving to assist Vega."

"Good," Aesop replied. He turned to Maggie so that her suit could pick up the laser communication. "Cover me."

Aesop tossed a second grenade, a stunner this time, through the hatch before he risked entering himself. After the thick *whump* of detonation, he swung through the opening with his rifle at the ready, drifting through the shattered glass of the desolated communications hub. A half-dozen Gavisari were within, two floating freely either dead or stunned, and another four huddled in the corner, muttering Kossovoldt prayers. The four lacked the curious weapons of the defenders so he dismissed them as an immediate threat. Civilians, survivors of the Gavisar Armageddon. Even as he watched, one of the stunned tripods recovered, shaking itself awake and latching on to both walls. Radiation warnings blared in his suit as the emitter swung in his direction, and he pushed off the bulkhead before it exploded where he'd clung. He sighted the Gavisari as it scrabbled after him, squeezing a half-dozen rounds into it. It took all six to stop the thing, and its momentum carried its body forward to crash into Aesop. They tumbled until the bulkhead knocked his shortened breath out of his lungs. Blood pounding in his ears, Aesop untangled himself from the mess of thick limbs and emptied half his remaining rounds into the other floating Gavisari before it could pull a similar act, also blasting apart the radiation gun. That first one had moved faster than he'd have thought possible, and he wasn't about to give the other one the opportunity.

Clearing his magazine and inserting a fresh one gave

him time to look around without concentrating on immediate threats. Aesop's time aboard the *Blessing* gave him ample opportunity to learn his way around the xenotechnology used to design the alien ships' systems. Scanning the room, he spotted a main power bus, and put three rounds from his rifle into the panel on the wall. The displays and tape reels dotting the compartment dimmed and faltered, leaving the Gavisari with no way to alert their comrades for help without significant repair. Repairs that, in all likelihood, Aesop himself would be performing.

"Stay here, don't resist, and you won't be harmed." Aesop offered in Kosso Standard before retreating. The doors were controlled with simple panels, and Aesop closed and locked the communications deck from the outside for good measure. If the four had rushed him, they could have swarmed him and overwhelmed him. The Gavisari were tough as hell, as strong and probably as heavy as a Grayling.

"Where was that cover?" asked Aesop, landing next to Maggie. There was no response from her suit's beacon. The pit of Aesop's stomach dropped as he gently shook her. She was completely limp in the microgravity, magnetic boots still latched to the decking gave the impression that she was standing on her own.

Aesop could hear the sound of his squad's rifles clattering down the passage, closer than he had left it. One thing to be said for microgravity, it made transporting wounded marines less risky. That might just be saving the girl's life. He disengaged her boots and pulled the unconscious marine along with him.

Vega was shouting obscenities in Portuguese through his helmet speaker back at the engine room, punctuating each taunt with a burst of rifle fire. Clumps of blood clotted into spheres decorated the air around him, and Aesop could see the vacuum suit had self-sealed over a nasty gash rent over Vega's right thigh. A section of bulkhead in front of him exploded, and Vega was pushed back into a set of pipes by the impact, helmet ringing like a bell. Aesop grabbed him and pulled him out of the line of fire as another shot twisted and ruptured the piping, spraying a gout of what looked like water down the passage. Deep, gravely Kosso shouts came from down the corridor, and an iris hatch slammed shut as the remaining Gavisari sealed themselves in the aft half of the ship. If they had pushed up any further, they would have cut off Aesop's return route. The xenos had control of the engine room, but for the moment Aesop wasn't interested in the engine room. Singh still had her weapon trained down the corridor.

"Vega, Vega! You still with me?"

The marine must have had a carbon fiber skull, because he shook off what Aesop knew would have been an impact hard enough to concuss, or a fracture for the unlucky skull. "Yeah, yeah Cohen. Let me finish them up, only a few left back there."

"Belay that. Did you find the medical suite?"

"What? Oh, yea. Shit, is that Mags?" asked Vega, looking at the prostrate marine. Alright, maybe he'd been rattled a little. The armored vacuum suits could only take so much punishment.

"Let's move, I don't think she's doing too well."

CHAPTER 15
IN THE HEAT OF BATTLE

RUNNING THE FIGHTER'S engine at full power in atmosphere would tear the ship apart in about thirty seconds, but a fusion reaction would tear it apart in a thirtieth of one. Still slow enough for him to feel every molecule in his body fraying at the seams. Slow enough to analyze his own subatomic demise. Individual lightning cracks illuminated his forward monitor, but all at once the clouds were shot through with a brilliance that made the lightning look like a child's captured glow beetle. Sothcide switched off his rear sensors to avoid damage to the delicate instruments, though his eye was already stung and bruised from the barrage of light flooding the often dim cockpit.

Two of his interceptors hadn't cleared the area in time. One of them had stayed until his death, refining the solution for Arda's missiles in an attempt to inflict as much destruction as possible upon the invasion fleet's detachment. Static filled his radio as the Gavisari missiles reached the battlegroup, and a second sun dawned along Wing Commander Arda's bearing. Sothcide reached out and braced himself against the forward bulkhead of the cockpit for the blast wave he knew was coming. Atmosphere robbed the exotic matter weapons of their kinetic energy that would shear a ship in half with the precision of a scalpel. But they traded it for incredible heat and a concussive blast wave that would overcome a cruiser's antigravity generators, and toss an interceptor around like a leaf in a storm.

The clouds betrayed its coming, beginning to rise at a pace that out-climbed his interceptor. They fled before the fury of the Maeyar weaponry. Then the blast hit him from behind, catching his ship and tearing it away from any effort to right its course. Sothcide tumbled nose over tail, helmet banging off the tight confines of his cockpit as a terrible rumble built underneath him. He had shut off his audio repeaters in anticipation, but the budding rumble that bloomed through his hull threatened to burst the fluid in his audial receptors. Behind the cacophony of the explosion was the blare of temperature alarms as the outside air baked the hull of the fighter, a fighter capable of nosediving through reentry. He could see similar heat rising on his thermal sensors from the rest of his wing as they were warmed by the infrared energy.

It might have been the tumbling, or maybe the bombs had scrambled his sensors. But Sothcide had counted an extra thermal signature on the scopes, one not associated with his interceptors. It was gone now, but Sothcide couldn't distract himself from the contact, despite the more pressing issue of the battle below as the reverberation from the shockwave faded and Sothcide wrestled control of his ship back, barely able to keep from blacking out. Something was up there. Something was shadowing his fighter wing.

"Riz, Did you see a thermal contact along axle six-two? Riz?"

No answer. Sothcide flipped one of his smaller screens to the after cockpit compartment recorder and saw his gunner slumped over in her straps, head lolling at an unnatural angle. He quickly cut the feed, sickened. None of the rest of his wing had reported it, it would have been all they could do just to avoid getting their own necks wrenched. And whatever brief glimpse he'd seen in Juna's ionosphere was gone.

Was that where Victoria would track them?

The humans were slippery, space walking killers. They didn't think like the Maeyar. Their tactics were almost Dirregaunt in nature. Could he think like one of them? That quandary would have to wait. With the area clear he had an attack to lead on the weakened Gavisari formation.

"See to yourself first, I don't need you bleeding out before you can help her. Singh, make sure they can't bypass that engine room door, then monitor the aft compartment. There's still a few sealed up in comms, too."

Singh's faceplate snapped in his direction, but she didn't comment. Her opinion on leaving any of the Gavisari alive was something she wouldn't discuss, but the scene that likely awaited him in the control center wasn't apt to be pretty. Aesop towed Maggie's limp form, pulling her along behind Vega as he navigated to the Gavisari medical bay. Medical closet would be a better description, as the three of them barely fit among the narrow stacks of supply compartments. There was nothing resembling a table or gurney, the Gavisari apparently performing operations while free-floating.

Aesop pulled off his helmet, inhaling the thick air, along with the scent of ozone and burnt gunpowder. His helmet he left in the air as he spun Maggie around and began pulling off her helmet as well.

"What do you need from me, Vega?"

Vega had already shrugged most of the way out of the

bottom half of his suit, a gash on his thigh oozing blood that clung to his leg hair. Oozing was a good sign, oozing meant he hadn't nicked an artery. "Pressure bandage," he said. "One of 'em nicked me around a corner, but I got him good. Let me handle Mags."

Pressure bandages were standard in every marine kit, stowed over the back left pocket. Aesop pulled it out and unrolled it. He had to get close to Vega to see what he was doing, and some part of him hoped Singh didn't choose that moment to see how the surgery was coming.

Vega was currently too busy to care, if he noticed at all. Using his knife he cut away a patch of Maggie's suit, pulling as he went to keep the material from self-sealing. As Vega tore off the section of suit, a sickly sweet scent hit Aesop's nostrils, and he saw Vega curl his lip up with a sharp intake of breath and pull the last morphine syrette out of his chest pouch. Aesop finished adhering the self-tightening bandage and pulled himself up for a look. He winced as Vega prodded the jagged piece of metal wedged into her abdomen. It had gone in at a shallow angle, but the suit rubbing against it this whole time must have been excruciating, and white pus ran from the puncture.

Vega, a veteran of combat in several systems, grew pale. "I uh, I need a scalpel, they'll have something like a scalpel. And forceps. And a spreader. Quick, the suit was keeping pressure on the wound. She's really bleeding now."

"Scalpel, forceps. Right," said Aesop.

"And a spreader!"

Antimicrobials too, if he could find them. Aesop didn't know if what Vega had would be sufficient. He pushed away from Maggie and Vega to the stacks of drawers and clasped cabinets. Blessed God, the Doc aboard the frigate had painstakingly labeled *everything* in a tight Kosso script.

How those hooks held a pen he couldn't wager, but he had probably saved Maggie's life.

And they probably killed him. It was a gruesome thought, but he shook it off. He was getting too soft on the xenos. That could get him killed. He pulled out a rack of surgical instruments, only a vague idea of what forceps and a spreader were. Everything was neatly strapped down, but Aesop ruined the careful arrangement by ripping out what he needed. He stopped for a moment as he saw a bright nova deep in the storms on the planet's surface through a translucent metal porthole. Someone had just blown up something down there. Something *big*.

"Aesop!"

"Moving," he said, clutching the tools to his chest and making his way back to Vega.

Vega had what few medical supplies fit in his pouch hanging in the air near him, and Aesop was careful not to disturb the air enough to send any of them drifting away. Thread, antimicrobial swabs, spray bandage, pressure bandage, and a suture kit hung around the marine like holy icons, completely counter to his chosen profession.

"Scalpel and spreaders, quick."

Aesop handed them over, instruments never designed for human hands or to be used on human physiology. Vega sprayed them with the disinfectant as he determined the best way to go about holding the treacherous hook-bladed scalpel. Despite the differences between the two races, medical professionals across the Orion Spur had seemingly universal commonalities. Doctors needed to be able to cut, they needed to remove foreign objects, and they needed solutions low-tech enough that the batteries would never die. Vega was clearly out of his element with the battlefield surgery. His hands trembled on the swabs as he cleared away the blood and pus, flinching as his patient twitched under his touch. Still, he knew more than Aesop. For all his ability to repair xenotechnology, he lacked anything more than the basic ability to repair the human body beyond applying a pressure bandage.

Vega's hands were almost a blur until they were suddenly still. He looked up at Aesop.

"Hold these here."

Aesop hesitated.

"Hold them, goddamnit, I need both hands."

"Alright alright, like this?" said Aesop, taking the perforated grips of the Gavisari forceps in his hands.

"Close enough," murmured Vega as he bent down closer and slid the forceps around the shard. Maggie moaned as he shifted it, and Vega flinched again as if he were feeling everything she was. "There's a second piece in there,"

"How can you tell?" asked Aesop.

"I can feel this one scraping it. Unless that's her rib, in which case pulling this out might leak marrow into her bloodstream."

"That could cause an embolism, right?"

"I don't fucking know, Cohen! But it's got to come out. Keep holding those."

Vega mopped up the blood which had oozed out to fill the wound and took a deep breath. With one hand flat against Maggie's pelvic arch he held his breath and applied a steady pulling pressure with his fingers white-knuckle tight on the forceps. Slowly, millimeter by millimeter, the shard of alien hull slid free, and blood welled up in its absence as the unconscious Maggie Chambers whined.

"I'm sorry Mags, I'm so sorry," said Vega as he probed the forceps deeper, for the piece of metal alloy that was still inside. The apologies weren't for the pain. Well, not directly.

'Vega," said Aesop. The marine didn't look up, but he was listening. "This wasn't your fault. The squad is my responsibility."

"Easy for you to say, mermão. You're not the one that landed that harpoon."

"And I'm not the one making up for it now. A thousand things could have put any of us out of commission, but you're the one that can give her a chance."

Vega grimaced again. "Holy…I think I got it." His fingers were quick and precise for such a big guy, and moving as much by feel as by sight, he adjusted the forceps an almost imperceptible amount, and then slid them out, with what looked like a radio receiver rivet between the tines of the tweezers. But the work wasn't done, and Vega didn't stop to gloat. Six sutures went into Maggie Chambers, then disinfectant, then layers of spray bandage to seal the wound. She would still need Doc Whipple, but Mags was through the worst of it. Aesop felt himself relaxing, running a hand through his sweat-soaked hair, and noticing for the first time, over the coppery tang of blood, the smell three days in a vacuum suit had imparted upon him.

He was still trapped on a xeno warship in a hostile system, but one had to learn to take the small victories where they could be found. Pushing off from the wall, Aesop left Vega to his work to revisit the porthole. The clouds had been pushed away from a substantial area on the blast wave of the nukes, but the speed of Juna's winds was already dragging fresh coverage across the gaps. The ECW frigate had communications that might be able to penetrate the storms, with the aid of some human modulators to refine the frequency discrimination. Aesop pulled his helmet close enough for the radio to pick up his words.

"Singh, grab the comms array and start patching it in.

Let's have a word with the holdouts about our friends on the communication deck."

―――――――――

Emerging from the clouds into the canopy cleared by the brief atomic exchange revealed the two fleets careening headlong into each other. Arda's smaller and more nimble remnant fleet against the comparatively slow but hard-hitting Gavisari cruisers. Without the mask of thick clouds, lasers lanced back and forth between the two. Only the Maeyar lasers fell within his visible range, but the searing metal and twisted gouts of venting gas betrayed the Gavisar arrays hitting home.

Sothcide pressed another burst of acceleration into his engines, switching to the fighter squadron frequency.

"Left wing, move in to support the *Vitacuus*. Right and forward, with me. We're going to make a pass at the lead ship's primary array."

With no gunner, Sothcide was limited by what dexterity steering the interceptor spared for weapons targeting, which was not much. Thus far the invasion fleet hadn't responded to his wing of fighters dropping down from the canopy, or they had their hands full. But that wouldn't last long. His squadron wings were practically skeletons, but he would make them work. Radio chatter between the Maeyar vessels failed to illustrate a favorable portrait of the tactical situation.

Barreling down at break-neck speeds, Sothcide opened up with tightly focused lasers. In atmosphere like this, they were visible to the naked eye and almost blinding even through the optical sensors. Violent cracks in millisecond bursts left glowing pinpricks on the hull of the lead cruiser. By the time he flashed past along with a dozen other ships, their presence had been noted and the anti-fighter stations began to deploy their own lasers and chaff to defract the cutting beams. But Sothcide was already headed back into the clouds, watching on his damaged rear sensors as the lines of the two fleets crossed each other, Arda with full engines burning trails in the atmosphere that snaked for miles, and the Gavisar fleet attempting to bring their cumbersome ships to bear. Two more Maeyar ships had left craters in the untamable mountains below, and they burned freely.

"Right wing, break off and provide fighter interdiction to the fleet. Forward wing, with me. Target is the Ridgebone-type missile destroyer aft of the main cruisers. Target the stress points amidships."

A kilometer-long ship was still built of parts, and swinging that much metal around in a tight arc was putting an unimaginable strain on an already damaged vessel. The Gavisari were getting greedy in their effort to stop Arda's escape once again, overexposing their flanks. With a half-dozen interceptors in tow, Sothcide navigated the web of defenses and dove down at the destroyer, funneling as much of his micro reactor's energy into his laser arrays as he could without blowing the linkages. Other lasers clicked on around him as his wingmates burned at the material joining points and the frame reinforcements of the destroyer. One of the sets of lasers winked out, and in a sideward monitor Sothcide saw a starburst explosion claim the unfortunate interceptor as a Gavisar fighter wing passed close to his formation.

His lasers weren't designed to take down capital ships. They were made to cut through the armor of a fighter, or into sensitive exposed parts required by any deep-space vessel to maintain combat readiness. But the concerted effort against already weakened material paid off as he watched a plume of venting gas billow from the breach, and the amidship compartments crumple like a ration can. The aft third of the ship swung out at an angle, still pushed into the turn by the powerful engine while the rest of the Gavisar destroyer nosed down and began to plummet from the skies above Juna. The Ridgebone class destroyers were one of Gavisar's prized artillery ships, and with its payload neutralized it would make it difficult for the Invasion Fleet to engage them without closing to almost point blank range.

As soon as Sothcide received the report that Arda's remaining ships were clear, he led his wing back into the clouds covering the battlefield. The Maeyar's positioning had given them the worst of the exchange, and left them three ships poorer to the Gavisari's two, including the destroyer Sothcide sent into the valleys below. Once again the violent lighting of Juna crept around his interceptor, welcoming it into the storm. Already communication was becoming spotty and distorted, but he knew where to find Arda.

His radio chirped, the local wing band light illuminating. "Wing officer, are we not returning to the battlegroup?"

"Negative, four. There's another ship up there somewhere, running quiet. Its feeding our course maneuvers to Gavisar. We have to locate and neutralize it."

If they could. Victoria was slick as river stone, and the way she spoke of this other captain . . . She didn't respect him, but she did fear him. If he were there, and that was still an *if*, then he was not to be taken lightly. Even as primitive as the Earth vessels were, there was a reason he personally had sought their kind out for this expedition. Now his decision may have cost the war if Arda couldn't return what was left of her fleet to Pedres in fighting condition.

"Passive sensors only once we reach the ionosphere," said Sothcide. "Assume all voiced radio calls are compromised. Use the light cipher when able"

This truly was a different kind of war. Sothcide cut his engines to just above idle, barely enough to stay aloft. *The humans rely on passive sensors and the reflected returns of radar in the vicinity.* Where would such a craft gain the most advantage? The lightning of Juna's storms followed the path of least resistance, likewise radio waves traveled with less resistance in Juna's overcharged ionosphere. The secondary band of the ionosphere was home to thick masses of increased ionization which would reflect the RF signals with stunning clarity. Sothcide tuned his passive receivers to identify likely parcels. It was likely Victoria's ghost ship would be in or near one, and he passed the message along to his squadron. The light array on his console blinked encrypted acknowledgements, and Sothcide silently cursed the necessary emissions.

The clouds were thinner here, but still ever-present in grand, sweeping brushes that would prevent visual detection. As Sothcide progressed, radio signals increased in strength toward his left front quarter receivers, and he swung his fighter around while keying the cipher transmission. *Two and Six, increase speed and array north of my mark, seven-hundred miles distant. Three and Four, left and climb another thousand meters. Five, with me.*

Four of his five wingmates keyed an affirmative. Number Four was silent. Sothcide sent an IFF interrogation toward his bearing. Nothing. Could be the storms, could be the radio interference. Could be the Privateer. *Six to Four's last known position. Three report.*

Four is unresponsive, Wing Officer the light panel

chirped at him, drawing his attention to the message.

Sothcide diverted his own interceptor, and as he approached he picked up a plummeting thermal signature. His fourth squadron mate. Cursing to himself, he climbed to a higher altitude and made an assessment.

Two and Five, deploy active sensors, he ordered. *Enemy vessel is present.*

The active radar nearly overwhelmed his receivers in the ionosphere, but radar returns weren't what he was looking for. Instead, he diverted his attention to the infrared sensors along his downed wingmate's last known bearing. A small contact appeared, barely above background levels. But it was there, and it was moving south away from the wreckage. Sothcide checked the prior thirty seconds of his radar returns. Nothing. His eye spun in its socket as he relayed the new information from his squadron and fell in line to pursue. The humans were still largely a mystery, but they had some way of preventing active targeting returns via radar. But it wasn't an infallible system. It generated waste heat.

Keep the active sweeps, narrow-field on incoming targeting data. Intensify output voltage. Ready point defense.

If they were confused at his orders to sweep what must seem like an empty swath of sky, the rest of the squadron gave no indication. These were Vehl's pilots, and they were used to the unorthodox. With the active emissions awash at his back, and there being less likely to betray him, Sothcide risked a bit more speed in pursuit of the fleeing thermal signature and continuing to give Two and Five updated bearings.

Three, return to Vitacuus. Advise Arda to press the attack. We will keep Gavisar blinded.

CHAPTER 16
RETURN TO PEDRES

VICTORIA WOKE, SPRAWLED on the sweat-stained gurney of Doc Whipple's office, the smell of it burning her nostrils. The memories of the Kossovoldt were already fading like a bad dream, and she struggled to hold onto whatever details she could. That giant space squid was like something out of a twentieth century horror classic, and had all but admitted a direct hand in humanity's development. In that false *Condor*, that *somehow* area existing between the physical world and that of horizons beyond the tears in time and space she had learned more about the Kossovoldt than the collective knowledge humanity had assembled over the previous century.

She wished she hadn't. The implications were less than ideal.

Behind her she could hear the hatch sliding open, and then Doc Whipple's voice on the growler. Victoria brushed off a probing hand, and pried open her gummy eyes to see what the pain in her arm was. An IV drip had been stuck in her, feeding her fluids while she slept.

"Doc," she said, panic rising from deep within. "get this fucking thing out of me."

It took all her restraint to not tear at the medical tape and yank the two-inch needle out of her vein. Whipple hurried over and Victoria grit her teeth as he performed the extraction.

"How long?" she asked, finding uncertain feet awaiting her as she stood up in the small medical shack.

"Easy, Vick. You've been out two days, ever since we fell into that hole in horizon space."

Two damned days. Gavisar could already be moving on Pedres. She thumbed open the door to the medical shack and found Red Calhoun waiting on the other side.

"Red, get me up to the conn."

"Easy there, girl."

Victoria scowled. "Stop saying that. Just get me up there."

Red offered the support of his arm, and though she was loath to accept it, Victoria felt like the bulkheads were spinning around her and the deck was buckling under her bare feet.

"Vick. We're stuck in horizon for two days now. Avery can't make heads or tails of the readings. We're flying rudderless and blind. We don't know that we'll ever hit enough mass to pull us out. Breaking your neck rushing yourself to the conn isn't going to help our situation."

Victoria shook her head as they passed the wheelhouse hatch. God, if only she could bring a bottle up with her. "No, we're going back to Pedres. The Kossovoldt," She stopped, clutching at the fading image of the Kossovoldt circling in her mind before it was flushed down the pipe all old dreams went to.

"We're going to Pedres," was all she could manage. The Kossovoldt were an issue too large for any one captain to handle. But the problem of the Pedres invasion was right before her, and that problem she could affect.

Red and Whipple looked at each other. "Alright. Then

we're going to Pedres," said Red.

"Stupid to argue when you get this stubborn," said Doc Whipple. "I can't say as how you're so damn certain."

The lighting flickered and the hairs on Victoria's arms began to settle. The tone of the *Condor*'s ambience took on a substantially muted hum as the horizon drive shut off and the ion engine ignited. The three paused, then pushed into the conn.

Huian twisted at her pilot's station, looking from Victoria to Carillo at the XO's chair. Never one to miss a beat, she turned back to her screens. "Ma'am, I'm running stellar recognition now."

"No need," said Red, offering a sly smile and a wink at Victoria as she settled into the command couch, "We're at Pedres. Captain Marin has the deck and the conn."

The computer confirmed his assertion moments later as it began identifying constellations and stellar bodies, including Juna at just a few million kilometers distance. They were staring right at the night side of it. Damn but Victoria would hate to play that Kosso at darts. It had thrown the *Condor* at a bull's-eye from two-dozen light years away. In another dimension. And *hit*. How did it even begin to calculate the math involved?

Whipple set Victoria's boots down by her chair with a hand on her shoulder, and then followed Carillo out as she tugged them on and engaged the magnetic locks with her coverall cuffs. She eyed Red up and down and scowled. The Scot was displaying his usual languid calm, but he only did it to hide his excitement.

"Something happen while I was out?" asked Victoria.

"Well I didn't think it mattered while we were stuck, but Avery decrypted the bulk freighter's logs. They received a warning of a Maeyar attack, *after* they'd already registered active missile tracking from the opposite vector. Jones provoked the Maeyar by making it look like Bullock fired on them."

"That little shit. If we pull through this I'll nail his dick to the wall with those logs so hard I'll make the Reformation look like a god damn sticky note. We're Privateers, not xenos, we don't treat our own like meat to slaughter when it suits us. It's time he learned that."

"Union Earth won't take too kindly to his attempts at sabotaging our alliance if it caused civilian deaths, either."

"No sir they will not. If they don't throw him in Leavenworth to rot he'll be lucky to pilot a turnip truck. Alright, let's go see how your boy Cohen is holding up."

———

The minimal thermal signature blossomed, the heat output increasing tenfold as Sothcide's interceptor became awash with targeting radar. After an hour of pursuit the active tracking of his two rear fighters had forced Jones' hand, leaving him no choice but to respond to the threat of the fighters closing on him close enough to engage.

"Anti-fighter missiles incoming, evade and engage with point defense. Contact is maneuvering to the southwest."

Relying on his wing mates to deal with the primitive, if plentiful, human missiles, Sothcide increased the thrust on his engines and banked to the right in a maneuver that would cut off the turn the Privateer was making and close the distance to visual range before Jones could escape to the night side of Juna. Advance warning had neutralized the greatest human weapon of surprise and allowed his interceptors to push in and buy Arda the time she needed. At his altitude, and under the pocket of dense ionization, he could hear snippets of radio chatter indicating Arda's intent to capitalize on the opportunity. Sothcide was some-what incredulous that she had actually listened to his ad-vice, but it did come from a position of validating her own suspicions about the humans' motives in the system.

On his screen, the thermal signature increased another four degrees as the active radar overwhelmed whatever mechanism was masking it. Still not sure enough for a weapons solution without Riz at the controls of the laser arrays.

Pushing through a bank of clouds, he entered a wide eye in the storm and got his first glimpse of the privateer before it disappeared into the shroud again. His battle re-corders were capturing every detail, but he could see the matte black shape with its stubby shielded wings at fore and aft. It looked a brother to the *Condor*, but different, more twisted and sinister. Like it was built for hunting, not ex-ploring. But now its captain had been thrust into the light, was forced to run like vermin. Now Jones would feel what it was like to be hunted through the storms of Juna. Soth-cide tightened his grip on the fighter's controls and pressed onward.

"Intensify signal strength. Give him nowhere to hide."

As his wing mates complied with his demands for higher wattage, additional contacts lit up his screen, awash with radar reflections deep in Juna's storms. Sothcide's eye looked from his battle scanner to his instrumentation. "Cut it off, cease all active emission now!" he yelled into his radio.

The radar return matched the cross section of the *Vit-acuus*. Jones had led them back through the clouds to their own fleet, and the Gavisari would pick up the reflections well enough to turn the surprise attack into a meat grinder. Thermal signatures bloomed as Arda was forced to alter course, unmasking the engine heat that had been vectored behind the massive ships. Before he could process what had happened, Sothcide's telltale track of the source he'd been following across the sky vanished. The Privateer, running only a few degrees above ambient, was washed out by the Maeyar fleet's temperature spike.

"Wing Officer Sothcide," his radio chirped. The voice of the *Vitacuus'* first officer. "Would you care to explain why you felt the need to bungle the attack you yourself advised?"

Victoria examined her main view screen as the *Condor* decelerated beyond Juna's moons. The only contacts left in orbit were those trailing the magnetic tethers too damaged to press on into the system. Which meant the bulk of Gavisar's forces had pushed on to siege Pedres. Ringed cloud formations on the surface told a tale of nuclear exchange. Had Sothcide's counteroffensive been driven down into the maelstrom of the planet? Juna's powerful magnetic field protected its atmosphere from solar winds almost to low orbit. You could hide a fleet in there for months. Either way, something had gone terribly wrong with the counteroffensive. Sothcide might already be dead. She needed a closer eye. Red had elected to stay with her on the bridge and she didn't have the will to send him packing, so Victoria made a point of ignoring him instead.

"Send the interrogation signal, let's see if anyone is listening."

The fraction of a second pulse would come across as stellar radio noise to any device not tuned to descramble the signal, in this case the marine communication dish that Aesop Cohen should have patched in by now, if he wasn't too busy twisting his throttle to all the xenotech floating down there. Sure enough, a return ping hit the *Condor*'s radio receivers within half a minute, and Victoria issued a shielded laser communication once her marine's transponder had been identified. First came a data burst of everything the squad's retinal contacts had marked and catalogued over the course of the previous three days. Then a voice-to-text transcript of all squad-level communication, and finally a black and white video transmission of Aesop Cohen himself. Presumably from his own helmet camera, since he wasn't wearing it. A few days beard growth didn't look too bad on the kid.

There was a small amount of latency in the signal, as soon as the squad leader was sure he was connected he offered a short salute in the IDF style and awaited her orders.

"Unless I'm mistaken, the hull we set you down on had no airtight integrity to speak of," said Victoria.

"Um, yes ma'am. Exceptional circumstances required that we commandeer a new vessel. We had need of a pressurized cabin to perform a battlefield medical procedure. We boarded and seized the *Oracle* from a crew of approximately sixteen, nine of whom were killed during the assault. The rest sealed themselves in the aft compartment of the ship with a host of civilian refugees. We're holding an additional four hostage in the forward compartment as insurance against the survivors irradiating us while Private Singh negotiates their surrender. One of them claims to be a higher-up in their priesthood that the others wouldn't willingly harm, something like a cardinal that can lay about two-hundred female eggs a year. Genetically engineered specifically for this Exodus. There's at least one on every surviving ship, as many as six on some of the bigger ones."

Busy little bastards. With numbers like that, the Gavisari would be on track to pass Earth's biggest colonies in just a few years. And naturally cave-dwelling? You'd never root them out without sucking the entire atmosphere into a tear in space and time. The Kossovoldt lamented releasing them on the galaxy. Now she knew why. Most of the encounter had faded, but she remembered the mournful speech. Victoria scowled as she read over the brief medical report Vega had included in the databurst. The Gavisari ship's higher air pressure and oxygen content had likely kept her alive. Better they'd have finished off all the Gavisari onboard, but that wasn't her way and it wasn't Red's either.

"Noted. With the majority of the fleet away I think we can slip close enough to pull Chambers off that wreck and rotate the rest of you."

Sergeant Cohen hesitated. "Ma'am, with respect, I would like to stay aboard to help the replacement team however I can. This frigate is equipped with advanced countermeasures and sensors, and right now Sothcide and the Maeyar need all the help he can get. The Maeyar fleet took a licking, and what's left of the forward guard is fighting for their lives right now while Jones runs recon."

Victoria muted the feed and decided to notice that Red had stayed on the conn. "Your call Red, you're the Major. Aesop is a marine first and an engineer second. If Jones is down there, the Maeyar are going to need a hell of an ace in the hole."

Red shook his head. "What he is, is the best xenotech specialist on this boat. I hate to make him stay on that frigate, but he's the only way we're going to get those sensors working."

Victoria clicked her fingertips on her console, considering. Then she restored audio. "Alright Cohen, you get your wish. But Vega, Singh, and Chambers are coming off. Rig for docking. And tell the surviving Gavisari that they have a ticket off when we take their priest with us."

"Aye ma'am. Oh, and one more thing," he said, allowing a grin to split across his face. "We have the codec Jones is using to talk to the invasion fleet."

———

Sothcide was at a loss. Somehow Jones had driven them back to Arda's fleet, revealing both the attack and their position and range relative to the invasion fleet. Only a full burn in atmosphere and the resilient nature of Maeyar ship design prevented the loss of another vessel from a Gavisari artillery salvo that Arda was unable to answer in kind with the *Slingray*'s arsenal of long-range missiles.

Whatever small capital he'd gained with Arda appeared spent. In the wake of her husband's wroth he'd been dressed down and reprimanded. Only the pressing need for an experienced wing officer to remain in command of her fighter squadrons had kept Arda from turning him into a space walker, and once Riz's body had been pulled from his interceptor and honored he was right back in the cockpit with a gunner of Arda's choosing.

If she did decide to eject him, could the humans have saved him?

Sothcide had seen the humans unpacking and distributing spare suits and breathing masks for passengers they carried without the rare physiological quirk of oxygen tolerance they shared with the Maeyar. That genetic anomaly of carbon-based life in the galaxy closed off a lot of worlds to species not capable of terraforming on a planetary scale, and competition within those worlds was fierce for their rarity. Gavisar had fended off more than a few attempts to seize it, consolidating power. The Maeyar had spread themselves, and now it appeared too thinly.

The communication bulb for the Privateer channel illuminated, and Sothcide's finger had brushed the circuit almost before he thought about what he was going to say. Human Aesop's intel had directly led to the confrontation with Jones and the subsequent demotion, but to pass the blame for that onto the human warrior would be nothing short of sheer cowardice.

"This is Sothcide, go ahead Aesop."

"Not quite," said Captain Marin. Sothcide almost fumbled his course correction. He lowered his voice on the radio, despite what a foolish and conspiratorial gesture it made. All communications on Maeyar fighter-craft were recorded locally and reviewed. But the logs wouldn't be downloaded until his next refit on the *Vitacuus*.

"Victoria. Did you scout Gavisar with the Malagath as the Wing Admiral requested?"

There was a humorless chuckle on the other end of the connection, a human gesture he had become familiar with as losing poker hands were revealed and the holders were relieved of their currency. "What's left of it. Sothcide, the Kossovoldt claimed the system, killed everyone on Gavisar and two-thirds of their fleet."

"Kossovoldt? This deep in the Paior's Bridge? What in the stars are they doing?" asked Sothcide. Paior's Bridge had been a no-man's-land for as long as the Maeyar had been a space-faring empire. The stretch of stars under contention from the Malagath, Dirregaunt, and Kossovoldt was the only link between the first and second blade of the galaxy without traversing the entire length, almost twenty-thousand light years.

In his mind's eye, Sothcide could practically see Victoria shaking her head as she spoke, running her small hand through that short crop of fur at the roof of her head.

"They're, something. I don't know. But they're trying to draw out the Empire and the Praetory. They tore a hole in space and wrung out the planet like a rag. No air, no water. Just a barren rock with the Kossovoldt hanging over it. Sothcide, the Gavisari in this system? They're the only ones left. *Anywhere.*"

Sothcide cursed to himself. "Then they have nothing left to lose, and we must be steadfast, Victoria, for Pedres and the light of my horizon are in graver danger than ever I dared believe."

There was a pause before Victoria responded, more-so than the transmission delay could account for. "My people have a word for stamping out an entire population. *Genocide.* I will stand with the Maeyar, but I cannot condone your action. Is there no way to make peace?"

Outside his cockpit the storms of Juna had calmed, and his interceptor was merely pelted with a rain of acetic acid. One star in particular shone on his view screen. There was a world set aside there. Uncolonized, untamed, rich with breathable air and drinkable water. The Gavisari had known of it, the Maeyar had made it a gift of sorts, when they realized their grave error. But the Children of Gavisar had come here to seek revenge for an ancient wrong. And peace was not their intent.

"Victoria. There is an episode in our history we do not share with outsiders. I learned of it upon becoming an officer, and it is not a proud moment for the Maeyar. Before your kind joined the rest of us, the Maeyar and Gavisar colonized a planet together. But we thought ourselves strong, our vessels were swift and deadly, and our great philosophers and generals had yet to tame our wild passions with the discipline of reason and humility before the vulnerable. The poem I told you of the pilgrim and the beggar had yet to be written.

"Out of jealousy we took Pedres from them, and out of fear sought to extinguish their flame from the stars. Our atomic weapons irradiated Gavisar, and it remains so to this day. But the blood of Gavisar did not lie on the surface of the planet as we believed, living on within its hollow veins and deep beneath its oceans. The Gavisar nearly perished, but through mastery of their genome, they survived. They hardened, turned to reclusion, which suited us, as to exterminate them would be too costly an undertaking.

"Over the centuries we became more enlightened while they hid in their caves amid their growing dogma. Neither of us are the same people we were during that shameful campaign. Now the Gavisari are in danger of spreading this poison my ancestors bred. And we must stop them."

A hollow welled up within as he spoke.

"Jalith stands in their path, Victoria. They cannot be stopped or deterred. Only wiped from the stars before they scour millions from the planet my ancestors stole from them."

A long silence followed, longer than any before. Then the human spoke. "Alright. But we're going to have to get you off that rock before you can be of any use to Jalith. We're coming down to Juna."

CHAPTER 17
A CROSS OF SWORDS

With Jones calling shots for the opposition, it would take more than luck and a few well-placed railgun rounds to crack the Gavisari's back at Juna. And even if they did, there was still the matter of a couple hundred warships making for Pedres. Most of which would make mince of the *Condor* in a fair fight, and do worse to the rest of the Union Earth fleet. The Pedres Defense Fleet was badly outnumbered.

The destruction of the *Clarke* represented the loss of a spacecraft comparable in size and cost to one of those brand new blue-water *Buchannan* class super carriers, with the complement of terrestrial aircraft thrown in. The Privateers were more expensive still, and collectively Earth could only maintain a fleet of twenty-seven of them, scattered across half the Orion Spur. All of Earth's collective space power wouldn't even slow down the Gavisar admiral's strength in orbit. Huian was right, they weren't ready.

But unparalleled tactics in stealth and information warfare made Juna the perfect playground for humanity's trickery. Trickery that Victoria quite literally wrote the book on. It wasn't unheard of for Privateers to play both sides of the aisle, but to be in direct opposition? That was an unusual circumstance indeed. Vick would never force

Jones out of Juna's storms. If it came down to it, she would never find him at all. Jones would fly circles around her. But maybe there was another way.

"Alright Skipper, magnetic clamps secured. Airlock seal is good, and no activity to suggest we were seen."

Victoria exhaled. "Just another hunk of space junk out here. Start cycling personnel and equipment, Red, but keep emissions to a minimum. It wouldn't do for anyone to see we've got a shiny new ship. Have Cohen report to the conn."

Victoria watched through the black and white feed of the Major's retinal implants as he surveyed the Gavisari warship, having to look away as he lurched through the microgravity. Retinal implants were not the most stable viewing medium. The marines had already done a number to the interior of the vessel, torn cabling and bullet holes riddled passageways twisted by the Gavisari small arms that the marine squad had reported. She saw Aesop Cohen salute the major as he drifted past him in the passageway, and under a minute later the boy was entering her conn along with a fantastic cocktail of vulcanized rubber, human body odor, and whatever additives were present in the Gavisari version of air.

"Alright I'll make this quick, Sergeant," said Victoria, holding back a gag. She would have to be quick. It was almost as bad as when they'd landed on Ersis. "Firstly, you are to report directly to the showers and then acquire a new suit. That one goes into a hazmat locker. Understand?"

"Yes ma'am."

"Good work on Chambers, you and Vega both. You turned a shit sandwich into a mud pie. Doc Whipple said he'd need a closer look on account of the electrical shock and infection, but from the reports Vega didn't mangle her too badly. I never gave that boy enough credit for anything but a bruiser. I'm glad to see I was wrong.

"Thirdly, I don't agree with your decision to stay aboard the *Oracle*. I think it's driven by personal feelings. But the Major is convinced that it's where you'll do the most good, and if we're going to get Sothcide and the others through this, we're going to need every ace in every goddamn hole we've got. Understand me?"

"Yes Ma'am," said Cohen, his helmet tucked under his arm. It was the same way that Sothcide had tucked his own helmet when Victoria had last seen him after the hearing under Arda, Vehl, and the Wing Admiral. His bearing would have put him at home with any of the militaries of Earth. If ever there was a xeno that resembled humanity, and not just superficially, it was the Maeyar. For all their faults and prejudices and suspicions, Victoria could see herself and her crew when she looked at the leader of the *Twin Sister*'s fighter squadrons. Humanity needed the Maeyar, they needed an ally that could show them a path forward through art and culture as well as military might. And if it started with silk and coffee? Well, then it started through silk and coffee.

Over Cohen's shoulders on the main view screen, Victoria watched as the Gavisari survivors were escorted off the *Oracle* and into the holding bunks in the *Condor*'s lower levels. They moved oddly in the unusual gravity that the ship's field-mass generators created, scrabbling for purchase on bulkheads and ceilings not designed for their physiology. Victoria sighed again. She couldn't even remember who they'd stolen the artificial gravity technology from.

The Major's marines had seized ships before. Xenos who weren't their enemies died every day that humanity fought to secure technology and advance their place in the stars. But this time that ship would be used in an attempt to protect the lives of xenos, and in doing so perhaps provide an alternative means of advancement.

"You understand what I need you to do up here, right Sergeant?"

"Yes Ma'am."

"Good," said Victoria. The little shit was a picture of military bearing. But he also had a mind for xenotech. "Rogers may outrank you over there, but you're the thickest dick on that wreck. If he tries to push you around, remind him that he may have a butter bar, but the old lady said he's still just an upjumped shithead sensor jockey with less balls than gall."

Victoria had, on occasion, wondered if you could make Israeli Special Forces blush. Revealing that she knew how he addressed her in private seemed to have answered her question. Victoria couldn't be sure, but it looked suspiciously like a smirk that Huian was trying to hide as Cohen left the conn. Victoria snorted, then keyed the engine room.

"Davis. How're the modifications coming back there?"

The conn was awash with the ambient noises of the engine room as Davis Prescott keyed his circuit to respond. All the little hums and whirs and whines that translated through the hull and ventilation of the *Condor* were magnified tenfold in the aft compartment of the ship.

"We're solid gold, Cap'n. The *Condor* can handle atmo, the systems are insulated from Juna's storms and the attenuator plates shouldn't trigger off the lightning. I knew it had to be possible, Jones has to be running the same setup down there to not be constantly caught in the open. Both the Maeyar and Gavisari use targeting radar. It will get a mite warm with all that active radiation flying around, but in atmo like that we won't have to worry about the heat sinks."

"Fantastic. Avery?"

"Conn sensors, my team is primed and ready. All my operators have been briefed on the *Howard Phillips'* unique identifiers, and on Gavisar classes and compositions and active radiation signatures. We know they have at least eight battle-strength ships down there, and a handful of fighters besides. We should be able to stay out of the line of fire if we want."

"Splendid. Carillo?"

"Tactical standing by, Vick."

One could never fault Carillo his brevity. But Victoria was already scanning through her systems readouts on her tactical repeaters. Short and long range missiles were locked and loaded, rails aligned and armed, point defense cannons updated with the latest firmware, and all countermeasure launchers freshly loaded with anti-laser rounds and chaff. Best executive officer she never had the pleasure of knowing.

"Red, finish up down there on that ship. Our orbit takes us day-side in 15 minutes, and that's our window to break atmo and link up with the battlegroup."

She settled back into her command couch as the major began to round up the technical personnel that were coming back aboard the *Condor* for the trip ahead. The *Condor* bristled with energy, she could hear it in the lighting and the eighty hertz power humming through the conn equipment. A ship knew when it was about to be pushed to its limits. A *good* ship got excited about it. Victoria was trying not to share that excitement. Two shots of bourbon burning in her belly went a long way toward helping. If she made it out of this system she wouldn't crawl out of that bottle for a month.

Until then, the *Condor* and her Vultures were ready.

Deep in the heart of the *Bulwark*, Admiral Raksava gazed upon the red stone and green seas of Pedres, on its frozen poles and harsh equatorial storms. The scouts had seen it first, obviously. And the spies, and the sensor operators and communications technicians. But to Raksava, it was as if his sensory band was the first to witness the sight since the Maeyar had chased them from it all those centuries ago. Now the children of Gavisar were hardened by the ancient Maeyar atomics, and what could the traitors do but succumb to a poison that they had inured their own enemies against? The Homeworld Defense Fleet would scour the surface clean before the survivors made landfall, burrowing deep within the caves under Pedres, never to be removed again.

Raksava had no hate for the Maeyar, as many of his brothers and sisters did. His grandfather's grandfather had not been alive to witness the theft of Pedres, and the subsequent burning of Gavisar that followed. Truly, his time in study of their fleet tactics and capabilities had given him a grudging respect for the martial prowess of a people who since their darkest hour had made efforts at reform. But they had also tried to tempt the children of Gavisar from the righteous path by offering an alternative world, and no sooner would it be settled than snatched away at the cruelest opportunity. No, their place in the stars must be earned, and it must begin here, on this multi-hued world of red trees and white sands and pearlescent ocean flora.

He looped a hook around the handle of his communications terminal. From this command station he could reach every ship in the Homeworld Defense Fleet. Raksava hesitated. He had never been one for stirring speeches or wit. His words did not rouse admiration or the courage of those under his command. His attempts at such often fell flat. In earnest, he was not the best choice to lead the survivors to their new home, but with the politicians dead, he was the most experienced and had kept the Maeyar away from two moons that would have offered a staging point from which to strike at the Homeworld. But he was no longer the captain of a warship, responsible only for a single hull. Now he was leading all warships that remained, even those left behind to safeguard his flank against Wing Commander Arda. They had not yet reported success and his human captain remained with them. Even the *Oracle*, the other ship in his fleet capable of faster than light communications, had been silent. Perhaps the Maeyar were hiding on the night side of Pedres, blocking transmissions.

Tightening his grip on the switch, he pulled it down two clicks into the radial broadcast mode, and began to speak in a slow and clear Kossovoldt.

"Begin the attack. The static defenses are concentrated over the population centers in the southern hemisphere. Be aware of surface to orbital batteries. Draw out the Maeyar admiral and force him to shield the planet. We hold the gravitic advantage, do not surrender it. First and second fleet, into assigned positions. Captains, assume control of your sections. Remember, brothers and sisters, this is the day we earn our place in the stars."

Raksava released the lever a moment, but left his hook looped around its contoured grip. Even with advance warning, the Maeyar interceptors had appeared suddenly, struck swiftly, and caused savage damage to the ships in Juna's orbit before splitting off or diving into the storms with Arda. It was uncharacteristically sneaky, bordering on what their admiralty would consider dishonorable. Perhaps when one of their worlds was threatened, all pretenses of valor disappeared from the Maeyar strategy books. But Raksava was doubtful. Perhaps there was an as yet unseen factor influencing the Maeyar fleet. He spun the lever to the strategic center and tugged it active again.

"Press the *Bulwark,* the *Aegis,* and the *Godhammer* to pressure the *Banner* and the other three carriers near the pole. I want those interceptors scrambling to protect their commanders, not carrying out their missions."

"My Admiral," his second officer responded, "That will put us in range of planetary defenses."

"Are we not a bulwark for the future children of Gavisar? We will sustain damage, to be certain. But our long-range defenses are up to the task of keeping the planetary defenses at bay. You have your orders, let us strike those carriers from the stars."

The winds and storms of Juna pushed harder at the *Condor* than Victoria expected, and with more howling ferocity. She had to admit, hearing sounds outside the bounds of the hull nominally surrounded by vacuum made for a disconcerting sensation. If she had hackles, they'd be raised. Multispectral cameras and lidar mapped the surface of the planet and offered the safest paths through winds that would have shamed any hurricane, but active emissions had to be kept to a minimum. Only laser-based communication with the *Vitacuus* and the tightbeam-encrypted channel to Sothcide's fighter squadron one hundred and nine miles ahead of the *Condor* kept her from being completely alone in the storms.

"Alright Sothcide, I'm climbing another three thousand

meters. Once I'm in the ionosphere I should be able to pick up a few open Gavisari communications and get a read on their bearing, but you can bet Jones will pick you up as soon as you get wind of him again. I can't take any actions that directly compromise his position or his safety, but don't expect him to show the same courtesy. He's way past weapons-free."

Jones would also stay in the shadows, he wouldn't put his own ship at risk unless absolutely pressed. Like by multiple fighters overwhelming his attenuator with active radar to force a trackable heat signature. Clever trick that, and Victoria wasn't sure she liked a xeno having that bit of information. It especially rankled that she probably never would have thought of it. Active emissions were ship killers. Attenuators were what kept privateers out of the crosshairs against xenos that relied on most forms of reflective sensors. It was almost a shame that only the Gavisari flagship carried gravitic distension sensing technology. Victoria would get no use out of her Malagath-enhanced gravitic stealth device. Not that she would complain about a ship like the *Bulwark* not breathing down her neck. But so many bits and baubles lined the *Condor* with the intent of hiding her presence, it was no wonder so many xenos considered humans almost mythical.

The clouds thinned with every meter, massive cumulus clouds giving way to sweeping bands of cirrus dozens of miles across that left her sensors frosted with glycol as she passed from one to the next. Lightning arced from cloud bank to cloud bank, even at this altitude, crackling pockets of pure ether that collected in localized troughs of low pressure. Wind howled against the hull, and the sound of the xenon ion engine translating through the metal and composite whined as the *Condor* fought against the push of the supersonic transit. Aerodynamics had been added only as an afterthought—Victoria's ship had never been designed for this type of flight.

Cresting the top of her ascent, Victoria tuned her command sensor repeater, watching her sensor team sweep for available communication signals. She picked up the Maeyar first, hiding low beneath a sweep of mountains that made the Alps look like barrow hills. They knew their communications were compromised, thanks to Sothcide, and were keeping radio transmissions at a level that severely impaired Jones' ability to range them. Reducing communications kept them out of the scope of the Gavisari for the moment, but the sharks were in the water. Pound for pound, the ships Raksava had left behind would still crush Arda's survivors if given clear opportunity and an advantageous angle.

The Gavisari were somewhere to the east, a general mass of radio and infrared radiation scattered by the atmosphere to the verge of uselessness. But the more Victoria climbed, the more her sensor team began to pick up snippets of communication, all of it now encrypted with the codec Aesop Cohen had acquired with his takeover of the Oracle orbiting a few thousand miles above.

"Sensors conn, what's the word from on high?" Victoria asked over the open microphone.

"Conn sensors. Sergeant Cohen is having difficulty integrating the sensors on the Oracle, but communications are active. Sounds like the invasion fleet has been warned against accepting unsolicited orbital communication and is using hourly passphrases. I think it's safe to say Jones suspects something has changed. He might have guessed we're back in the area of operations."

"Or his paranoia spiked when our boy managed to

flush him out from under his rock. Any sign?"

"Negative Vick. Sothcide's wing reports clear skies, aside from heat put out by enemy fighters. If Jones is up here, he's looking for the Maeyar same as we're looking for Gavisari."

He was up here. Victoria could feel the chill of him watching her, almost as bad as if she was still in a horizon jump. Hell, the bastard might already be picking up her scent, and she wouldn't put it past him to break the Privateer pact and relay her position if it wouldn't cause a mutiny aboard the *Howard Phillips*. His sensor operators would be looking for the tell-tale ionic xenon that marked Victoria's presence. Jones was propelled by a reactionless emdrive, another piece of technology humanity had stumbled upon before seeing its practiced applications in the hands of other xenos possessed of a deeper universal understanding. Almost as eldritch as his vessel's namesake, it left no detectable propellant for her hyperspectral sensors to track.

"Alright, keep monitoring those reflected returns and the bands for sonics put out by his drive. This atmosphere is so thick and layered we should be in a good position to pick them up," said Victoria. She leaned forward and lowered her voice. "Huian, give us another half percent of thrust. Their engines are barely above idle but the squadron is still running away from us."

Her navigator nodded. There was no perceptible change in the attitude or activity of the *Condor*, but the ranging solutions offered by the computer's IFF tracker began to reverse their trend. The interceptors were running at barely above idle and still leaving the *Condor* in the dust. She could see the holes their wake turbulence was tearing through the cloud banks, massive spiraling vortexes that dragged the frozen cirrus bands a mile or more before the winds of Juna's upper atmosphere swept away any trace of their passage.

"Conn sensors, one of the fighters is sweeping north. She's reporting positive bearing rate on a Gavisari cruiser."

Victoria zoomed in on her main view screen, the computer highlighting the fighter's trajectory projected through the intervening clouds.

"Understood. Huian, swing us four degrees port. I want us to be covering that gap she's leaving in the formation."

The heat signature on the fighters was only a fraction of that generated by the larger ships. Both the Maeyar and the Homeworld Defense Fleet were using them to scout ahead of the main battle groups. Following the pattern of Sothcide's wingmate, the other four interceptors began to drift north, and Victoria considered. Some small amount of active radar was being picked up, but not enough to present a cross section to the technicians on the low-flying Gavisar ships. But if Jones wanted to pick up the most direct bounce, he would be keeping pace ahead of the wing, maybe three or four hundred kilometers distant. Victoria keyed the laser intership comm connection that she maintained with Sothcide. Jones would have no way to intercept it without directly transposing his ship between the two, a feat of which even he was incapable.

"Primary wing, this is *Condor* Actual. Recommend dropping your number three, four, and six about six-zero-zero meters below your azimuth."

"Confirmed and complying, *Condor*. Expect further maneuvers to develop ranging solution on errant Gavisari vessel."

Victoria nodded as she followed the general path of the maneuvers. She had been out of the system, but the last time the Maeyar had pursued what they believed to be an errant ship it had cost them half their forward fleet. Even with a superior force remaining here, the Gavisari did not need to draw out and destroy the Maeyar remnants, only keep them from striking at Raksava's rear flanks while the real battle was fought elsewhere in the system. On the flip side, if they did get a ranging solution, it could provide means for a long-range strike by the *Slingray*, the first Maeyar ship she'd identified at Ersis before this mess started.

"I wish I'd landed on the other side of the planet," muttered Victoria.

"What was that, ma'am?" asked Huian.

"I said steady as she bears, we're passing under strong reflection. Avery, now's your time to shine."

"Roger conn, hailing the *Oracle*."

It took monumental force of will to resist adjusting the propulsion feed line closer to the intercept power setting. An interceptor should have been the fastest thing in the sky, not creeping around with an engine purring like a house pet. It was a distraction, at a time when Sothcide was attempting to both lead his wing of fighters and keep his eye glued to the thermal scope. It was obvious why Victoria would not be direct with her knowledge of the human captain who opposed and defied her, least of all revealing his position. But the request to alter the tails of his wing put him in mind of his attack run on what he suspected to be a Gavisari cruiser prior to the destruction of Wing Commander Vehl's battlegroup. Victoria tightened his squad's radar signature, oriented to cover the patch of sky that she expected the other privateer was lurking. Only a few hundred kilometers away.

For the moment his thermal sensors read clear, washing out momentarily as flashes of lightning overwhelmed the apertures.

His number two had swung north. Putting herself fifty kilometers off his port bow and realigning with magnetic east had provided enough of a bearing drift on a Gavisari contact to triangulate the engine heat and active radar from one of their warships within a few hundred miles. Not nearly accurate enough for a firing solution to beam back to the *Vitacuus*, or anything beyond general awareness of its proximity really, but it presented an opportunity that Sothcide knew Arda desperately needed. Now down two frigates and a destroyer, Arda was at a firepower disadvantage.

The *Condor* had weapon systems that struck like the marine slug throwers on a spacecraft-sized scale. It was the same principle behind the interceptor launch systems aboard Maeyar carriers, if a brutish and primitive application of it. They were completely dumb-fired, and badly affected by the high winds over long distances, but emitted less light and heat than a laser and less traceable electromagnetic waste than an excited particle cannon. The projectiles were also smaller than missiles, small enough for most radar systems to overlook or dismiss as a harmless meteor. Jones had shot down one of his squad mates with one, Sothcide was sure of it. Would they do much against the smaller Gavisari vessels? Perhaps, if she knew where to fire them. The *Condor*'s advanced optics would count for little in this soup.

Sothcide angled the nose of his interceptor. Dipping below the rim of a hailstorm sounded like someone pouring out a sack of grain the size of the entire sky. Victoria had confided in him that the sounds of atmospheric activity unsettled her, and Sothcide had to admit a similar vulnerability. He was used to the relative silence of space flight, hearing only the sounds of his own engine and instruments. The thick hail disrupted his sensors, but he still saw the signature of the overexposed Gavisari vessel shift two tenths of a degree, corroborated by his number three flying twenty miles to the south. Their target was on the move. It was time to put the Privateer's plan into motion.

CHAPTER 18
CONDOR DESCENDING

"SOTHCIDE'S ON THE move, Vick. I'm seeing engine heat output increases all across the board. The adjacent squadron is moving in to support."

"Thanks Avery. If Jones is watching you can bet he saw them too. Huian, climb us up another two kilometers while his sensor operators are distracted. I want a height advantage. Carillo, launch a pair of tightbeam relays."

The *Condor* shuddered even harder for a brief moment as the two small missiles carrying communications equipment sped toward low orbit on plumes of frozen propellant. A blinking light on her comms repeater showed that her operators on the *Oracle* had successfully connected to them as well when it turned to a dull magenta glow. The relays would let her communicate without compromising her own ship's position.

Victoria drummed her fingers against the arm of her command couch. "Let him know we're right behind him."

"Roger that, Vick. I'm intercepting a communication between the Gavisari using Jones' codec. He's put them on high alert. I don't have a fix on his position, but he's reporting the fighter positions within a thousand kilometers of the formation. Expect our boy to maneuver soon. His active EM radiation signature matches recorded light frigate systems. Designated Primary."

The main view screen lit up with the new designation, replacing the overlay for an unknown contact with the double crescent moon shape of a light frigate. Similar in size and profile to a Privateer, but likely more than double the tonnage with all the armor plating and active defenses that Gavisar liked to slap on their hulls.

"Light frigate. Perfect. Any word of us on the waves?"

"Negative, either Jones hasn't caught our scent or he's keeping our secret. Whatever else, he's still a Privateer."

Victoria caught herself drumming on the arm of her couch again and stilled her hand with an effort. Some of the Privateer and Union Earth Naval captains came from blue water backgrounds where they had gone head to head with the minds of other human officers. The previous hundred years of human history had not been without wars and skirmishes, despite the extra-planetary efforts of Union Earth. But Victoria had never been part of any country's navy. She was an explorer and a pioneer. Maybe a bit of a pirate, but not a military operative. It was a new sensation, knowing there was another human mind working against her. Somehow more sinister even than meeting the Malagath, being pursued by the Dirregaunt, or even kidnapped by the Kossovoldt.

Victoria had witnessed terrible acts committed by individuals and governments alike. Humanity was her cause and her life's work, but it was also capable of unimaginable cruelty. Some rough patches maybe got smoothed over along the centuries, but the malice to perform it and the guile to confront and resist it through blood persisted through each generation, and never had she found herself faced with that utterly *human* miasmic threat. Sometimes the devil you knew was goddamn worse than the one you only pretended to know.

Victoria eyed the tactical grid on her sensor repeater, watching as expected contact positions were pushed and pulled and bearing rate began to increase measurably on a few more contacts. They were closing on the formation. "Huian, put us on an east southeast heading."

"Aye Skipper."

East southeast increased the crosswind component of the storm buffeting them, a massive storm cell over six thousand kilometers in diameter. In the lower ionosphere they were out of the worst winds, but the *Condor*'s rattling intensified. Sometimes high-frequency vibrations could be worse for a spacecraft than the pressure wave of an explosion. Hopefully Davis Prescott wasn't slacking his fat ass off in the engine room.

"Tactical conn, I'm maneuvering to shallow up our dive so we don't plow into a mountain side, and to try and keep our bow pointed at the quadrant of sky where I expect Jones to be. Be ready to readjust firing solutions."

"Aye Vick."

Carillo must have been feeling talkative today. A few rare moments passed with no chatter on the open circuit, then the communications notice blinked in her retinal implants. Sothcide was initiating. Victoria thumbed the activation switch on her command couch.

"*Condor* Actual. Go ahead."

"Captain, Wing Commander Arda has been monitoring our progress through the other fighter wings, and gotten wind of your plan. She has ordered the fleet out of hiding and is preparing for a long range attack based on our intel. I am patching you through to her now."

"Shit. Okay, go ahead."

Passive sensors lining the aft third of the ship spiked

when active sensing radar passed into line of sight from the *Vitacuus* and her sister ships. Victoria eyed her thermal scope reading the most likely bearing of the *Howard Phillips*, directing the Gavisari ships, but even at max sensitivity the field remained barren. However, several new contacts sprang up on the main view screen.

"Conn sensors, active reflection, cross section suggests fighter-type craft. Two squadrons to the east transitioning north."

"Sensors conn, aye." said Victoria. She had known they would be out here, but the Gavisari fighters were taking pages out of the Maeyar playbook by reducing their engine output as much as possible. Or maybe from Jones'.

Her main view screen overlay still painted the light frigate as an unreliable range when a portion of it was taken up by Arda's severe onyx features. The bridge behind her was a carefully controlled chaos of orders and department heads directing the actions of the massive command carrier and the remaining fleet. She was broadcasting in raw radio, despite the warnings of who else may be listening, with her husband and first officer resting a hand on her shoulder.

"Human Victoria. I see you have rejoined the defense of Pedres. I do not know if you betrayed or abandoned the Malagath duchess, but you will not have the opportunity to do so with me. I am pulling my forward fighter squadrons back. I will not risk exposing them for a solitary frigate. Our situation is too dire."

"Commander, if you just give me a chance to explain the plan."

"Negative, human. We are pushing over the mountains now, climbing to high altitude. Vacate the area of operations and do not engage. If you are here, you will follow my directives and follow the fighter wings away from the coming battle."

"Let me guess," Victoria said, an edge of venom creeping into her voice, "You can't guarantee my safety if I persist?"

Arda's eye jerked clockwise in its socket, the iris narrowing as she let her temper get the better of her. Arda was cunning, ruthless, quick, and indomitable. If they weren't at such odds Victoria might have even liked her.

"This is a war, human. I will not vouchsafe, nor do I particularly care for, your safety either way."

The connection was severed, and she opened up a tightbeam radio link to Sothcide. "We won't get another chance at this," she said.

"I am with you, Victoria Marin."

Sothcide had never gone against the orders of a superior officer, let alone purposefully interceded in a planned fleet-level offensive push. But Victoria had seen things at Gavisar that would give her more insight than the mistrustful commander of the Pedres defense fleet. And she had her eyes in the sky with their spacewalker-captured vessel. The fighters in his wing and those moving to support were the remaining sixteen pilots under Vehl's command, and with deft fingers he linked their communications together in a single circuit and their transponders under his command, ignoring the protests and threats of his gunner, placed by Arda to watch him.

"All fighters of First and Fifth wing. Form up and position for an attack run."

The leader of the fifth wing, Allid, responded almost immediately. "Wing officer, we are going against Arda's orders?"

"Yes, Allid. Arda is a brilliant commander and a sound

tactical mind. But sound conventional tactics will not over-come a fleet with half again our strength. We must embrace the unconventional, as Vehl Ku would have done. Trust in me."

Time was running out, they were drawing closer and closer to the frigate, and though radar was being scattered by clouds, Sothcide was sure they were closing inside of a hundred kilometers. Even the stunted lasers would be effective under twenty, but visual would be optimal in Juna's unrelenting storms. Somewhere behind and above him, Victoria was preparing her heavy weapons as well.

There was silence on the channel. Sothcide waited while his counterpart wing officer considered.

"Vehl chose you to lead us. We will follow."

Sothcide flipped his engine from a high idle to an attack profile. "Then cover the eastern approach. Keep those fighters away from our attack run."

The light frigate was changing course again, realizing the intentions of the fighters too late. Even a ship of that size carried more mass than was convenient to move, and the Gavisar ships had little in the way of aerodynamic aid. Overhead, Allid and his wing had increased their intercept speed, burning hot and accelerating at a breakneck pace. His radio blared in his ear as Arda's gunner in the back of his fighter overrode his communications and Arda's voice filled his cockpit while her face and the frantic bridge crew behind her filled his monitor.

"Wing Officer! Pull back now, I cannot launch with two wings in the target area."

The bearing on his sensors was coalescing, and Sothcide turned on his localized targeting sensors. They were inside of two hundred kilometers now, and closing fast on the fleeing frigate. Its engine heat blazed like a guiding star.

The active radar swept and returned, offering ranging information within five hundred meters tolerance. *Still not close enough.*

"I cannot, Wing Commander."

"Sothcide, we are committed to this attack run."

"So are we, Arda."

The Wing Commander hissed through her proboscis, which turned into a low growling order to break off the attack, declaring ship position orders and trying to salvage the wreck of her formation. She could not lose a third of her remaining fighters to friendly fire. Several thousand feet above his dive, Allid had engaged the tough-skinned Gavisari fighters. Lasers lit up the sky, carving linear paths distinct from the lightning that staggered its way across Juna and crackled against the damaged hull of his fighter. The clouds robbed it of almost all its range. It was like an ancient planetary duel fought with the lasers of pre-space-traveling Maeyar ships that still relied on lift and aerodynamics to achieve flight instead of fusion engines and anti-gravitic generators. Even if these interceptors weighed a hundred times as much as their jet-driven counterparts.

"The rest of Gavisar's fleet is on the move. We will have one opportunity, Victoria. Be prepared."

CHAPTER 19
TRUE COLORS

"L ET SLIP THE Dobermans, and send a few missiles to cover our approach."

Shrieks echoed through the hull of the *Condor*. Victoria's will was made manifest by the myriad armaments pouring down past the Maeyar fighters and into the Home Defense Fleet frigate. Warnings began to dot her screen, noting Sothcide's contact with the frigate's active fighter defenses, as well as the medium-range ship-to-ship missiles that the rest of the Gavisari was slinging their way to cover the frigate's retreat. Sure enough, her missiles began to be cut down as well, but the Doberman rail mines storming toward her target had yet to be targeted. Admittedly, her own missiles were disappearing from her combat network at an alarming rate.

Confirmation of successful hits from Sothcide's wing came in the form of light brighter than any bolts of lightning Victoria had yet witnessed at Juna. The laser energy scored grooves through the storm and that energy, normally invisible, was allowed to propagate through the atmosphere, carving off armor plating and penetrating existing damage on the frigate.

"Conn tactical, fifteen seconds to firing range. Have good solution, one of the pilots laid eyes on through a break in the clouds."

A micro-nuclear burst created a tiny sun off her starboard bow for an instant. Two of the IFF beacons from the fighter winked out, struck by an exotic matter payload more suited to cracking a destroyer's back than to taking out fighter-type craft. It must have come from one of the cruisers in the main formation. Her radio crackled to life again.

"*Condor*, this is Sothcide. Target is breached. Dorsal spine, just aft of the twenty second frame. Two of my pilots reported it before they were taken."

"Make the adjustment," Victoria shouted over the open mic. In the corner of her eye, for the first time, a new identifier icon appeared on her communication screen. A warped, 5 pointed star shone on her screen, with a flame burning in the center. But there was no time to think about that now.

The *Howard Phillips*.

"Fire," said Victoria. Lights dimmed aboard the *Condor*, and for the first time Victoria was treated to the deafening roar of the twin magnetic rail cannons running the length of ship being fired in atmosphere. The forward view-screen was so overwhelmed with brightness that for an instant Victoria worried that she was looking at an unlucky missile that had found the *Condor*, but the rails continued to bark and rattle the deadly gout of metal shards at speeds beyond hypersonic. They left vacuums behind that collapsed so violently that the air ignited in their wake, and the Doberman rail mines, miniaturized versions built into a mid-sized missile housing, added to her thunder with their own.

"Holy shit," said Victoria, though no one who was listening could have heard her profanity over the report of the railgun rounds. Huian was already lifting the bow of the *Condor*, banking with what power the ion engine could produce to halt their forward motion. Now on their port side, the reduced heat signature for the Gavisari engine was decreasing quickly on the azimuth, and accelerating toward the surface of the planet.

"Primary is down, repeat, primary is down. Zero bearing rate on multiple contacts, Vick."

Sothcide had seen the kill, and was pulling his fighters out of the dogfight, trying to minimize losses. But two more fighters had been struck from the sky. Victoria opened the channel to Sothcide again. "Alright, target down. What's Arda's status?"

"Human Victoria, the battlegroup is a mess, exposed, still attempting to reorganize without crashing half the ships into the eastern face of the Jodaeyar Mountains. If the invasion fleet were to find them, we would be lost. We cannot continue, we must return."

Once again the icon for the *Howard Phillips* illuminated on her communications display. "Hope you're paying attention, kid," she murmured before accepting the video invitation through one of her remote comm relays. A portion of her main view screen was filled with a mirror of her own conn. Same pilot's bench, same command couch wreathed with consoles, switches, and command repeaters. Jones looked out at her with the same metallic glint in his eyes, reflecting the bright light of his own view screen on a face otherwise steeped in shadow.

"Pawn takes bishop," said Victoria.

White teeth appeared in the shadows. "So it's chess we're playing? Very well, Victoria. You may have taken a piece, but you exposed your queen in your haste to strike the first blow. Your pieces are out of position, and you've shown your strategy to be full of holes."

"Not as full of holes as that frigate."

Jones leaned forward, rolling his shoulders he looked like some fairy tale monster with white glowing eyes and a Cheshire grin.

"And to punch those holes you tore a rift in the entire Maeyar command structure. Fighter captains mutineering against their commanders, your entire fleet clustered and disarrayed like a flock of sheep."

"Keep talking, asshole."

Jones laughed, but it was true he seemed to be in no hurry to terminate the connection.

"Face it Victoria, you've lost here. You tried to shut me out of Pedres out of spite so you could foster your little pet project. But these waters aren't the East Indies. Empires aren't built on coffee and cloth anymore. Tech div wants tech, not a few lousy minerals. You think long-range trade is profitable for Union Earth?"

Not after he got the trade freighter killed. A single line of text appeared on her retinal display.

Keep him talking.

"No, but alliances are built on trust. And I earned that trust, a trust you tried to sidle in to and swindle like a con man," said Victoria. She leaned forward in her chair as well, staring at those stark white eyes.

"Trust? That Maeyar commander can barely stomach you. Hell, do Maeyar even have stomachs? Never mind. She distrusts you so much that she would rather broadcast her intent and position over radio waves than rely on the secure communication channels that you provided. Your fighter captain sure had faith in you."

Avery was staying silent, but her sensor repeater was being constantly updated with the evolving situation. *Zero bearing rate, emissions increasing, radar up-doppler.* Victoria eyed the panel. The Gavisari were arrayed in their arrowhead formation again, driving west into Arda's remnant fleet, and all the heat her straining engine was putting out painted her signature in the skies.

"And how the fuck would you know anything about what Sothcide thinks?"

"Your emission discipline lapsed when things began to fall apart. Even tightbeam comms aren't a one hundred percent secure method. If you can get between the source and the receiver, adaptive beam forming will do the rest. You should have stuck to the laser. Oh, and if the Gavisari don't pin your ship to a storm, get that portside ablative wing fixed back there. It's an eyesore."

Victoria tried to control a shudder. A predator like Jones was tuned to pick up signs of weakness. Victoria expected to be outmaneuvered, for the privateer to fly circles around her, be where she wasn't expecting. But the fact that he'd gotten a *visual* on her ship and none of her operators had picked up on it? Well, that was unsettling. She was right to fear him. But she had also pegged him for a gloater, eager to soothe his ego after she had emasculated him in front of a xeno military officer. And in that, Jones did not disappoint.

"Now I suggest you vacate the area. Once I relay the Maeyar positions to my xenos, that mountain range is going to get a bit warm."

"Don't bother, I took care of that already."

The vulpine smile faltered.

"Come again?"

"That'll be the day. I said don't bother. I already told them exactly where to find the Maeyar. Or rather, you did. And how to position themselves to best take advantage of their disarray. Very clever of you, Jones."

Victoria swung the main view screen one hundred and eighty degrees with a wave of her hand. Ahead to the west, pinpricks of light were growing in the storm, hidden by occasional gouts of iridescent lightning.

"Victoria, what have you done?"

Victoria sat back in her command chair as Jones frantically swiped through his command repeaters. He would be seeing the new Gavisari positions for the first time. "Amazing what you can do with a spoofed crypto codec and a xeno-tech specialist aboard a compromised electronic warfare ship. You always did disregard your marines. The last little thing I needed was your emission profile. And I knew that if I messed up, you couldn't help yourself, you little shit."

Ahead, above, and all around, missiles burst from the cloud bank. Mid and long-range missiles whipped past her ship, rocking her with sonic shockwaves as they thundered louder than any lightning. Two, from the *Slingray*, were almost as long as the *Condor* herself. Victoria scowled at Jones. "And yeah, I knew you could fly circles around me. But you forgot I'm the meanest bitch you've ever fucking seen. If you're not where I would be then of course you're shadowing me, hiding in my wake and intercepting my comms. You can't resist showing how much better you are. And you know what? You're still fucking listening to me when you should be telling the tripods to get the hell out. There's a storm coming. Batton down and get ready for the thunder."

"This won't change what happens here. Remember that, Victoria. Remember this hollow victory when your precious defense pact burns down with the ashes of Pedres.

On her view screen, Jones reached down to the comm

circuit panel in the arm of his command couch. Then the connection went dead and the icon for the *Howard Phillips* disappeared from her view screen. Bastard probably wouldn't even try to warn the invasion fleet, more likely he'd already be climbing with the intent to break atmosphere and reconnect with the Gavisari Admiral.

"Good work Cohen. Keep the destroyers in low orbit jammed, they won't even see those birds coming."

The comms panel lit up again, tightbeam-encrypted radio from the *Vitacuus*. Victoria opened the channel.

"*Condor* Actual, that is how you humans address captains, yes? I am pleased to report that missiles are away and should be arriving on target in three, two, one, mark."

The rear sensors on the *Condor* deactivated and shuttered to avoid damage as soon as they detected the fierce light at the center of a dozen or more exotic matter detonations. A handful of speedy nuclear tipped missiles were a preamble to a pair of the *Slingray's* fleet-killers that had put the other warheads to shame. It was so bright that Victoria could see clearly the ridgeline horizons in all directions, despite the miles-high storm banks being swept clear by the force of the blast waves. Maeyar artillery was truly terrifying.

"You won't have gotten them all, even with the *Oracle* running interference."

"Perhaps. But the ones who remain are in no position to follow. We make for high orbit, the path to Pedres stands open."

Through the dissipating clouds Victoria could see the sleek profiles of the surviving members of Arda's battlegroup, flying in perfect formation. Six warships, Arda's carrier, the *Slingray*, and another dozen lighter craft. They were climbing faster than the rockets that carried man first to the moon, then beyond. A force like that, striking from behind, could break a formation like the Invasion fleet and turn the battle. If it still raged.

"Aye, let's go give Raksava a taste of the Maeyar military. Huian, take us up. Nice job on the radio speech, Wing Commander. Hell, you almost fooled me. And I was in on it."

Arda's eye spun lazily. "Yes, well, it wasn't much of a stretch, if I were to be honest. But you did come back, though no one forced your hand. You could have collected your men and left without detection. But you did not. Perhaps Yadus was not in error."

Victoria was disinclined to mention the eleven Gavisari in her holding deck, including one of the hyper-fertile priests. Union Earth would prevent their total genocide, and take the fully-functioning *Oracle* as a prize to boot, if they could get it back to Earth in one piece. Or rather, in however many pieces it was in now. The video signal buzzed with interference from the nuclear events, but Victoria couldn't keep up with the Maeyar's climb anyway, so she signed off. She would have to catch up with the Alcubierre after she broke orbit. With the time it would take to break from Juna's gravity and reach a safe space to drop the compression shell, Pedres was only a couple hours away.

The skies above Pedres loomed, dotted with the fires of a half-thousand vessels. Some were locked in a desperate attempt to cast off invaders, others viciously fighting for the survival of their species. Sothcide emerged from the launch tubes of the *Vitacuus* to the horrible revelation that the Maeyar were barely holding on to the line of defense and the anti-bombardment network on the surface was under heavy attack. The Homeworld Defense Fleet, originally designed as protection for the world of Gavisar, made an indomitable siege force.

Before the static from the launch rails had faded from his monitors he was relaying orders to all eight fighter wings, newly returned to his command. His eye spun as he swiveled his visual sensors, analyzing the battle from every possible angle. *Jalith, Jalith, where is Jalith . . . there!*

He found his wife's carrier locked in battle near the northern pole of Pedres, locked in a standoff slug-out with the *Bulwark*, the Gavisar Flag Admiral's personal battleship. It dwarfed any two of the carriers, hull seeming to shimmer as dozens of active defenses cut down wave after wave of missile. Lasers carved away layer after layer of ablative plating but the *Bulwark* had it to spare, and was giving better than it got. Somewhere in the heart of that beast, Raksava was directing his wife's murder.

But that was on the other side of the field, a quarter of a million kilometers away. And between he and Raksava lay an entire armada of deadly ships. After days stuck in the limited visibility of Juna, Sothcide was almost overcome with the lack of claustrophobia over the clear sight lines. The entire time in Juna's storm, the thought of crashing into an undetected peak had terrified him. Now he could see clearly again. The Gavisar admiral had divided his forces to tackle the clustered orbital defense platforms, the gravitationally advantageous territory above Pedres' first and second moon, and had moved a main wedge in to threaten the planet with lethal bombardment to force Maeyar interception and rob the advantage of their maneuverability as they struggled to screen the planet's surface with active defenses. So far they were successful. The main front of the Gavisar assault could not spread thinly enough to penetrate the screen without the flanks losing the critical overlapping defenses of the formation. But they were slowly gaining space.

The long-range missile boats had been held in reserve near the starward edge of the armada, slinging their heavy payloads at the robust orbital defense platforms and leaving craters on the moon where previously stood stationary defensive installations. Raksava had left light defense around them, perhaps expecting his flank to remain unabridged by Maeyar forces he thought trapped at Juna. Well Victoria and her devious ruses had set them free, loosed like arrows into the vulnerable hindquarters of the Homeworld Defense Fleet. And while Arda labored to connect with Wing Admiral Yadus, Sothcide led his attack on the valuable, and sluggish, formation.

"Wings two and eight, flank on the positive azimuth and draw the escort's attention. One four and five, with me. Stay in the engine wash, they shouldn't see us coming until the fighters report it. Three and seven, cover our strafing run," said Sothcide, filtering sensor contacts and assigning target designations with deft finger tips tapping away on his communication panel. On his side monitor he could see the laser arrays cycling through their various configurations, one last pre-firing operational check before settling on a focused array for system penetration. The artillery ships were not heavily armored, with the exception of the magazines containing the missiles and their automated loading systems. And it was engineered to protect against the missile fire and excited particles an artillery vessel was expected to encounter. Terrible damage could be done at the right angle of incidence with short-wavelength lasers.

"Adjust course, drop six degrees on the negative azimuth and come in below the magazines. We won't get through those, but we can hit the aft couplers energizing the autoloaders. Adjust for a pass at sixteen degrees to minimize reflection."

"Sixteen degrees will spread the beam, it's shallow, wingboss," said his new gunner. Ganyo, one of Vehl's whose interceptor had been damaged beyond repair covering their attack run on the light frigate with Victoria. His accent betrayed his heritage from the furthest north reaches of Maeyar, where the howling winds drove away men's senses.

"We want shallow, we're aiming for internals. Anticipate their reaction."

The roar of the engine intensified as Sothcide lowered the reducing rods in his micro reactor. The cockpit warmed noticeably with the action, but the artillery ships would never read it through the backwash of their own thrust. Some of the escorts had begun to react as they detected the diversionary wings approaching, fighters and corvettes accelerating to intercept and protect the artillery from Maeyar fighter craft. The artillery ships, for their part, kept up their fire while they made to maneuver away, slowly traversing their bow and exposing the couplers to his attack run.

The bulk of the artillery ship loomed ahead, brown and green with the animalistic striping of the Homeworld Defense Fleet. Their target was slightly bigger than the other artillery ships, roughly the size of a destroyer, with a hunched shellback magazine and four forward-facing launch apertures. The engines burned to counteract the kinetic force of the missile launches, and every few seconds another appeared, flaring briefly before distance turned it into just another pinprick of light.

"The light of my horizon shines like aurora over the

roof of the world, and you are blocking my view of her," said Sothcide, giving the dorsal thrusters a kick to drop their sight-picture. His gunner just laughed, a series of rapid clicks as his lower jaw clacked. The instant it came into view, Ganyo and the other six fighters in their formation cut loose with a salvo of ultraviolet lasers. The response from the artillery ship was instant, realizing immediately the maneuver that had carried Sothcide's fighters into the formation. Anti-fighter lasers stabbed back, attempting to keep up with their evasion program, but it was too late. The combined barrage penetrated the hull, venting atmosphere, and what looked like missile propellant, into space. The ship began to yaw uncommanded on this new axis of thrust so far from its center of gravity, the opposite side thrusters unable to overcome the forces.

Ganyo howled over the radio as the attack run carried them past the artillery ship, and swung the lasers to rake the hull of the damaged vessel. His shots had little effect of course, the capacitors not even returning to full charge between each triggering of the array, but it didn't look as if that mattered. The artillery ship must have been barely holding together after its escape from Gavisar, and the remainder of the missile propellant exploded, shearing off the magazine, and the entire shellback assembly from the vessel. Reports began to chime from the other wings on attack runs claiming similar successes, if not so spectacular. Arda and her battered battlegroup joined the fray as well, bearing down on the now weakened line of six artillery frigates and providing cover for the interceptors engaged with the escorts.

Without those missiles, Raksava might not have enough pressure to keep the Maeyar from maneuvering. He had made a risky play, reducing the defenses in his rear line to increase pressure. And while more formations of artillery ships existed, it would take time for the admiral to withdraw ships to protect them, and lives. Less time than it would take Arda to sweep through their rear lines. The ships would be climbing against the gravity of the planet to come to the aid of the missile boats. And every Homeworld Defense Fleet vessel destroyed was one fewer hurdle in his road back to Jalith.

"Wings Two and Eight, withdraw and regroup, anticipate formation advancement to following coordinates, adjust for an attack run. Wings One and Five cover. Wings—"

Sothcide was cut off as the battlegroup circuit overrode his communication. *"Superluminal contact, mark, contact subluminal, Human IFF identified."*

Victoria. Damn, but what was she doing? It was clear from the Gavisari positioning that despite the success of their attack, their presence had yet to propagate through the invasion fleet's command channels. The armada was too large and unwieldy, made up of more armed civilian vessels than warships. Part of that surprise attack's effectiveness had been dropping compression early enough to prevent photon doppler anomalies. That maneuver was uncharacteristically clumsy of a Privateer, and had probably tripped the superluminal sensor alarms on half the Gavisar ships. She had just. . . .

"Additional superluminal contact. Mark subluminal . . . Human IFF."

Sothcide's orders fell flat as he adjusted his battle scope to the area in question. Before he could puzzle it out, another Human vessel dropped out of compression, and then two additional vessels, and then four.

What in the stars were they doing?

CHAPTER 20
TO FALL AMONG
VULTURES

VICTORIA WATCHED the battle unfold as she approached. Arda was already engaged, plowing into the rear line of the missile boats like a starving man at a seafood buffet. That first run had been easy, but even with the defense fleet aware of their presence, the bitch was going to do staggering harm to the Gavisari back-row artillery.

"Huian, take us in closer. UEN Intel is going to want to analyze the Maeyar fighter tactics. Damn that boy is good."

"Aye ma'am, currently one hundred and fifty KK from rendezvous with Arda's battlegroup.

There was a brief starburst on the screen as something big exploded in the Gavisar line. Victoria cringed and hissed, then grinned. "I bet they'll be missing that guy soon enough."

"Conn sensors, multiple superluminal contacts bearing one-seven-eight!"

Victoria slid her command repeater around. "Shit! Is it another Gavisari response? We have to warn—"

"Negative, conn, I'm getting human IFF."

"That doesn't make any sense," said Victoria. Her retinal implants were alerting her to a half-dozen new designations while she looked at her battle grid. More populated as she scanned.

"*UEN Missouri, Elbe, Colorado, Mississippi, Thames, Yangtze.*"

Those were all Union Earth heavy destroyers, with the exception of the *Yangtze,* a cruiser, and the most advanced ship in the Union Earth Naval Fleet. And they weren't alone. Five more dropped Alcubierre compression in the middle of the formation, the *Zumwalt, Iliad, Trebuchet, Prometheus,* and the *Longinus.*

"Vick, I've never heard of any of those five ships," said Dan Avery. Victoria hadn't either.

"Avery, get me a better visual. Laser link to the *Yangtze,* I don't want us getting blown out of space for not broadcasting our transponder."

The main view screen zoomed as the optical sensors refocused, bringing the *Zumwalt* into focus. The ship was the full length of a destroyer, but like one that hadn't been fed. Frame spars hung down beneath like ribcages, shrouding a series of reactor housings. The forecastle and cylindrical front third of the ship, flanked by two huge ablative plates. It looked like—

"Holy fuck!" shouted Victoria. "That's one of the *Spring-dawn's* main fucking lasers!"

An open radio broadcast from the *Yangtze* took over the bottom left quarter of her main screen. Admiral Chadha in full battle dress, three stars blazing on each side of his collar, made an address to the battle at Pedres, and any radio receiver in line of sight on the surface of the planet.

"To all forces in the area. The destruction of the *Union Earth Clarke* and the *Union Earth Yakima* at the hands of the Maeyar will not go unanswered. Union Earth stands with GaviSar. Let it be known here today what happens to those who threaten Earth."

"That's not what goddamn happened!" Victoria screamed, rising to her feet.

Alarms blared across the conn as detected heat and electromagnetic radiation made the computer believe a Dirregaunt battleship was about to fire. Each of the five new ships had been built around a laser pulled from what was left of the *Springdawn*, that much was obvious. Victoria had seen the front of the dreadnaught torn off by the Malagath's ramshackle emergency engine, but it hadn't been ripped to pieces as she had expected. At least not until Union Earth got their hands on it. The Big Three weaponry was far too advanced for humanity to recreate, but all the technology needed to operate was voltage, and control of the firing aperture. The Dirregaunt rare elements and their stimulation process would do all the heavy lifting.

Someone must have noticed Victoria's laser, because the screen showing Admiral Chadha flickered, and she found herself in a private comms channel.

"Ah, Victoria, it is good to see you. I did not know if you would be in the immediate area. I am glad you are, these new frames are a direct result of your handiwork with the *Springdawn*. It is good that you are witness to the first live test of their weapon systems."

"Admiral, there's been a mistake, the *Clarke* was shot down by Gavisari forces, and the *Yakima* was a false-flag attack. I've just secured a mutual defense pact with the Maeyar!"

Chadha shook his head of gray hair. His Kosso Standard was thickly accented. The admiral was old enough to not have had to learn it in primary school.

"No mistake, I am afraid, Victoria. Jones contacted us through the *Bulwark*'s onboard FTL channels some days ago, and Director Sampson has been in contact with the

Gavisari admiral ever since. The Union Earth declared the *Clarke* to be an unfortunate misunderstanding, a terrible tragedy by a desperate people. The captain and crew's sacrifice is to be honored. But the *Yakima* was a deliberate betrayal, possibly an attempt at piracy, and a direct attack on Union Earth sovereignty. And for the first time, thanks to you, we have a way to answer it. Long range laser artillery, ships each built around a single emitter of the latest Dirregaunt design. Here, let me patch you in, but I must ask that you stay back. This is a military action now, not a Privateer matter."

Chadha's retinal implants gleamed as he reached out to his own communication display, making the connection with the flick of a finger. Suddenly Victoria's conn was filled with the battlegroup cross chatter.

"*Iliad* capacitors at eighty-five percent, number two reactor at reduced output."

"*Zumwalt*, ready to fire."

"*Trebuchet* at ninety-five percent."

"Rail mine picket deployed, Admiral. *Missouri* standing by."

"Excellent. Assignments per battlefield arrangement, screen and provide support for the *Zumwalt* class artillery. Weapons free. Fire as ready."

"Aye aye, Admiral. Priority targets are carriers and missile cruisers. Deconfliction assignments by *Yangtze*. *Zumwalt* firing."

The ablative fans at the forecastle of the *Zumwalt* flared out, massive servo arms forming a black-mirrored dish to reflect the backwash of the stimulated Dirregaunt lasers away from the human elements of the ship's construction. Victoria could see a ring of a dozen or more thrusters fine-tuning the heading of the ship by what must have been hundredths, if not thousandths, of a degree to track a distant target.

"Conn sensors. *Zumwalt* preparing to fire, recommend disabling optical sensors to prevent possible damage."

"No Avery. We need to see this," said Victoria. She wanted to see. She wanted to watch the Union Earth shit all over everything she fought and bled for, everything she risked her ship and her crew for. Ice ran through her veins, curling her lips up in a snarl.

The majority of the light escaping the aperture was outside the visible spectrum. The human adaptation had lost the careful tuning of the Dirregaunt scientists and engineers, and so waste light blazed at the point of emission, dimming the main view screen as it forced adaptive contrast to narrow the iris apertures on all sensors. Even so, the bow of the *Zumwalt* was too bright to look directly at, and Victoria had to avert her eyes from the screen. Thick layers of ablative plating charred and baked off, shrouding the *Zumwalt* in a black haze. The intense light clicked off after an eighth of a second, leaving a greenish afterimage in her vision. Almost a hundred thousand kilometers away, and almost a second later, the *Slingray* exploded.

The *Zumwalt* had carved a basketball-sized hole through the entirety of her reactor compartment, breaching containment and spilling the contents of the fusion reactor into space and the inner compartments of the ship. The detonation claimed the remaining missiles in the *Slingray's* magazines, bright blue spikes of exotic matter striking out and cleaving through two small frigates held in defense of the valuable missile boat. In under two seconds, the ship which had dwarfed the *Condor* by several orders of magnitude could boast no pieces larger than a fist.

"Five minutes, fifty-two seconds to recharge."

"*Longinus* preparing to fire. Targeting the holdout carriers above the northern latitudes."

Sothcide watched helplessly as the *Slingray* ceased to be. In his mind he replayed the message given by the dark human admiral again and again. "Earth stands with Gavisar."

That laser, that impossible range, nearly a hundred thousand kilometers away and it had only taken a single shot to wipe the missile boat from the stars. The immediate threat of battle and the imposing line of Gavisari artillery was left almost forgotten while Sothcide watched the pieces of the *Slingray* shine in the light like stardust. The humans, the primitive, sluggish humans, reliant upon computers to breach interstellar space, had just struck his battlegroup's hardest hitter from the stars at a range matched only by the Malagath, Dirregaunt, and Kossovoldt.

The Maeyar could not answer. They had no answer. Even with the human's primitive weapon systems, attempting to cross the interim space would be a death sentence. And if they had been capable of this all along, who knew what dirty tricks the rest of those vessels could be hiding?

Sothcide's radio clicked on in his cockpit, the all-fighters frequency of the Maeyar. "The Senior Wing Admiral has ordered a general retreat. Pedres is untenable. All elements are to make their way starward to—" Sothcide saw the bright flash in the sky of another of the human vessels firing. The Admiral's command carrier blossomed with fire, then began to drift. Missiles, lasers, and point defense went dead. The Gavisari missiles held barely at bay began to strike home, and without the active defenses to thin the bombardment, the ship was torn completely apart in minutes. Maeyar ships at the periphery of the battle began maneuvering to pull back, and then individuals in the defense picket started to abandon the line. The gaps they left in the defense overlap were holes that Gavisar was more than happy to exploit, the main wedge of the invasion fleet pressing forward.

It wasn't until Sothcide saw the first dark red cloud of atomic power flaring over the second largest city, that he abandoned the line and released all limiters on is engine.

"Ay, wingboss, where you speeding?" Goya asked from the rear compartment of the interceptor. "They just sounded the retreat. We got to get out of here."

Sothcide growled into his helmet and keyed his transmitter. "All fighter wings, support the retreat and cover the remaining carriers. Direct orders and assignments by Second Wing Officer Allid."

"Acknowledged, Sothcide. I'm assuming control of all fighter elements for Battlegroup *Vitacuus*. You're going after her, aren't you?"

Sothcide didn't answer. He didn't have to, there could be only one thing driving him deeper into the hell of battle instead of away to the safety of the stars and a jump closer to Maeyar. One single connection in all the stars that could sever him from his years of service and discipline, and that was the order to leave his starward sky to die in the Gavisari onslaught. No force of terrestrial or cosmic power could deter him from this. His gunner whooped and hollered, taking potshots at everything in range.

Another of the impossible human artillery ships fired, reflected light blinding from a heavy destroyer holding off the line of advance over a hundred kilometers ahead. The laser scored a glowing metal rift from the dorsal dampeners to the undercarriage laser arrays, and the force of the escaping gasses pushed the two halves of the ship away from each other. The hit had been too far forward to rupture re-actor containment, and aft of the launcher magazines so its crew would suffer as they either froze or suffocated. Kinder to have killed them outright.

His own cabin was getting hot as he continued his ac-celeration. Without Yadus' support, the remaining two carriers were hard-pressed to hold off the advance of the *Bulwark*, and Jalith was losing ground quickly to the ham-mering assault of Raksava's flanking attack against her point defenses. Sothcide wasn't sure how he intended to intervene, his interceptor was one tiny spacecraft weaving among giants, still alive because the Gavisar ships had dis-missed or ignored his wild blaze across Juna's orbit. But he would find a way. He would disable the point defenses on the *Bulwark*, or strike at Raksava's battle-damaged frames, or . . . or. . . .

A sunburst blossomed on the bow of the *Twin Sister*, as if a bright glowing eye had sprouted in the center of the carrier's forehead between the deployment rails, red-hot veins snaking out across its outer laminate skin. The light of the cutting laser reflected off the *Bulwark* and the doz-en missiles en route across the interim sky. The port-side point defenses fell silent, as did the maneuvering gravitic thrusters. With no way to correct her left yaw, Jalith's carri-er slowly exposed a broadside profile to Raksava's ravaging lasers, and they finished the vicious carving that the hu-mans had begun. Metal and composite boiled off the sur-face of the *Twin Sister*, scoring holes in the hull that vented gas, and presumably personnel. Several missiles closed to within a kilometer of Jalith's bow before detonating, and the pressure wave of the expanding exotic matter crushed the weakened and compromised hull like an empty ration can.

Sothcide's hands went limp on the controls, and for once Goya seemed to have nothing to say. All of his work, all of his faith placed in the humans, had led to this. The Maeyar fleet in a full rout, Pedres lost. His wife, Jalith, betrayed and murdered by the very people Sothcide endeavored to enlist in their cause. The weight of all that he had distanced from himself fell heavy upon his shoulders. Millions were dying below, and he had abandoned his post only to arrive helpless. There was but one thing left to do. Sothcide cut the acceleration to reasonable levels, and keyed his communications array.

Victoria watched the destruction unfold. Pedres had fallen to the staggered attacks of the *Zumwalt, Iliad, Trebuchet, Longinus,* and *Prometheus.* The staggered fire was resulting in a fleet-critical Maeyar ship disabled or destroyed roughly every sixty to seventy seconds. And it was accomplished from a position of complete safety, a hundred thousand kilometers from the battle. It was barely more than a third the range Dirregaunt had squeezed from the lasers, which they had fired in concert. But it was more than almost any armor of the lesser races could withstand.

And she had helped it happen. She had led Jones to this hunting ground, and now that ground was littered with the bones of countless hulls, ripe for salvage while the Gavisari focused on their advanced breeding program in the tunnels and caverns of irradiated Pedres. While pyrocumulus storms would blanket the surface, the Gavisari would repopulate and rebuild their defense fleet with the empty mines and manufacturing facilities the Maeyar left behind. She could see it now; this day would be considered the greatest human victory in space to date. Chadha would add another star to his collar, Sampson would get enough new tech to *swim* in. All it had cost was the crew of the *Yakima* and her own integrity.

On the main view screen the *Longinus'* ablative fans extended, preparing for its second shot. Enormous gyros held the aperture steady while thrusters made micro-adjustments with the aid of the computer's targeting system. Once it had run sufficient simulations to declare a positive firing solution it triggered the xeno laser hooked into the multiple reactors.

Victoria looked away as the emitter clicked on and off, dispersing another cloud of vaporized ablative plating. Without it, even the comparatively miniscule ambient wash from the laser would cause serious damage to the ship firing it, and burn out dozens of sensor modules on the other ships in the formation. Reflected light took almost a second to return from the target, painting a new star in the sky above the north pole of Pedres. Victoria winced as her tactical team confirmed that the target was the *Twin Sister*. Seconds later the ship disappeared from her tactical repeater entirely. The *Bulwark* had moved in and finished the job. The Maeyar were in full retreat now, harried by the Gavisari invasion fleet descending on Pedres. Their line was in shambles now, the *Zumwalt* class artillery breaking the back of Maeyar resistance with its picked shots. Chadha's interdiction had come at a perfect time to counterplay her deliverance of Arda's battlegroup and nullify any advantage it might have gained the Maeyar.

A radio signal emerged from the tumult of distress calls, desperate requests for orders, and electronic countermeasures. A signal unique in that it carried the private identifier she used to communicate with the marine detachment sent down to that Gavisari derelict what felt like years ago, though it had only been a few days. The identifier she gave to Sothcide before her expeditionary trek to Gavisar to identify the cause of the interstellar exodus. Victoria reached for her comms panel, then hesitated. There was half a bottle of scotch left in her rack that she would sorely like to pull from before she had this conversation. Her hands were shaking, centimeters from deciding whether to accept or refuse the transmission. She should refuse it. Her duty was to humanity, not any xeno officer. She owed him nothing. And yet. . . .

The cold exterior of Sothcide's flight helmet appeared on her main view screen. Hidden from view was his onyx skin with its monolithic, starscape-patterned eye. The way he moved was subtly different, stiffer, betraying his alien biology. Were it not for that, it could have been a marine or a human fighter pilot under that mask.

"Sothcide, I—" Victoria began. But the Xeno cut her off with a slash of his hand.

"Is this what it means to make pacts with humans? Betrayal, sabotage, and the murder of two billion Maeyar families?"

Victoria shook her head, tears stinging the corners of her eyes. "I didn't mean for any of this."

"Spare me, Human Victoria," said Sothcide. "This was no chance interdiction. Was this planned from the start? Were your Union Earth forces already dispatched by the time we set off from Ersis? I came to you for help because I believed your people of similar spirit to mine. I believed you to be the Samaritans of your story. Now you willingly commit the very sin we have spent half a millennium trying to absolve, and I see that you are not the beggar by the road. You are no Samaritans. By enlisting your aid we have fallen among robbers. And there is no one coming to dress our wounds with oil and wine."

Victoria opened her mouth to respond, but no words

came out. Over the transmission she could hear the hum of the interceptor's powerful engines and the radio transmissions of the dying Pedres defense fleet. She wanted to apologize, wanted to shift responsibility to Jones and Sampson and those assholes in the Union Earth government that had decided to sully humanity's reputation just to test out some shiny new toys. But she couldn't.

"What happens next?" asked Victoria.

Sothcide slumped in his cockpit. Righteous anger could only carry a body so far through the numbing shock of personal loss he had experienced at the destruction of the *Twin Sister*.

"Next? If I am not executed as a traitor for my role in the fall of Pedres, or exiled for abandoning my post then I will be assigned a new command. Likely under Arda, if she survives. She is now the senior wing commander for Maeyar's defensive fleet. And someday, stars willing, I will return with her and repay humanity with the same brand of *kindness* that you have shown us. One day humanity will answer for this betrayal, as we answered for ours. And I will be there to see it."

"For what it's worth," said Victoria, "I thought we were better than this. I thought we could be the good guys, but we're the same squabbling backstabbing creatures we've always been."

The communication signal was overcome with static as Sothcide's ship carried him around the orbit of the planet, away from the battle and beyond line of sight. Victoria watched the feed degrade, until the screen flashed a *no signal* alert and the communication window closed permanently. Victoria dropped back into her command couch, and her tearstained face fell into her open hands.

EPILOGUE

THE AIRLOCK OF THE *Yangtze* opened, and Victoria stepped aboard with Red Calhoun and the dozen Gavisari pulled from the remains of the *Oracle*. It smelled of fresh paint. Naval ships always smelled of fresh paint. Overhead lighting ringed the corridor, and not for the first time Victoria cursed under her breath the bright halos the scotch had decided to leave with her when it left. Red had found her half passed out fifteen minutes before they were set to dock, shoved her in a cold shower and practically dragged her to the airlock.

The Gavisari survivors gathered behind her lumbered and milled. Occasionally one would reach up looking for a handhold that wasn't there, then warble or mutter something in Kosso before continuing. They weren't happy finding out that Victoria would suffer no repercussions for her marines storming their ship, and was in fact being lauded as a hero by the Gavisar High Command. But all in all, they were just grateful to have survived the exodus. Victoria would turn them over officially to Raksava's high priest aboard the *Yangtze,* to formalize the agreement between the Union Earth and the Children of Gavisar.

A parade detail waited on the other side of the threshold, six enlisted led by a saluting chief petty officer and an ensign.

"Condor, arriving," the ensign belted out into the ship-wide announcement circuit, next to a ship's bell which he rang twice.

"Fuck off butterbar," Victoria grumbled, and pushed her way past and off the quarterdeck. "Main briefing room, yeah?

"Umm, yes ma'am. This way please."

"I know the goddamn way," she shouted over her shoulder, then winced as twisting her head straight renewed the throbbing in her head and the retort reminded her how dry her mouth had become. The last time she'd been in it she gave a lecture to the Union Earth officers on just how fucked they were if they actually had to go to war. Luckily the briefing room, which doubled as a ceremony room as it was the only compartment aside from the galley that could comfortably house a sizable portion of the crew, was only a few minutes from where she was. Doubly lucky, it did not require the coordination necessary to climb or descend a deck ladder to access.

Crewmembers gave her a wide berth, also skirting the Gavisari filing behind her. The tripod footsteps sounded unsettling with their asymmetrical three-legged gait on the steel decking. The arrhythmic tapping was somehow making her queasiness worse. Too much more and she'd have to find the nearest head. But she was spared the experience when they came upon the entrance to the briefing room.

Nominally filled with folding chairs for the various divisions and crews attending award ceremonies, pre-horizon jump briefings, and general military training, a large segmented conference table had been assembled. Admiral Chadha stood at the head, having traded his battle dress for a more formal set of dress blues with gold-trimmed epaulets. A slew of brass stood to his left, and a trio of Gavisari to his right, one festooned in similar cloth wrappings as the holy man she'd pulled off the *Oracle*, if more elaborate.

Jones was also present, and in his disheveled uniform, he looked as haggard and out of place as Victoria. He was sulking. Despite the victory, he had not taken well to being outsmarted and outmaneuvered by her. Nor the fact that she had somehow gained a majority of the credit for the events taking place. Only Red's hand wrapped around the hem of her coveralls at the shoulder kept her from launching across the table and landing a fist in his lopsided gob, which would really give him something to frown about.

"Ah, Victoria. Please come in, we were just discussing the formalization customs with the Gavisari delegation. I see you've brought the crew of the *Oracle*."

"What's left of them," said Victoria. Hushed gasps and a look of warning from the admiral brought some small color to her cheeks. She didn't want to be here, wanted no part of credit for the butchering of Pedres. Being scandalized by remarking upon the death of a handful seemed laughable. Everyone seemed to be ignoring the fact that they'd been complicit in the *Bulwark*'s assault and bombardment of the planet before the battle was even truly over. Even if Gavisar had lost the battle, they would have rendered the surface uninhabitable for the millions still living there. Union Earth had participated in the extermination of a lawfully recognized civilian population. Xeno or not, the Maeyar were a sovereign power.

"Peace, Human Victoria," said the bedazzled Gavisari beside Chadha. It lifted a single forelimb, unfurling its curled hook glistening with enamel and invited her closer. "I am Jessad. I speak for the Admiral Raksava. For obvious reasons, he must stay aboard the *Bulwark*. Pockets of resistance yet hold in the shipyards around the second planet, shipyards critical in repairing the Homeworld Defense Fleet. And the Maeyar darkspace vectors must be girded.

Victoria took a seat, pointedly as far from Jones as was possible. "Is it still the Homeworld Defense Fleet without a home?"

"Pedres is our home now. I know you witnessed the reality of Gavisar, and returned to deliver us. You have seen that the Kossovoldt have reclaimed the planet for their own ends. This was the only path forward, and now our people can forge it together."

The only forging was the events of whatever peace treaty they cooked up. How much of it did Jessad know was bullshit? Or whatever they had instead of bulls. Union Earth had played both sides, backed two horses with a pair of Privateers at odds. By rights the Gavisari should be blowing her from the sky.

"We need only your provisions to complete the treaty."

"Excuse me?" said Victoria, leaning forward in her chair.

Admiral Chadha looked somewhat nervous, his fingers kneading the podium from which he presided. "There was not time to inform you, Victoria. The Gavisari are an individually meritocratic society. They recognize that you fall under higher authority, but request that your *personal* mark is left on any lasting accord."

"What are the existing tenets?"

The Gavisari holy man pressed a sheet of paper across the table. "A summary," he said. "It outlines a mutual defense agreement that includes five of your *Zumwalt* Class artillery vessels remaining here to bolster the Homeworld Defense Fleet during the reclamation."

Personal. Her ass, she knew exactly what *personal* requests the Union Earth would expect her to make. Salvage rights, Gavisari missile, and point defense tech. Maeyar fusion reactors, inertial dampeners, and lasers.

"I want the bombings to stop. I want all Maeyar citizens still on Pedres or onboard ships in the system given a chance to withdraw and evacuate using whatever unarmed cargo and transport ships remain on the planet or in orbit."

Victoria heard Red stiffen behind her. Jones almost retched. Admiral Chadha looked stern, but she could see the tiny corners of a smile creeping out from behind his gray mustache.

Jessad drew up to his full, considerable height. "Human Victoria, you must know what you are asking. The Maeyar would have had us dead to the last child. We were told you would want total salvage authority, weapon schematics, shipyard access."

Victoria held up her hand. "If you want to repay humanity's contribution to your continued existence and the presence of our *defensive* Union Earth naval assets, that's my price. Feel free to toss in salvage and tech too. But there is no need for the continued butchery of civilians. Get the Maeyar survivors off of Pedres."

The priest looked at his fellows gathered around the table. "I will need to confer with the Admiral. The remaining ships necessary for such an evacuation were part of his plan for the Reclamation of Pedres."

Victoria chuffed. "Do you speak for him or not? Maybe we ought to put these talks on hold until Raksava is less occupied."

The Gavisari muttered in a low, guttural Kosso Common. Jessad reached for the paper, crossing out the expected provisions and scribbling Victoria's new ones at the bottom. Those hook hands were surprisingly dexterous. Victoria supposed she shouldn't be surprised. The Gavisari managed to build space ships with them. Considerably better space ships than humans could. And they'd done it in caves, after being pushed to the brink of extinction. Union Earth would still get their salvage. There was so much debris between Pedres and Juna that the Gavisari couldn't *pay* them to haul it out as fast as the tripods would like. They might lose out on the most choice bits, but it was worth reclaiming whatever shred of humanity she could. That was the real salvage.

Jones stood so violently that it tipped his chair back. He cast a dark look Victoria's way, then stormed from the briefing room. Victoria allowed herself a small smile, her headache seemed to be clearing.

"I also want cohabitation on the planet the Maeyar staked out between here and Gavisar," said Victoria.

Now Chadha frowned. "I'm afraid such a request would rightly have to come from the Department of State and Colony. Victoria lacks such authority to direct colonization efforts. This cluster of stars is awkwardly placed with our current horizon limitations."

Jessad scribbled more. "Regardless, we welcome such cooperation. Now that the children of Gavisar are free to expand, one of Raksava's hopes for this alliance was such an effort for a joint colony. Humanity has more than proven their dedication to our cause. I look forward to presiding over such an event personally, should you wish it."

The Gavisari hesitated. Chadha's smile returned, this time with effort made to suppress it.

"Is there a problem?" asked Victoria.

"Typically," said Jessad, "among the Children, an accord such as this is ratified with . . . the joining of two bodies, and the fruit of that union."

Victoria blushed at very few things. The suggestion of copulation with a two-meter alien amorphous tripod turned out to be one of them.

"With that in mind," Jessad hurriedly continued, "I think on this occasion it is permissible to indulge in the human method of marking a written contract with your verbal identification."

"You're goddamned right it is," said Victoria Marin.

Defeat.

That word spread through the light-speed channels across the worlds of the Maeyar before the battered and broken fleet emerged from the darkspace passageways to the homeworld systems. It raced beyond the Maeyar borders, to those who looked upon their resources with covetous eyes. Pedres had fallen. With the second largest Maeyar world proven to be so vulnerable, what outpost, or colony for that matter, was safe? So much of the fleet had been committed and lost in its defense, it would take years if not decades to undo the damage the Union Earth and the Children of Gavisar inflicted. All the while, the rich mineral assets in the Pedres system, and those harder to reach stars accessed by its avenues would be exploited by their enemies.

Sothcide heard reports of skirmishes on the rimward edge of the territories. Pirates, opportunists, warbands probing for weakness. With almost a third of the Maeyar's warships destroyed or disabled beyond repair, the remainder would be spread too thin to manage their most remote holdings. There would be a pullback. Thousands more would be evacuated, or left to the mercy of the stars. That was, to die.

Once back aboard the *Vitacuus*, Arda said nothing about his excursion during the battle. Such a lapse in discipline was tantamount to desertion, but Jalith was an old friend of Arda's, and she could not, or would not, fault him for his actions. Instead, he sat in the council chamber as the high command conferred upon the present situation of the fleet.

"Pedres is a black hole. Any response we send, we send to their deaths. Especially with those new human ships skulking in the system. We simply do not have the forces to send without leaving the homeworld inadequately defended and risking the loss of critical fleet assets."

The Wing Admiral spoke for the rimward theater, even now forced to withdraw in defense of Pedres. Arda now stood his equal, promoted into the upward vacuum left by Yadus' death. The loss of four command carriers had left a planet-sized hole in the fleet command hierarchy that had seen a slew of automatic advancements realized. Some deserving, others less so.

"Agreed," said Arda. "By now Gavisar has entrenched themselves deep underground, and radiation prevents recolonization for several decades. Throwing loss after loss only diminishes us further. I propose a course to demonstrate our strength, a statement to Maeyar fleet power. The humans have made us look weak before our enemies. They played and betrayed us, all so they could pick the bones of our war and steal our advancements for themselves."

Sothcide did not contribute to the debate. Still numb, he wished for the simple escape of sleep and intoxicants.

"These humans hide. They hide their ships because they are weak, they hide their worlds because they are afraid and because they are few. Those five ships notwithstanding, their fleet cannot stand and fight. A small force dispatched with the objective of locating and destroying their holdings would show the Bridge our resolve."

The admirals nodded. A small battlegroup could do untold damage to a primitive race such as the humans. If their worlds could be located. "The *Vitacuus* sustained minimal damage at Pedres, did it not?"

"It did," said Arda.

"And here in this room with me are the two foremost experts on human customs and tactics?"

"I think that's fair to say."

The leading wing admiral turned to Sothcide. "Wing officer, what say you?"

The admiral had to repeat his question before Sothcide realized he was being addressed. He quickly recounted the conversation in his head, realizing the implication of what they were suggesting.

"The humans are as ghosts. To believe you know them is to believe you can court death. But I have courted death before, and will do so again. Hunt them all down."

"How do you hunt ghosts?" asked the admiral.

Sothcide considered. "The humans are not without enemies. Tell me, in your travels have you encountered the Grah'lhin?"

In the skies above a barren world, Ea dreamed. She dreamed of the past, the worlds she had visited and the ether through which she swam. She dreamed of creation and destruction, the rise and fall of civilizations across countless worlds. Ea dreamed of the first meeting of the Dirregaunt and the Malagath, between the twin suns of Yon and Appali. Would that she could dream of the future—what would she see? The ashes of a war ravaged between the hunters and the scholars? Or the darkness claimed by their covenant's pursuit? Or perhaps even one of the lesser empires rising to usurp them? Someday, perhaps soon or perhaps in another hundred thousand years, someone would surpass the Kossovoldt. No one could see the future, but one did not need to pierce the veil of time to see that the younger races were becoming more than they had before.

If only they knew how little they knew. If only they could learn how little they learned. Perhaps it was a mistake to allow the Malagath and the Dirregaunt to grow and flourish in those early years, but such things were not for Ea to judge and no longer within her control. Her task was deciding what to do next, and by now the news of her presence spread to waiting ears. Though the Most Wayward Children and the Unveiled Children did not recognize the significance of such an event, others had longer memories and even now Ea dreamed of the forces amassing to answer her call.

I am ready.

Ea awoke.

The children must be protected, even if doing so required some die that the rest might live. The children must not break the line of the Kossovoldt.

"It goes without saying, Victoria, that the Union Earth will not be pleased with your decision."

The *Yangtze* drifted away on the main screen as Huian deftly maneuvered the *Condor* clear of her docking ring and eased back into the steady orbit above Pedres. The sensor team was idly tracking and cataloguing space junk for potential salvage. The Gavisari would take the choicest bits for their Reclamation, but there would be plenty of bones to pick through. The salvage freighters were only a day or two behind the battlegroup.

Victoria scratched at her nose idly. Chadha addressed her from his stateroom, as close to privacy as the admiral could get. "Haven't any idea what you mean, Admiral. We prevented not one, but two genocides with that agreement. Union Earth should be thrilled."

Chadha allowed her a small smile. "Outwardly perhaps, and many will agree with your actions. Myself among them, Victoria. Sometimes I envy the Privateers their ability to act without constraint."

"But. . . ."

Chadha sighed. "But I am a creature of duties and loyalties, and this our union cannot survive without men like me to carry the orders. Even if I do not agree with them."

The bow of the *Condor* swung, putting the star front and center. The computer dimmed the light of the system's core star while superimposing the rest of them in the daytime sky. Victoria swung the view around with a gesture, bringing one last time the planet of Pedres into view. From this angle it was split between day and night, and fires still ravaged the night side. The Gavisari stopped short of causing a total nuclear winter, and estimates of the Maeyar refugees already numbered in the tens of millions.

Not refugees, survivors.

"Victoria, it was good to see you. I am sorry it could not be under more pleasant circumstances. If I may ask, where are you headed now?"

Victoria considered. A few horizon jumps away, the Kossovoldt had lit a signal fire for the Malagath and the Dirregaunt, and too close for comfort to human territories. Things were promising to get more interesting around the

Orion Spur than she preferred. What exactly the Kosso-voldt were doing in Gavisar's night sky Victoria couldn't say. She had managed to get down in writing the parts of the conversation she could remember, and looking back at her notes jogged the memories enough to get a picture of the thing in her mind's eye. She couldn't hedge a guess as to the bits she'd let slip, but she knew it had already dictated her next destination. It wasn't exactly home, but it had probably been, at some point.

"Earth," said Victoria.

ACKNOWLEDGEMENTS

When I realized that I was now under a book deal and expected to produce a novel-length book in just under four months, and not just any book, but the sequel to *Vick's Vultures*, I'll admit that I began to feel the heat.

Union Earth Privateers began with a simple premise, followed by a straightforward novel. Now as I look at the last round of edits on *To Fall Among Vultures*, I can see the release date on the horizon and I would not have made it here alone.

First and foremost are Colin Coyle and Eric Ryles, the masterminds behind Parvus Press. For all the trust I placed in them to handle my book with care and attention, that trust was a two-way street and they believed in my writing enough to offer at least two more books a spot on the shelf before I'd fully intended to write them.

I'd also like to say thank you to my tag-team of editors, John Adamus and Jennifer Melchert, who helped hammer my rough manuscript into a tight, well-punctuated interstellar adventure. In the same vein, Tom Edwards provided an eye-catching cover that perfectly encapsulates the tone of the book. It is especially difficult for me to surrender artistic control, having illustrated the cover of my first novel, Devilbone, myself. But I know I am in good hands.

And lastly, I would be remiss in not mentioning you, the reader. Thank you for spending some of your valuable time choosing to read this one book among untold thousands. I hope you have enjoyed the adventure as much as I have, and I hope to see you in the next installment.

Until then,
Scott Warren
July 27, 2017

ABOUT THE AUTHOR

Scott Warren got his start in writing while living in Washington during the summer of 2014 when he entered the world of speculative fiction by writing *Sorcerous Crimes Division,* followed shortly by *Vick's Vultures.*

Scott blends aspects of classic military fantasy and science fiction with a modern, streamlined writing style to twist tired tropes into fresh ideas. He believes in injecting a healthy dose of adventure into the true-to-life grit and grime that marks the past decade of science fiction, while still embracing the ideas that made science fiction appeal to so many readers.

As a UAV Pilot and former submariner, Scott draws on his military and aviation experiences to bring authenticity to his writing while keeping it accessible to all readers. Scott is also an artist, contributing his skills to board games, role playing games, and his own personal aerial photography galleries.

Scott currently lives in Huntsville, Alabama. Visit Scott on the web: *http://scottwarrenscd.blogspot.com/* and follow him on Twitter: *@ScottWarrenSCD*

BOOKS BY SCOTT WARREN

The Union Earth Privateers:
Vick's Vultures
To Fall Among Vultures

The Sorcerous
Crimes Division:
Devilbone

COMING SOON FROM PARVUS PRESS

PERIDOT SHIFT BOOK ONE:
FLOTSAM
by R J THEODORE

A fantastical steampunk first contact novel that ties together high magic, high technology, and bold characters to craft a story you won't soon forget.

Captain Talis just wants to keep her airship crew from starving, and maybe scrape up enough cash for some badly needed repairs. When an anonymous client offers a small fortune to root through a pile of atmospheric wreckage, it seems like an easy payday. The job yields an ancient ring, a forbidden secret, and a host of deadly enemies.

Now on the run from cultists with powerful allies, Talis needs to unload the ring as quickly as possible. Her desperate search for a buyer and the fallout from her discovery leads to a planetary battle between a secret society, alien forces, and even the gods themselves.

Talis and her crew have just one desperate chance to make things right before their potential big score destroys them all.

January 2018
www.ParvusPress.com/flotsam

DO YOU LIKE FREE BOOKS?

We give away advance release copies to our loyal readers!

www.ParvusPress.com

Join the mailing list at ParvusPress.com and we'll let you know when we have new releases or free books to share. Give-aways are always announced to mailing list subscribers first. And we hate spam as much as you do, we promise to only mail you sparingly. Sign up today:

http://bit.ly/2undtWN

(Or head over to ParvusPress.com and use the sign-up form at the bottom of the home page).

Thank you for supporting independent publishing and being the best part of Parvus. We couldn't do this without you.

Oh, and don't forget to take a minute to stretch. *TO FALL AMONG VULTURES* is a great read and you've probably been at this for a little bit, now. We wouldn't want you to bust a hammy.

GLOSSARY

CHARACTERS
Union Earth Privateers, crew of the *Condor*:

Avery, Daniel – Rank: Senior Sensor Supervisor. Nation of Origin: United States.

Cohen, Aesop – Rank: Sergeant - Privateer marine and xenotech engineer. Former Mossad (special forces). Nation of Origin: Israel.

Carillo, Cesar – Rank: First Mate – Executive Officer of the *Condor*. Leads the Tactical Division. Nation of Origin: Argentina.

Calhoun, Red – Rank: Major – Commanding officer of the *Condor's* marines. Nation of Origin: Scotland.

Marin, Victoria – Rank: Captain. Commanding Officer of the *Condor*. PHD in Xenotechnology, specializing in sensor analysis and avoidance. Nation of Origin: Northern Ireland.

Prescott, Davis – Rank: Chief– Chief Engineer of the *Condor*. Nation of Origin: United States.

Marines – Vega, Maggie/Mags, Singh – A squad of UEP Marines under the command of Sergeant Aesop Cohen.

Union Earth, other:

Bullock, Garth – Rank: Captain. Commanding Officer of
the *Hudson River*.
Jones, Terrance – Rank: Captain. Commanding Officer of
the *Howard Phillips*, a Privateer vessel. Nation of Origin: United States.
Sampson, Ethan – Rank: Civilian. Director of the Union
Earth Technology Division. Nation of Origin: Canada.

Maeyar:

Allid – Wing Officer and senior pilot aboard the *Starscream*.
Arda – Wing Commander in command of the carrier *Vit-
acuus* and friend to Jalith.
Edrus and *Kal Vaan* – Assigned to Listening Post 121.
Jalith – Commander of the *Twin Sister*. Wife of Sothcide.
Sothcide – Senior Wing Officer and fighter/interceptor pi-
lot. Husband of Jalith.
Yadus – Senior Wing Admiral in command of the flagship
Banner and the Pedres defenders.

Others:

Grace Tora – Malagath noble investigating anomalous sen-
sor readings from Gavisar.
Raksava – Gavisari Admiral. Leader of the Homeworld
Defense Fleet and the Children of Gavisar.
Jessad – Gavisari chaplain and personal advisor to Raksava.
Tavram – First Prince of the Malagath.

SHIPS
Union Earth Navy:

Artemis – Privateer
Clarke - Destroyer
Colorado - Destroyer
Elbe - Light Cruiser
Hudson River - Light Destroyer. Captained by Bullock.
Iliad - *Zumwalt*-Class Artillery
Jackdaw – Privateer
Mississippi - Light Destroyer
Missouri - Missile Destroyer
Prometheus - *Zumwalt* -Class Artillery
Longinus - *Zumwalt* -Class Artillery
Thames - Heavy Destroyer
Trebuchet - *Zumwalt* -Class Artillery
Yangtze - Cruiser
Zumwalt - Artillery

Union Earth Privateers:

Condor - Specialized for stealth and salvage. Captained by
   Victoria Marin.
Howard Phillips – Specialized for enhanced stealth and
   communications. Captained by Terrence Jones.

Non-Human:

Apex – Lereigh light cruiser.
Blessing – Gavisar wreck above Pedres.
Bulwark – Gavisar Homeworld Defense flagship
Kreshna - Vautan vessel salvaged by the *Condor*.
Oracle – Gavisar Electronic Counter Warfare light frigate

Slingray - Maeyar missile boat.
Starscream – Maeyar carrier.
Twin Sister - Maeyar carrier.
Vitacuus – Maeyar carrier

PLACES AND RACES

Dirregaunt Praetory – One of the "big three" races in the
known galaxy, along with the Kossovoldt and the Malagath. The Dirregaunt Praetory is ruled by a Primarch.
They are fearsome hunters who excel at ambush tactics.
They are tall, clawed humanoids with four eyes.

Ersis – A trade, fueling, and refit hub located on a moon in
orbit around a gas giant. Ersis is a neutral city and its
dense, nitrogen-rich atmosphere makes it a welcome
environment for many life forms.

Gavisar – A subterranean, tripod race inhabiting the world
of Gavisar. Their religion has a complicated history
with the Kossovoldt.

Gavisar - Homeworld of the Children of Gavisar.

Grah'lhin (Graylings) – A race of arthropod predatory hunters with an interest in humanity. Individual Grah'lhin
consciousnesses are spread across multiple bodies.

Humans – Bipedal ape-like creatures that are relatively new
on the galactic scene. Not a military or colonizing power of any note, they are considered insignificant by the
rest of the galaxy if they are considered at all.

Jenursa – Amphibious, migratory race. Waist-high to a human and move via pseudopod. Allied with and share
colony worlds with the Union Earth.

Kallico'rey – A world at the edge of Malagath territory beyond which is the vast emptiness of the Orion Spur.

Kossovoldt – The most enigmatic of the "big three" races in
the known galaxy, along with the Dirregaunt and the

Malagath. Theirs is the common language of the galaxy, enabling interspecies written and verbal communication. They reside in the Sagittarius arms of the galaxy and ferociously guard their borders.

Maeyar - Bipedal, tall and solidly built with skin ranging from gray to black. Trading partners with humanity.

Malagath – One of the "big three" races in the known galaxy, along with the Dirregaunt and the Kossovoldt. The Malagath Empire contains over 8,000 known planets. They are ruled by an imperial dynasty and have a large aristocracy. The Malagath are blue humanoids with three fingers on each hand.

Orion Spur - The bridge of stars connecting the Sagittarius and Perseus Arms of the Milky Way Galaxy

Pedres - A system that shares a name with the inhabited planet contained within.

Tallidox – Interstellar arms manufacturers and dealers

Thorivult – Allied with the Union Earth and have established shared colony worlds.

Union Earth – A unified spaceborne human government comprised of representatives from all spacefaring nations on Earth, as well as all established human colonies. Their priority is the continued survival of the human race in the Milky Way.

Vautan – A race in the midst of a war for mineral rights.